THE
DEEPEST
KILL

THE
DEEPEST
KILL

LISA
BLACK

KENSINGTON
PUBLISHING CORP.

www.kensingtonbooks.com

KENSINGTON BOOKS are published by

Kensington Publishing Corp.
119 West 40th Street
New York, NY 10018

All Kensington titles, imprints, and distributed lines are available at special quantity discounts for bulk purchases for sales promotion, premiums, fund-raising, educational, or institutional use. Special book excerpts or customized printings can also be created to fit specific needs. For details, write or phone the office of the Kensington Special Sales Manager: Attn. Special Sales Department. Kensington Publishing Corp, 119 West 40th Street, New York, NY 10018. Phone: 1-800-221-2647.

Library of Congress Card Catalogue Number: 2023947407

The K and book logo Reg. U.S. Pat. & TM Off.

ISBN-13: 978-1-4967-4965-9
First Kensington Hardcover Edition: March 2024

ISBN: 978-1-4967-4967-3 (ebook)

10 9 8 7 6 5 4 3 2 1

Printed in the United States of America

To my (numerous) cousins
who made any day fun

Chapter 1

"He's lying," Rachael Davies said.

"What?" Ellie nearly spilled the cup of overly warm coffee she'd so carefully carted across the terrazzo. Her new boss, Dr. Davies, sat in the cafeteria, absently eating what looked like cold pasta primavera and watching the twenty-inch monitor perched on the counter next to the coffee-maker. They were two of only five people in the large room, built to hold the entire lunchtime crowd of a DC-area boy's school but now utilized only when sessions of forensic training were being held. The last two had ended the week before. Until more started the following month, the cafeteria provided only coffee and use of a microwave. For anything more, the Locard staff were on their own.

The television monitor replayed the interview of Greg Anderson appealing for the return of his wife, Ashley. Ashley, four months pregnant, a white twenty-five-year-old, apparently went boating one day two weeks previously and disappeared. After one week, local fishermen found the empty boat bobbing in the Gulf. Though boating accidents were hardly unheard of in coastal areas, Ashley's case stayed in the news—mostly because of her father.

Martin Post, the third-richest man in the United States. Genius of OakTree software and hardware design—there were few computers in the world that didn't churn up cyberspace using his components. And now, a mere mile from his opulent Florida fortress, his only child had washed up on a beach among the seaweed and discarded water bottles.

On the screen, Greg Anderson pleaded for any information about his wife. "If anyone saw her, if anyone was on the water that day, please call the tip line and let us know. Ashley w—is the joy of my life. And that we were about to have our first baby—" He broke off and put a hand to his mouth, his eyes screwing up into tight knots, apparently overwhelmed.

"Totally lying," Rachael said again.

Again Ellie's gaze swung from her to the television and back again. "How do you know that?"

"First, he speaks of her in the past tense."

"She *is* in the past tense."

"Not then. That interview was shot on the day after she disappeared." Her new boss tore open a bag of chips, chewed one with a thoughtful air, then set the bag down to position her hands with all five pairs of fingers touching. "Second, he held his hands like this."

"Like he was praying."

"Not exactly. The palms aren't touching, the fingers aren't interlaced. It's called *steepling*, and is a huge indicator of confidence. One of the biggest."

The gesture did seem familiar. "Like a supervillain in a movie."

"And he's sweating."

"It's Florida."

"Even at this time of year?" Rachael said, and glanced through the windows where a Chesapeake Bay fall had already begun to bluster, ripping the dying leaves from the surrounding forest.

"At every time of year. Trust me on that."

Ellie and the assistant dean of education had already been through much more than most coworkers, and in a short amount of time. This had made the two women intimately familiar in some ways and left them total strangers in others. Right now Ellie had no idea what her new boss might be thinking as Rachael waved a chip and said, "Exactly! Third, his facial muscles are all relaxed. His lips aren't compressed, his eyes are wide—until he scrunches them up at the end, because on some level his body knows that his skin isn't matching his words. He even tilts his head to one side, something you don't do unless you're relaxed and, well, *happy*. Usually, anyway . . . there are always exceptions."

The news story moved to a new clip, and Rachael continued. "Here, the interview after her body washed up, he doesn't seem so chipper. His chin is trembling, he's pressing his lips together hard, he seems to pant when specifying on which beach the body was found. To be fair, it doesn't necessarily mean he's lying about any part of it. It only tells me he's worried."

"Huh," was Ellie's less than eloquent comment. The TV coverage continued its recap of the saga with a clip of a news reporter in a motorboat. Ominous clouds gathered overhead as she described the water search after Ashley went missing. "You think he killed her? Or somehow drove her to suicide?"

Rachael crunched another chip. "Not necessarily. I just think he's glad she's gone."

"Martin Post's daughter? She was young, beautiful, filthy rich—"

"It's a marriage, which means the dynamics are not always logical. And a lot depends on the prenup."

"Wow. Can—can you teach me how to do that?"

Rachael laughed, heartily enough to be flattering. "Deception detection? Sure—sit in on my class next quarter. But you probably already know a lot of it, maybe had it in other training?"

Ellie shook her head. "I know how to interpret the crime scene, fingerprints, bullet casings, inanimate objects. Human beings remain a mystery."

The Locard secretary materialized between them and the television set. "Phone call, Rachael."

The assistant dean gave her a pleading look. "This is the first time I've sat down all day. Can you scribble a message?"

"I think you'd better take this one."

Ellie watched as Rachael's interest perked up along with her eyebrows. "Who is it?"

"He says he's Martin Post."

Chapter 2

The coast of southwest Florida did not care to be convenient, refusing to progress in one solid line of beach from Tampa to the Everglades. It dipped and swirled and created pockets of bays and lagoons and estuaries and mangrove paddies and marshes. There were miles of sandy beach, yes, but also miles where the pockmarked land declined to provide a consistent foundation.

Martin Post, Ellie could see, had gotten around that by sinking a fortune in concrete and making his own. His property formed, more or less, an island in a sea of undeveloped coast, surrounded by soupy bunches of mangrove trees and unstable shoals. This provided an effective but beautiful no-man's-land between his family and the rest of the world. Paparazzi or corporate spies would have to wind through the marshy, bramble-like growth in a flat-bottomed johnboat, risking alligators, water moccasins, and exsanguination by mosquitos in order to reach even the border of his property. And *then*, Ellie noted as she approached the security shed, scale a twelve-foot wall equipped with cameras and topped with spikes.

Much easier to make an appointment.

Which, apparently, the fifteen or so news channel and print media vans parked along the street did not have. They had pulled to the side of the public thoroughfare rather than on to the Post property, burning gallon after gallon of fossil fuel to keep their air-conditioning running while they waited, waited, waited, for something to happen. Each occupant sat up like a meerkat sensing a tasty scorpion as she drove down the otherwise empty street, and poured from their doors with cameras running when she pulled into the drive. They started up the pavement after her, then paused, slowed, as if held back by an invisible forcefield of money and a possible trespass charge. No doubt the back of their rented sedan would be on the evening news, unless something more interesting happened before air time.

Ellie had peppered Rachael with questions during the flight down, questions she couldn't answer as to why the third-richest man in the country wanted to talk to them about his daughter. Clearly the third-richest man in the country wanted to hire the Locard as forensic consultants on his daughter's death—but what he expected them to do, neither could guess.

"It's getting cloudy," Rachael said.

"Rainy season." Ellie had once lived there. She had once lived in a number of places, since her mother died when Ellie was four and her father had no interest in being a single parent. She lived with her grandmother until the age of nine, spending most summers with her mother's cousins in Nevada. After the grandmother got sick, it was Aunt Rosalie's until twelve, Uncle Terry and Aunt Katey in West Virginia until sixteen, then Uncle Paul and Aunt Joanna in Naples. College in California and vacations with her mother's cousin Tommy and Valeria, recruited to the bureau in DC, and a now-ended marriage to fellow forensics expert Adam. So yes, she knew the local weather. "Florida has two seasons. It rains every day during the rainy season. And then one day it stops, and then it's dry season."

Rachael glanced at her as if she might be kidding. She was not.

The security guard at the gatehouse, politely dour, ignored the cameras one hundred feet away and asked them for ID. He took their Locard badges into his workstation, so well air-conditioned that condensation trickled down the open glass door, through which he kept an eye on them. His work space appeared to have enough electronic screens and equipment to operate the space station, an overstuffed couch, and a full kitchen. Nice that Martin Post provided pleasant working conditions, even for an apparent ex-WWF bodybuilder who looked as if he'd have been equally at ease chowing down an MRE in an Afghan desert.

She also noticed no less than three cameras aimed at them and their car, undoubtedly beaming their photos to the main house for confirmation that the two women were expected. Only one lane leading into the estate, and one to let a car back out. Not a drive designed to welcome a crowd and without a chance to dart around another vehicle while the gate lifted. The gate itself went far beyond a single wooden stick across the lane, made of thick stainless steel bars with only enough gap between each slat to allow Florida winds but not a human being. Of course, if Ellie had more money than the GDP of many first-world nations, she would consider security worth paying for too.

The guard gave her the go-ahead and she drove forward into the masses of greenery. She only knew a house existed at the end of the two-lane road by a glimpse of its uppermost floors over the tops of the mangroves. It took longer than she expected to get there, but at last the wild vines parted and a campus of concrete and glass appeared to spring up from the ground. The drive split into three directions with no indication of what might be where, so, true to form, she continued on the middle one.

Boxy, concrete garages sat on either side, more like an industrial park than a home. The door of one stood open with a lithe woman visible inside; she stood in front of a workbench holding a belt sander. "That's the wife," Rachael said.

Ellie stopped the car and they got out.

The woman was not alone. A man, also thirtyish and attractive with dark, perfectly cut hair and a slender form. But he wore a suit complete with tie while she had on a white tank top and crumpled khaki shorts that probably would cost Ellie a week's salary.

The young man's hand rested on the woman's arm, gently, an almost pleading look on his face. "Are you sure you even want to do this?"

"It's too late for that."

He dropped his hand. "You're right. It is."

They both noticed the Locard women at the same time. Before they got close enough to greet, he added, to the woman, "Please get the time to me as soon as you can. I've got everyone's schedule coordinated for that one narrow window, and if we miss that he'll lose the opportunity to bid at all."

"I understand."

"And I'm very sorry for your loss."

"Thank you, Tomas."

Rachael's shadow on the floor alerted the woman; she set the sander down and turned. The young man nodded to them as he left the garage, while the woman wiped her hands on her clothes and tried for a smile, starting with Rachael. "You're Dr. Davies." A statement, not a question. "And Dr. Carr. I'm Dani. I'm Martin's wife."

Ellie shook the hand offered, the firm fingers lightly coated with dust. "What are you building?"

It seemed a safe bet for a conversational gambit. Ellie had

negotiated so many "news" in her life that a careful approach had become second nature. Stay quiet and polite, don't tick anyone off, don't choose allies too quickly. Get the lay of the land first. Keep a pleasant expression glued to your face at all times. Good advice for infiltrating unfamiliar families or second grade or world-class teaching institutes. Or the households of the ultra-rich.

"A bookshelf." The woman's smile deepened a millimeter or two, as if embarrassed. "The last thing we need, but this is how we cope with stress. Martin writes code, and I work with wood. Come this way, I'll take you to him."

Martin Post's wife had ice-blue eyes under a shock of artfully cut blond hair that swished with each step, and stood about Ellie's height but at least fifteen pounds lighter. Her skin, figure, nails, the arch of each eyebrow were all perfect, yet she didn't seem to care that her stress-release hobby had left her with two deep scratches on her right forearm and an angry patch at her left wrist, perhaps where the sander had jumped its board. Or that she trailed sawdust from her bare feet as she guided them through a door to a cool interior corridor. She hadn't said anything about being Ashley's mother, which seemed likely only if she'd given birth at ten. Maybe fifteen.

They entered an elevator. When Martin Post had asked them to come "to the house," Ellie had expected a mansion, a sprawling example of *Million Dollar Listing* with gold-plated faucets and a fountain in the curved drive. But perhaps "house" was only OakTree slang for "headquarters." Even the elevator consisted of four blank steel walls.

Dani said nothing, so neither did they.

According to the indicator they had passed three levels when the doors split to reveal yet another cool corridor, but at least this one had artwork hung at uniform intervals. Dani moved forward and the two women followed.

The photos were of Martin Post, sometimes with Dani,

sometimes with Ashley. They carried water bottles on a cliff overlooking the Grand Canyon or hiked in Machu Picchu with backpacks and walking sticks, all matted and framed to coordinate with the creamy taupe walls. This family, Ellie thought, values experiences more than gold-plated faucets. Good for them.

They turned the corner and came to the mansion part of the "house." The single room would encompass the entire footprint of her bungalow near Chesapeake. With an outer wall of glass from floor to twenty-foot ceiling, ash wood floors, a kitchen area in the back left corner, a group of seats facing a cold fireplace, it seemed all straight lines and minimalist elegance and smelled faintly of lavender. The muted shades and a spare coffee cup left by the sink didn't make the place much more homey, but homeliness wasn't needed, not when the blue expanse outside the window immediately captured each last synapse of your attention. The Gulf of Mexico churned and flowed and took any human back to their basic, vital foundation, rooting them to their planet and their place on it. *No matter how strong you become*, the water seemed to say, *I'll still be stronger than you. And bigger, and deeper. Eternal.*

Directly below the window she saw part of a pool, then high-end patio furniture scattered across lush green grass, then a spread of mangroves and trees with one wooden boardwalk winding through it. After the trees stopped came a swath of beach; she could only see the thinnest line of sand before it sloped down to the water, the exact edge out of sight. These sections of landscape extended as far as she could see to the right and left. Neighboring houses did not exist.

The waves of the Gulf were rougher than usual, the first tremors of an approaching tropical storm. Fall was the hurricane season, after all. But when she looked down to the ground level, the picture seemed to distort ever so slightly. She realized the glass must be thicker than normal, inches thicker, hurricane and maybe even bullet resistant. Such a calm environment, but then details like that reminded one never to take this oh-so-serene environment at face value.

Nature dominated the view so fully that Ellie almost missed the slender, quiet man standing to the side of it. He came forward and, as his wife had, held out a hand. "Dr. Davies? Dr. Carr?"

He shook Rachael's hand and turned to Ellie, who banged a shin into the sharp corner of the coffee table as she reached him. She had to stifle a grimace while saying, "I'm so pleased to meet you." Then she remembered *why* they were meeting. "I'm sorry it's under these circumstances."

"Me too," he said simply.

The man looked exhausted. Dark hair flecked with gray hung in neglected clumps, and his thin face seemed all the thinner, its lines elongated by grief. Shoulders sagged under a heavy T-shirt and the sinewy arms twitched. His lips were dry and cracked from the dehydration common to fatigue. Though Ellie had never had a child to lose, she knew grief. But she'd known it at an early age, with limited comprehension. Martin Post now knew it in all its myriad, multilevel implications, and it might devour him whole.

"Please sit down," Dani said to them, gently handling the social niceties that he could not.

But Martin Post didn't have time for niceties, and didn't pretend to. He visibly shook off the fog and spoke. "Thank you for coming. I realize it's short notice, but time *is* short. The medical examiner's office is about to release my daughter's body. They've ruled her death accidental."

"Yes," Rachael said.

"My son-in-law will have custody, since he's technically next of kin."

"Yes."

"I need you to examine her body." He took a deep breath, steeling himself to say the next words, the stuff of every parent's most crushing nightmare. "I need you to examine every factor in her life. I don't believe my daughter died in an accident. I believe she was murdered."

Chapter 3

Rachael Davies, in her former life as DC medical examiner, had had many similar conversations with similarly grieving family members. She modulated her voice into the perfect combination of sympathetic and professionally brisk. "What makes you say that?"

"Ashley hung out in boats all her life, motorboats, catamarans, sailboats, you name it. She knew everything about them, had experience with every vagary of the weather—which had been fine that day, a little rain in the afternoon but no particularly high winds. It wasn't as if she'd been in a sailboat, where a gust could have caught the sail. There's no way she'd just fall out and . . . drown." He said the last word reluctantly, as if still unwilling to concede that Ashley had died at all.

"Was it common for her to go out alone like that?"

Martin Post paced as he spoke as if his energy, fueled by grief, would not allow him to stay in one place. Dani silently folded into a leather love seat with a fresh water bottle, and watched him with sad eyes.

"Utterly. She did it almost every day. She said the water was the only place she could think."

"Could Ashley swim?"

Martin said, "Like a shark. We're all pretty big swimmers. Dani's practically a pro. Ashley led the swim team in high school."

"What *is* her medical history? Any chronic illnesses? Hereditary issues? Surgeries?" Asking questions of family members not only gained information, it gave them a chance to focus, could temporarily diffuse the tension of grief.

But Martin only shrugged. "Nothing, really. She had chicken pox in the fourth grade, strep throat a couple of times. Broke her arm when she was eleven—"

"How?"

"Riding. Never was crazy about horses after that. But the worst time . . . we were climbing on Mount Denali—just a low climb, doing a bit of the West Buttress, not going anywhere near the top. Ashley was only fifteen. We started off from the Kahiltna Glacier, but on the second day she fell into a crevasse. She only fell twelve feet and onto snow . . . it wouldn't have done much except knock the wind out of her if she hadn't hit an outcropping on the way down. It cracked her femur."

"Wow," Ellie breathed.

He glanced around as if he'd like to sit and then realized the futility of it, took another step in another direction. "The doctor said later we could have just splinted it and she could have walked out, but we didn't *know* that. She felt sure it was broken, and I believed her, kept thinking about blood clots from the marrow going to her heart or lungs, so I didn't want her to move. It took almost eighteen hours for rescue to get there and rig up a way to lift her out of the bottom of the crevasse. I lay with her the whole time, trying to keep her warm, thinking this was it, I was going to lose her." He put one hand over his eyes, but didn't cry. Rather, it seemed a gesture of utter hopelessness, as if the despair he'd been holding off for the past two weeks had finally eaten its way in. "And when we made it to the hospital, were warm and dry and her leg in a cast and the doctor said she would be fine, I thought, 'At least I'll never have to go through that again.' I guess I was wrong."

The room grew so silent that Rachael could hear the miniature *thumps* as insects collided with the glass windows.

"She's perfectly healthy," Martin said, as if realizing this point needed to be made clear. "She . . . *was* . . . The doctor gave her a gold star every visit. No gestational diabetes, anemia, hypertension, nothing. She had just had the amniocentesis—that was fine too. She hadn't found out what gender it was, yet . . . said she wasn't in a hurry. She said she liked considering the possibilities." He smiled at the memory, lines deepening in his thin face.

"Do you have the autopsy results?" Rachael asked, even more gently. "I haven't seen anything about them."

"They said there was a linear cranial compression leading to a hematoma."

A bump on the skull with some internal bleeding, in other words, possibly from slipping and hitting the head on a hard surface. Perhaps just enough to cause unconsciousness, and if she'd sustained the injury during a fall into the water, fatal since it would cause her to drown. "And"—Rachael chose her words carefully—"you don't agree with that?"

"I've spent hours and hours on boats with her, and never saw her slip. She has the balance of a cat. But she would never take any chances, either—especially in her condition."

"Pregnancy can change things. Babies can shift, throw off one's balance, press on nerves . . ." Not that she would know from personal experience.

"Not her," Martin insisted. Across from Rachael, Dani made the tiniest sound. It could have been a sigh, or it could have been the shift of her slight weight against the leather.

"But—murder," Rachael said. It was quite a leap, but Martin Post wouldn't be the first to make it. She'd been over this ground before. Usually in cases of suicide, where the harsh reality that they couldn't save their loved one sent family members on a desperate search for other explanations, but also in cases of natural death or misadventure. The popularity of forensic-based television shows, of both fictional and true crime types, had only made it worse by portraying every death to have hidden complexities. Rachael could well understand wanting to believe a suicide had only been an unfortunate accident, but it had always escaped her why a parent would want to believe their child had instead been purposely killed by another human being.

At least, it had until Danton came into her life. Now she wasn't so sure.

"There's a number of possibilities." Martin Post's voice became calmer, more methodical, a keen analyst delineating the variables, and she pushed thoughts of her own toddler from her head. "Obviously, I have a lot of money."

Which was like saying the universe had a lot of stars.

"I've made sure our home here is well guarded. Ashley didn't go out often by herself—no reason to, she'd never been much of a shopper, didn't golf, didn't have a club. The water would be the best, maybe only, place to catch her alone. It could have been a kidnapping attempt, she fought too hard—and she would have. They might have been after ransom or access to one of a couple of new products I'm developing. I'm working on a processor that will be the only one used in every device within five years. I'm also finishing up a new strategic defense initiative—a Star Wars–type missile defense system. Corporate espionage or actual espionage, they could have tried to grab Ashley as a bargaining chip."

That sounded like it would make a great movie plot . . .

but it also sounded possible. Even a fraction of Martin Post–type money could make people do extreme things.

"The plan could have been murder from the outset," he went on. "This has put me behind schedule on CurrentSDI—that's our system. Both Donec and EntreRobotics are trying to come up with a competitive design and there's a congressional hearing coming up. If OakTree doesn't have demonstrable, positive test results to show, if I lose even a day's progress, we don't get the contract and the U.S. misses its chance for true physical security during the next fifty years. I know that sounds extreme, but believe me, if you dealt with this world every day—sorry, don't mean to be condescending—but you have to trust me, it's not out of the realm. It really isn't."

"Okay."

"Then there's Greg."

She had wondered when they'd get to him. The grieving young husband, the one she already didn't trust.

Now, Martin paused. Now, he spoke carefully, at least at first. "Let me be clear. I have nothing against my s—Ashley's husband. He would have no financial motive, thanks to a prenup, and as far as I know, he's never been violent or cruel toward her. But he's certainly seemed indifferent. Ashley's—an amazing person. She's been one of my best programmers since she was in high school. Z-Stream? L.A. Pac? The Ch card? She was the founding designer on all of those. But Greg acts like, like he's mentally patting her on the head, isn't she cute thinking she's actually contributing something? Meanwhile, he's only *on* my payroll because of Ashley."

Dani's head made a nervous swivel left and right, as if concerned the not-so-valued son-in-law might be around to overhear.

And Martin backpedaled. "Okay, maybe that's not fair—I did hire him, that's how they met, and he is very talented with video card interfacing. It's been instrumental with the design for this defense contract."

But, Rachael thought, and waited. She glanced at Ellie, seated at the other end of the couch, preternaturally still. Also waiting, and watching.

"But not as talented as he thinks. And he certainly didn't seem to care one way or the other about this baby." He turned to Dani for validation. "Did he?"

"No. He—he'd smile back at her and pretend to be enthused about planning a nursery, but didn't even seem to care about picking out a name or finding out the gender," Dani admitted with apparent reluctance. "He acted as if she were buying a car he'd never drive. As if he were willing to be supportive and do the whole good husband thing even though the whole issue had nothing to do with him. I don't know how else to describe it."

"I see," Rachael said, though she didn't. She didn't so much that perhaps she should cut to the chase. "Mr. Post—"

"Martin."

"—what exactly would you like the Locard to do for you?"

He didn't seem offended, might have been relieved by this return to practical matters. "I want you to examine my daughter's body and see if you agree with the county's conclusion of accidental death. Maybe they're right, and it was just a tragic, freak accident. Maybe the pregnancy or a bad breakfast caused her to get sick or dizzy on the boat and she fell overboard. If so, that's fine, that—would certainly be more palatable than knowing someone did this to her deliberately. But if I don't make absolutely certain, if I don't inspect every last line of code, then . . . I've failed her, as her father."

A hard admission, clearly, from the choke in his voice. Rachael understood. But she also knew that absolute certainty rarely came about in forensic pathology. A human body formed an incredibly complex megaplex of systems, the balance of one affecting all the others while at the same time prodded and influenced by its mechanics, chemistry, and that unprovable entity called emotions.

Rachael was dying to look at Ashley's body, deeply curious about what might have happened to the young woman. But she also needed to be honest, and to protect the Locard by throwing out a few disclaimers. "The Locard appreciates your confidence in us—"

"You've been in the news a lot this past month. I'm impressed that—both of you—could deal with crimes so close to home. I need someone who's going to tell me the truth, no matter what. Even if it's not what I want to hear." A puff of exhaled breath and the ghost of a smile. "*And*, Ellie's uncle used to be my doctor—"

This was a surprise.

To Ellie as well, whose mouth fell slightly open before she snapped it shut. "My uncle? Paul Beck?"

"Indeed. Point is, the Locard does good work. I thought we'd begin with a fifty-thousand-dollar retainer."

"Mr. Post—"

"Martin. Seventy thousand? That's just for your visit today. After that you can charge the same amount by the hour. Any amount, I don't care. Call in any other of your colleagues that you need, get all the minds possible working on this. I'll be frank." He checked his watch. "You responded, and you got here, and I scheduled your examination at the ME's at three. That gives us a hair under one hour. I know evidence disappears the more she decomposes—"

"Martin," Dani protested, very gently.

"It's true, honey. It's biology, and I have to accept its rules. So, Doctors, in the interest of time, may I be so bold as to suggest a division of labor? Dr. Davies could please accompany me to the medical examiner's office—I have to be there, I don't know how territorial they might get—while Dani can take Dr. Carr to examine the boathouse and Ashley's apartments. Is that acceptable?"

Hesitation would be pointless. They *were* the Locard, the Locard *could* use the money, and, Rachael knew, she and Ellie were more than capable of answering questions. Surely the dead young woman deserved that, the girl ordinary in many ways and yet caught in such extraordinary circumstances.

She glanced at Ellie, who clearly couldn't wait to get started, and said, "Yes."

Chapter 4

Ellie thought better of it on her way to the elevator, and suggested to Dani that since the boat resided on the property, she should take a look at it first. Then they could go to the apartment.

"Not a concern," Dani said as she tapped the button. "Ashley and Greg lived here."

"Here?" Ellie squeaked, and the young woman gave her a smile, half amused, half pitying—*you really don't know where you are, do you?*

It turned out, after they'd passed through a living room on the lower level that made the upstairs one look like a break room for staff, and beyond an indoor pool with a long glass aquarium suspended over it like a fallen redwood, that Ashley and Greg had their own wing of the estate. It connected to the main house on the first and third floors, the third containing five guest bedrooms, each with bath, in case the young couple wanted to have friends over, Dani explained. They headed to the second, which consisted of the master bedroom suite plus an office for each, a kitchen, and their own workout room with equipment, matching bikes and treadmills, sauna, steam room, and Jacuzzi.

So yes, the young mother had lived with her parents — but they were hardly talking about a basement rec room with 1970s paneling and cast-off furniture.

Aunt Katey would have tut-tutted. She never actually said so, but Aunt Katey seemed to feel that wealth was wasted on the wealthy, who surely should be able to think of better things to do with it. A low-key revolutionary was Aunt Katey, and the most talkative in a family where questions weren't encouraged . . . except she had certainly never mentioned her brother treating the third-richest man in the country.

Knowing Uncle Paul, he'd have never told his sister, or anyone else. And Martin hadn't *been* the third richest at that point in history.

"Bedroom or office?" Dani asked.

"Bedroom."

She followed Dani into a room of opulent and unmade bedcoverings of silk and fine cotton in sage green, cherry furniture, and the now expected wall of windows overlooking the Gulf. Books and papers cluttered both nightstands, but she assumed the messed-up side of the bed belonged to Greg. His surface had a tech magazine and a can of peanuts. Ashley's had a tube of lip balm, two small bags of Cheez-Its (original flavor), a bottle of hand lotion, a half-empty bottle of water, and the latest Grisham thriller. The room smelled the way it looked, of a faint woodsy air freshener, maybe sandalwood, but with the emptiness it made Ellie think of dust.

All the furniture had been firmly and fairly divided, or so she assumed. Ashley and Greg each had two dressers, one wardrobe, one low chest of drawers topped by mirrors and more shelves, one walk-in closet of apparently twenty by twenty feet at a glance, and a fifty-inch flat screen mounted near the ceiling in opposite corners. Each had their own bathroom. *If we could have had separate bathrooms,* Ellie thought, *I might still be married.*

The room sat awash in white tile, broken up here or there by other muted shades, the countertop along the sink and dressing table a creamy marble. A glass shower stall took up most of one corner, but a perfectly round, white porcelain bathtub sat in the center of the room like a throne. The faucets, Ellie noted, were not gold. More floor-to-ceiling windows—she couldn't help stepping over to them to see how easy it would be to flash the neighbors before slipping into the water.

Not easy at all, since there were no neighbors. But anyone around the huge outdoor pool with its own slide and lazy river could get more in their eyes than the sun.

As if reading her mind, Dani spoke. "It's one-way glass. Clear from this view, but a mirror from outside. It can blind us if we're taking a sunset swim."

The windows faced west, over the Gulf, so Ellie could well imagine. Still, as much as she liked a view, she couldn't quite picture having such a reverse fishbowl for a bedroom.

Dani went on, dropping words like sand through her fingers, in a hopeless, absent conversation with no one. "It also makes the place distinctive when you're out on the water, like a beacon. That's how we know she couldn't have gotten lost, but of course she could have used the GPS if she did."

Beyond the impressive pool and a relatively small yard, the estate turned into a forest of mangrove trees. Their twining branches packed the estate from side to side, a solid green block with only a few boardwalks snaking through the marsh like veins. After perhaps six hundred feet the green turned into the blue of the Gulf and Ellie could see the top half of a small building. From her vantage point, it felt as if no one else existed in the entire state. If you wanted to get far from the madding crowd, you couldn't do much better.

She turned away, focused on the interior once more. "Cool bathtub."

"Thank you." Dani smiled, brief but genuine. She adjusted the sage-green towels on one rack, sliding the fluffy terrycloth a half inch along its pole. "I designed this house. It's how Martin and I met, when he decided to move software operations here and keep hardware in California."

"You're an architect."

Dani smiled again. "I was with an architectural firm . . . more on the artistic design side of things than the structural, but yes, I set the layout of the rooms, the plumbing, most of the landscaping. A big job for a kid from Cat Lake Community College. I was trying so hard to be sophisticated, but that bathtub—totally impractical, and I just had to include it."

Ellie relaxed just a smidge for the first time since approaching the guardhouse. They might be outstandingly rich, but they were still people, with their own tastes, goals, baggage, and whims.

She turned away from the windows and went to the sinks—two of them, for a one-person bathroom, but who was counting? You might be soaking something in one while using the other.

A person's bathroom forms an archive of their health, beginning with the most obvious: prescription medications. Did the person suffer from high blood pressure, colitis, depression, or bronchitis? Then the OTCs—a bulk-size bottle of aspirin, antacids, or sleeping pills? Homeopathic remedies only? Were the bottles recently stocked or near their expiration date? Then, did supplies indicate any chronic issues like dry eyes, bleeding gums, sore muscles? Ellie examined the mirrored cabinet and all the drawers.

No surprises. The very, very rich young woman had the medicine cabinet of the most ordinary citizen. Ibuprofen, bandages, antibiotic cream, clear-skin treatments—most of which, it tickled Ellie to see, were the generic, store-brand versions. Makeup components were slightly more upscale, pricey eyeshadow mixed with cheap, impulse-buy lipsticks. Shampoo decisions seemed to vex her since no less than eleven full-size bottles rested under the sink. Ellie wondered if the maid or housekeeper had to keep track and occasionally clean out the oldest ones, to make room for a new selection. This family *must* have maids, right? No way they were scrubbing their own toilets.

As far as prescription medications went, Ellie found only a hefty bottle of prenatal vitamins with folic acid and DHA.

She turned to ask if Ashley had been having any problems during the pregnancy, but Dani had disappeared.

Four months. She wondered how much Ashley had been showing. In photos she'd appeared pretty slender but that could vary. Some women might only look a little pudgy by this point, others as if they smuggled a football under their shirt. Ellie had learned a lot about pregnancy, what to expect at every stage, studying for it the way she did her homework before every challenge. She had wanted to be completely ready when she went off the pill, when she began charting every cramp and temperature change. When she went on the chlomiphene. When they tried the artificial insemination. When she had been on the phone making an appointment to have her eggs harvested prior to IVF and Adam had walked into the kitchen and said, "Stop."

She finished the cabinets. No illegal drugs at all. This could mean Ashley didn't use them or that she had better sense than to leave them in the room the aforementioned maid must clean daily.

Dani returned, as silently as she had left. "Do you want to check Greg's bathroom?"

What for? she thought, unable to think of any fact about Greg that would assist her in Ashley's autopsy, unless he had some unusual drugs that Ashley, for some reason, had been taking. "I don't see a need. I'm not one-hundred percent sure that would be legal, anyway."

"It's not his house," Dani said. "It's Martin's."

Not *Martin's and mine.* Just Martin's? "Yes, but . . ." Search and seizure laws could get a bit murky with owner's rights, tenant's rights, houseguest's rights, though in any event they weren't particularly relevant since she did not work for a law enforcement agency investigating—what, exactly? She was technically a guest of Martin's, and it seemed clear that he owned the property. Ellie made herself speak more firmly, toeing a legal line she wasn't sure existed. "I only need information potentially relevant to Ashley's physical condition."

Dani sighed, tossed a hairstyle made for tossing. "Just as well—Greg would keep anything incriminating at his man cave anyway. I'm not even sure where that *is.*" This last realization seemed to surprise Dani. People were often stunned by how little they knew about the day to day of their own household. But if there wasn't a reason to ask, a reason to find out, a factor could easily be forgotten—smoke detector batteries, a call-waiting feature, a password.

"Man cave?" Ellie asked.

"It's a storage unit, really, not far away, but he's got it outfitted as both a workshop and a place to hang with his bros and watch sports. I guess I don't blame him. People want a place of their own, you know? And this one is a fishbowl."

But who's tapping on the glass? Ellie wondered. *The news media? Or Martin?*

"I've played with the idea myself. It can be stressful to be filthy rich." She grinned with full knowledge of the insanity, leaning back against the wall as if her back hurt. "But it's even worse knowing that millions depend on your products making their lives better, not worse. Sometimes I want to run away from the enormity too."

When she said nothing more, Ellie asked, "Where *is* Greg, anyway?"

"At the funeral home. Making the arrangements."

Technically correct, since he *was* the legal next of kin. But—"If you don't mind my asking, where is Ashley's mother?"

Dani seemed surprised by the question, almost stunned. "Deborah died when Ashley was seventeen. You didn't know that?"

"Uh—no, I hadn't. I'm sorry—"

"Don't be! I can't tell you what a relief it is to meet someone who doesn't know every single aspect of our lives, from the grade I got in biology to Martin's shoe size." The woman seemed genuinely delighted. Her shoulders relaxed and she said almost cheerfully, "If you're through in here, we can go see the boat."

Chapter 5

Rachael knew a few people with Teslas, but those had been more or less stripped models compared to Martin Post's. The leather seats were butter soft and seemed to form to her back, supporting the lumbar while cooling with more than just the A/C. The car seemed to shimmer over the ground as it parted the media sea with its nose. At least if a reporter got run over it wouldn't be by her.

The crush of paparazzi gave her technicolor flashbacks to the uncomfortable amount of media attention she'd gotten during the murders at the Locard. Messages had come in fast and furious until she'd been forced to turn off her phone and ignore her email. Reporters had camped, literally, on her doorstep until the local cops came by to issue citations. She'd had to push through crowds and learned that polite statements of "can't comment on an open investigation" would be totally ignored, and they would continue shouting questions no matter what—sometimes right in her ear. She never resented them for it; they had the job of asking, and she had the job of not answering.

But that had been nothing like this. There had to be at

least sixty people overwhelming her vehicle, heedless of its damage deductible, forcing her to focus on getting out of there without being consumed whole, as if they were a flock of ravens in *The Birds* and at the slightest spark, would attack, and kill.

When it became clear the car would not stop and no statements would be forthcoming, they dashed to their own vehicles and gave chase. But when all reached their destination twenty-five minutes south, the medical examiner's office had been prepared and waved only the Tesla into their gated parking, locking out anyone else. Amazing, the doors that money could open—and shut.

FBI agent Michael Tyler had also been made keenly aware of the doors that money routinely opened. He and his partner had been dispatched in case Ashley Post Anderson had been kidnapped, a purview of the bureau under these circumstances—Martin Post had been preparing a new piece of national defense equipment. Michael wasn't a super techy guy, but it seemed to be a vast refinement on the Strategic Defense Initiative, or SDI, or Star Wars. That space-based missile defense system had never really become reality due to the astronomical—no pun intended—costs involved. So Post designed a program to bounce signals off every bit of space junk already out there to pinpoint incoming threats, whether they were missiles, nuclear weapons, errant spacecraft or, it sounded like, a reasonably effective slingshot. This also meant that enemies couldn't simply take out satellites installed for this reason prior to the attack, because there would be no such designated satellites. Sounded like a great idea—if it worked. Whether it did or not might not matter. Just as Reagan had freaked out the USSR by acting like we had it, if foreign enemies or business competitors even *thought* Post could produce it, what better way to get him to cough it up than threaten the life of his only child?

"Coffee, partner?" Luis Alvarez asked him.

"Thanks, but . . . I'm not really down with eating or drinking anything in this place."

Luis fired up the Keurig with an unnecessary flourish. "Don't be such a baby. I think this is the cleanest government facility I've ever been in. And all the dead bodies are up the hall, behind an airlock."

They sat in the break room at the medical examiner's office, waiting for the second autopsy of Ashley Post Anderson to begin. As Luis had pointed out, the white surfaces gleamed, tidy and scrubbed. A dish drainer held washed mugs and the counters were lined with a prodigious array of teas, sweeteners, creamers, and other mix-ins, granola bars, disposable cups, and a school program's candy bars sold on the honor system with *$1* scrawled on a manila envelope.

"There's airborne stuff. Tuberculosis. Meningitis. Hepatitis."

"Hepatitis isn't—"

"And no matter how much Tyvek you suit up or how you take your gloves off, it can never be perfect."

Luis shook his head and drank his coffee. He seemed to live on coffee, existing as a constant hum of barely suppressed energy. He made a great yin to Michael's yang, apparently outgoing and apparently friendly and diving in to every interview with every victim, witness, or suspect as if they might be the most fascinating person he'd ever met.

This left Michael to stand back, observe, maybe intimidate a little with his height and his muscles and his much-less-approachable face.

None of that would help now. Ashley Post Anderson had passed the point of being either intimidated by him or comforted by Luis. And since she *hadn't* been kidnapped, Michael didn't see why they were there at all. Certainly there was no reason for the FBI to be involved in a boating accident. Even if she was murdered, that would be a case for the local cops, not him.

But little jurisdictional facts like that didn't matter when Daddy had more money than God, and couldn't accept that his little girl fell out of her boat. Tragic, yes. Michael had two children with his ex-wife, shared custody, and if he had lost one of them he would probably have to be sedated into a coma for six months, so he got it. He definitely got it.

But if Ashley Post Anderson had been killed by foreign or domestic agents bent on possessing the nation's next great defense—yeah, that warranted FBI interest. He needed to figure out if that was the case, and figure it out quickly because such an attack would need a good chunk of FBI resources and not just the two agents currently wandering around Florida wondering what the hell they were supposed to do.

One of the doctors—Michael stupidly wished they'd wear tags, since he'd have to list everyone's name in his report—poked her head in. "We're ready to start. I'll have to get you suited up."

Luis dropped his half-full paper cup into the trash with an expression of deep regret.

The doctor provided them with disposable masks, gloves, gowns, and booties to go over their shoes—PPE, Personal Protective Equipment. Michael felt like a badly dressed clown, but any barrier between him and the dead seemed like a good idea and at least they didn't need to wear face shields, the clear welder-type masks, or goggles, or sleeves. They wouldn't, he resolved, be getting that close to the action.

The staff, so far, had been courteous and helpful while not exactly friendly, which Michael found unsurprising. No workplace appreciates having outsiders watch over their shoulder and interrupt their daily routines. But there was crazy money in Naples, and they had no doubt gotten used to catering to people like Martin Post.

Another doctor awaited them in the autopsy suite, swathed to the eyeballs in disposable white garments so that Michael could only vaguely tell that the person was female, until she said, "Michael."

"Rachael? Dr. Davies? What are you—"

She seemed as surprised as he felt. "What are *you*—oh, that's right, you're in violent crimes now. I suppose you could turn up anywhere in the world."

Before he could respond, the other pathologist muttered, "Great, Old Home Week," and ordered the body brought in.

Rachael explained her presence in a few brief and quiet sentences, leaving Michael in a flood of mixed feelings. Post had not only called in the FBI but the Locard? Who else might turn up? Michael knew the Locard, and trusted it. But this situation looked to be either a grief-crazed, overrich father or a sort of terrorist action, and he lacked experience with either. Therefore he didn't even want this case, and he certainly didn't want it if it came with a bunch of outside interference.

But of course what he wanted didn't matter, so he took a breath and focused.

He had seen the other doctor giving a brief statement to the media; she had done the original autopsy. Michael wondered if she considered it a professional insult that Rachael had been called in, but they seemed to chat amicably enough. Doctors conferred with other doctors all the time, after all, so it must not be a big deal to them. He wondered if Ellie Carr had arrived as well.

After these observations, he had no choice but to look at the victim on the table—what had been left of Ashley Post Anderson, a beautiful, bright, healthy, pregnant twenty-five-year-old.

It barely looks human. He banished that thought as if someone might overhear it.

The face had bloated beyond recognition, the lips and nose oversized, cheeks bulged out. Small aquatic animals had been nibbling around the eyes and mouth as well. Only the hair seemed the right color and length or he might wonder if they were looking at a different person entirely. Thick black lines ran under the skin like a loose tangle of strings, the veins having darkened as the blood in them became solid. And the *smell*. He used to wear swimmers' nose plugs under his mask, but quickly learned that they hurt and also made him look like a total weenie. Still, they were the only thing that really worked.

Luis, he noticed, stayed near the door, perhaps regretting that half a cup of coffee.

The skin on Ashley's hands had wrinkled so much it pulled away from the layer beneath it, forming tattered gloves. Rachael brought these hands close to her face mask.

"We did scrape the nails," the other doctor said, as if wearily anticipating an obvious question. "The three-carat rock on the left hand was returned to the husband. It was our first point of ID."

"Immersion creates so much difficulty," Rachael said. "My General Chem teacher, Dr. Wolff, always told us: 'Water is the universal solvent. Given time, it will dissolve anything.'"

"Even a body?" Michael asked, forcing himself to breathe through his nose. Breathing through his mouth, even behind a mask, still might pull in too many contaminants and the throat didn't have cilia to protect it like the nose did. Also, breathing through the mouth unleashed too many flavors of that morning's breakfast, and not in a good way. He should have brushed his teeth.

"We'll never know," Rachael answered him. "Flesh doesn't last long enough in the water to prove it."

"Because it decomposes," Luis said from his spot near the door.

"Yes, exactly. The cells break down, lyse, fall apart. So it is dissolving, but from the inside out."

Luis added, "One week in air equals two weeks in water equals eight weeks in the ground. See, I paid attention in your class."

Rachael promised him a gold star. "And once out of the water, putrefaction takes off at an accelerated rate, as if making up for lost time. Even refrigerating the body won't put the rate back to normal. The process is even faster in stagnant fresh water, without moving currents or salinity. But this was the ocean, so the bacterial growth would be somewhat retarded. And it's deeper? Colder?" She looked to the other doctor for confirmation.

"It's the Gulf. It's still pretty warm, having had all summer to absorb those rays. Clearly she's been dead the whole two weeks."

Michael wondered why that was clear.

Rachael asked the other doctor, "You don't see any defensive wounds, do you? I don't, at least nothing significant."

"Yeah, they all appear postmortem—my guess. I can't be sure."

"There's scratches," Michael said, pointing to the numerous small gashes along the blackened arms. He had moved forward despite himself.

"Yes, but that's common in water deaths. Though the salt in the water increases buoyancy, a dead body will usually sink. They'll eventually move upward as the tissues start to bloat, but regardless of all that, no matter how or when or where they went into the water, the usual position for them to assume is facedown. The extremities sort of dangle, and as the current moves them around, their hands and feet brush against rocks and coral on the bottom. Thin, soft tissue areas like the hands or neck would disappear the quickest, so the body starts falling apart at the fingers and toes and moves inward." As she spoke, Rachael continued down the length of the body, the thighs, the legs, noting how the feet showed the same scrapes and shallow cuts.

"But she didn't lose fingers, if you still found her wedding ring," Michael pointed out.

The original pathologist said, "She lost some—see?" She seemed to take a wicked delight in holding up the partly dismembered right hand and watching Michael's reaction. The fingers were missing, the smallest one chewed off at the second knuckle. Bile rose in his throat.

"Did she have any clothing?" Rachael asked—maybe because the question just occurred to her, maybe to buy him time to get his stomach back on the non-puking line.

"Shorts," the other doctor said. "Panties, sports bra."

"No shirt?"

"Nope."

Michael said, "So she was walking around in her bra." He found that a little odd, but then he'd never been a twenty-five-year-old pregnant woman alone on a hot Florida afternoon.

Luis said, "Post released a video to the media, apparently the boathouse camera, that showed Ashley driving away. It was hard to tell, light-colored fabric and so bright out, but she seemed to be wearing a shirt. You can only see a glimpse of her under the roof of the boat."

"Hardtop," the first doctor corrected.

"Yeah—that. You can see her hair and her arms. It *looked* like she had on something, with sleeves, like elbow length."

The original doctor spoke to no one in particular. "So she probably had a shirt but took it off because of the heat, and it then blew off the boat. We have a monsoon, high winds, just about every day during this season here—you know that, right?"

She made eye contact with each of her three guests until they acknowledged that yes, Florida weather differed greatly from DC.

"She and the boat had been floating around for a week. It would have gone through a number of storms during that time."

Rachael continued. "No shoes or socks?"

Luis said, "Sandals. They were found in the boat."

"Huh. So they found her shoes but not her laptop . . . weird. Bare feet could have made things slippery, if it rained, if she spilled her drink, if she stood on the back edge, or the tip."

The first doctor muttered, "Stern. Bow." Then the two doctors moved on to the head, poring over a shaved patch of skin on the scalp. Their conversation involved "linear compression" and "hematoma" and Rachael found a tiny fleck of something caught in the hair that interested her.

"We found a piece of that too. You can keep that sample—there's envelopes on that tray behind you," the first doctor told her, and was thanked as if she'd turned over a box wrapped in shiny paper and tied with a bow. Michael wondered about people who chose to spend their lives slicing up dead bodies.

The scalp had already been cut and separated from the skull, the skull already sawed open and the brain removed. "This is the only evidence of hematoma I found," the first doc explained, pointing to a dark red patch within the dark red underside of the scalp. And you can see the bone reaction here—hard to tell, but there's a very slight fracture."

"Would it be enough to knock her unconscious?" Michael asked. Both doctors turned to look at him.

"You know they hate it when you ask that, bro," Luis spoke from his perch at the doorway.

"I know. But I still have to try."

Rachael smiled under her mask. He could tell from the way her eyes crinkled at the corners.

The other one did not. "I couldn't make such a conclusion based on that. It's a very tiny fracture."

Then—reluctantly, it seemed to Michael—they moved on to the abdomen. Or rather where the abdomen, and the baby that had been inside it, was supposed to be, because nothing remained except flaps of skin. Michael already knew from the first autopsy that everything had been missing up to and including the bottom of the lungs. If Michael looked, something he'd been avoiding, he could see the woman's spine. "What would eat her like that?"

"Lots of things," Rachael said absently. She and the other doc were using their hands to spread out the remaining skin, trying to reconstruct the covering, but too much of it had disappeared. "Turtles, fish, crabs, shrimp. Sharks. Some eat carrion, but most sharks eat only live prey."

"Will any kind of fish do that?"

"No, some are herbivores."

"So there's meat-eating fish in the Gulf?"

Rachael said, "They don't have to be big fish. Minnows can make a good dent in animal proteins."

"But why just her stomach?" Michael asked.

"It's a large mass of soft tissue. Or she could have received some injury as the waves tossed her around, maybe ripped her skin on coral, and that gave the animals an entry point. You didn't find any nicks on the ribs?" she asked the original doctor, who said no. The breastbone and front half of the ribs had already been removed in the first autopsy. It sat to one side, resting against a thigh.

"Is it possible someone took the baby from her?" The idea made Michael queasy, but it had to be considered. It had happened more than once in the world's history, and maybe someone thought the rich guy's grandchild would be an easier hostage to control than his strong, fully grown child.

Or maybe someone really wanted a baby.

Rachael said, "It would certainly explain the damage to the abdomen when the rest of the body is basically intact."

The original doctor was shaking her head. "Four months? It would never survive. Maybe in pediatric ICU, but out somewhere on a boat?"

Rachael nodded. "It would be *extremely* risky. A baby born at four months in the best hospital NICU would face tremendous hurdles. Out on a boat somewhere, well, that would be a very bad plan." She had become interested in the dead woman's backbone, bending so close that her face shield knocked against a cut rib. "What do you think this is?"

The other doc bent with her, and they discussed a small cut in one of the lower vertebra. Michael listened to them trade terms like perimortem, plastic deformation, sharp right angle, beveled fractures, and other unintelligible stuff. It seemed to add up to a possible injury close to the time of death, an injury to Ashley's spine. From the inside.

His interest in the case had been dragging its feet, but now it picked up the pace to a low trot. "What does that mean? She was stabbed?"

"Maybe," the first doctor said. The way she drew out the word made her disinclination clear.

"Maybe," Rachael said. "It's a stretch. The damage seems smooth and with an obtuse angle, indicating perimortem—about the time of death. It would be unlikely to look like that if due to damage sustained after decomposition, such as from waves crashing her into objects on the sea floor, and there's no sign of healing, so not antemortem—well before death. But it's almost a squarish indentation, not sharp like a knife. It *would* explain the disproportionate animal predation."

"So—someone stabbed her? With something?"

The two doctors exchanged a look. Rachael said, "Possibly. But I can't be sure."

"That's not helpful, Doc."

"I know." She seemed genuinely sorry about it.

Chapter 6

In the disrobing area—which Luis had fun pointing out, as in "Let's meet in the disrobing area"—Michael ripped off all the gowning like Prometheus shedding his chains, and with about as much relief.

Luis did the same. "So whaddawe got, partner? A murder, or not?"

"Don't know. But Rachael knows what she's talking about, and—c'mon, we've seen bodies. Animals eat where there's already an opening. But we don't know how she got overboard. There could have been an injury and that's what invited in the animals . . . but even Rachael isn't sure it's from a weapon. So what we have is a towering load of 'maybes.'"

"And we're going to err on the side of caution and assume murder?"

"Temporarily."

"Who the hell would stab a pregnant lady in the stomach?" A storm brewed across Luis's face, no doubt picturing his own wife, glowing while expecting any one of their three children. "What do we do now? I say we—"

"Get a jump on it."

"Talk to the—"

"Husband."

"If even a hint of this comes out—"

"In the press. Or, worse, to the family, before we can pre-pare them—"

"Total nightmare. And, it's always the husband."

"Almost always. The rich father gives off weird vibes too. So—good/bad cop? Or *someone can't afford to act uncoop-erative?*"

"Latter. He's got Daddy breathing down his neck." Luis pitched his last bootie in the designated bin. "That's why we get along so well, partner. We think alike."

Rachael came into the room and, like the men, wasted no time in pulling off the disposable protection, now smeared with decomposition fluids and oils, and Michael appreciated that she didn't come too close.

He asked her: "You think she was murdered? Or at least received an injury due to a weapon?"

"I think she received an injury—" Rachael began.

"Can you describe the weapon?"

"Sure—if this were a TV show. But out here in reality, no, I can't begin to guess. It's very small and, without the sur-rounding flesh . . . it doesn't look like any knife nick I've ever seen. But an injury would explain the massive predation to her abdomen." She bundled the PPE and stuffed it into a biohazard disposal bin.

"What does Post expect you to do?"

"What parents usually want from medical examiners—closure. It's his child. He wants to know he did everything he could."

"I doubt what you found will be very comforting."

She spoke with regret. "I know. It doesn't have to be a man-made injury, even as acute as it—Ashley could have been bounced out of the boat on a wave and caught in the propeller, though I don't see how it could cut all the way to her spine without hitting any limbs. I've texted Ellie to look for anything in the boat that could cause such a deep injury."

So Ellie Carr had also arrived in Florida. "She's at the boat?"

But Rachael was still theorizing. "Ashley could have been tossed in the water, and then impaled on something. It's a big ocean—who knows what's out there."

"Killer octopuses," Luis said. "Or should that be octopi?"

"Octopuses," Rachael said.

"Or a stingray," he went on, more serious now. "Like what killed the Crocodile Hunter guy."

Rachael appeared to give this some thought.

A murderous animal would make everyone happy, Michael knew. A freak accident with an unthinking beast, not a malicious entity threatening the Post family and beyond them, the nation's security.

Problem was, he couldn't see a stingray making off with Ashley Post Anderson's laptop.

Chapter 7

Ellie followed Dani through yet another set of elevators and hallways and out to an outdoor pool large enough for professional athletes to train in. A three-story cage of mesh screens protected the area from dead leaves and wildlife and mosquitos. Tasteful and extremely comfortable-looking lounge chairs lined the edge—four chairs, Ellie noticed. Four and only four. A round teak table under a canvas awning rested at the shallow end, with, again, four chairs. This place existed for Post's core family, not staff, not parties, not press junkets. Clearly, the people who lived there craved privacy above all, and it took murder to let a stranger like her cross the threshold.

Or, they just had no social life.

"Deborah, going to the boat."

Dani spoke these words in a firm, clear voice as she pushed open the screen door leading to the yard, holding it for Ellie, as Ellie's brain tried to sort out this last comment. Who was she—

A disembodied tone, two pleasant notes, tinkled through the air.

"What was . . . who—"

Dani didn't slow, her feet—now clad in flip-flops kept next to the rear door—crunching the mulch underneath them as she headed up a path toward the boardwalk. "It's a smart home. The assistant app is wired throughout. If you need anything, just tell her."

Ellie skipped to catch up. "Something like Alexa?"

"Basically. Only, because Martin designed it, much more complex," she added with a smile of either amusement or pride. "It's mostly a safety thing. All of us wind up being alone here a lot, doing things you're really not supposed to do alone, swimming, bathing, boat—Even hiking through these trees. So we tell Deborah where we're going."

He named the smart assistant voice after his dead *wife*?

Ellie stole a look at his current wife, but Dani's face remained the same gentle blank, not so much adhering to the party line as simply thinking about something else entirely. Maybe she had enough self-assurance not to be threatened by constantly hearing her husband speak to her predecessor. Maybe she thought it would be a comfort to Ashley, as if her own mother were still looking out for her. Maybe she had suffered loss as well, and understood. Ellie understood too. She'd have talked to even an electronic version of her mother, Claire, all day and all night if smart assistants had existed in her youth.

Ellie also wondered who insisted on as much solitude as possible—Martin, a reclusive genius? Dani, who'd probably had a normal existence until she'd married into tech royalty? Greg, who had made it inside the gates and now wanted to raise the drawbridge? Maybe Ashley hadn't wanted to share her father with the world? Or a stepmother barely older than herself?

Maybe all four. Ellie didn't know much about being rich and famous, but she knew that that sort of pervasive, unrelenting attention could have disastrous effects.

They plunged into the mangrove forest, through a tunnel of spiny, twining branches, all green leaves on top and a tangle of bare sticks on the bottom. The foliage created a bit of spotty, claustrophobic shade, but Ellie still felt the sweat begin to slide out of her pores. Wood-colored planks of reconstituted plastic wound through the trees, sometimes over earth, sometimes over pools of brackish water. Clumps of mangroves not only protected the coast from erosion and helped scrub the environment of carbon dioxide and trace metals, they provided an ecosystem for a truly incredible amount of life. The roots were rich in tannin and could turn a smaller canal to the color of tea, so that water appeared dirty or polluted while actually healthy.

"Is it recorded? D—the smart assistant's information?"

Dani anticipated Ellie's question. "Yes. Ashley told her she was going to the boat at nine fifty-three a.m. on Friday, two weeks ago. Fifteen days ago. It was Deborah who first alerted us that she hadn't returned within her usual window of time. That's what I mean by a more complex program."

Interesting. "What about cameras? Surveillance video? I saw the bank of monitors at the guardhouse—"

"No cameras," Dani said, switching her water bottle from one hand to the other. "Those are the security feeds of the perimeter. Not the interior of the estate."

"None at all? The house, the pool? Boathouse?"

"Of course not," Dani said with a touch of annoyance. "This is our *home*, Dr. Carr."

They were so concerned about security . . . but it made sense. People who were incredibly sick of the world following their every move would hardly want their own household doing the same thing.

A gust of wind caught the branches and they gave a mighty shake, a tropical storm named Hazel making its way from the Caribbean. Unlike the tornados from Ellie's early childhood, ocean disturbances usually gave plenty of warning. This allowed one a few days to put up shutters and bring more lightweight items in from the yard—or do nothing, depending on one's personal level of alarm.

Dani checked a text message, then shoved the phone—an OakTree product, of course—back into her pocket.

Ellie said, hoping to prompt a more helpful conversation, "I'm sorry, I know you must have a million things to do right now."

Dani gave a sharp shake of the head, though at what, Ellie couldn't guess. "This takes priority." Then, perhaps realizing that sounded harsh, she went on. "It's the scheduled test. Tomas has to herd all the cats on his side, and I have to do the same with OakTree. Believe it or not, Martin has never had a government contract before, and he had no idea what he was getting in to."

"It's complicated?"

"It's *beyond* complicated. It's—have you ever been involved in government contracting?"

"Nope. That's always been above my pay grade."

Aside from the distant cawing of a seagull, she could hear nothing over the breeze, no cars, lawn mowers, conversations of neighbors having a pool party. Ayn Rand had to be right about one thing: what common folk like Ellie craved was privacy, and the rich could afford it. Martin Post could have as much peace and quiet as he could stand . . . well, quiet, at any rate. Peace, maybe not so much.

Into this quiet Dani explained. "It's a highly regulated process, and for something this major, spanning years. When DOD put out an RFP—that's a Request for Proposals—about missile defense, Martin got interested because he'd been daydreaming about using satellites for a while. I had to boil his daydreams down to the specific spaces on the proposal form . . . but we should have started the year before when they put out the RFI."

Birds, ever-present in Florida, chirruped and tweeted away. More than once Ellie caught sight of a snake beating a hasty retreat through the marshy pools. Most area snakes were harmless; there were only four venomous varieties in south Florida and of those, only diamondbacks and cotton-mouths were likely to be found around salty water.

Best, however, to stay on the path. She focused on the issue at hand rather than fangs and venom. "RFI?"

"Request for Information. That's what the government does when it wants to know what's out there, what's possi-ble, and how it can solve their problem. Most companies pay attention, and when there's something that falls in their wheelhouse, they'll respond. Of course, what they advise the government needs is what their company provides— which is perfectly legal. But it gets the contracting agencies familiar with you, a foot in the door. Martin skipped all that—not intentionally, but . . . it left us with a huge learning curve."

Her voice dipped in a way that made Ellie think a lot of that curve had been draped across her shoulders. "I can understand that."

"Government contracting is a relationship game—and I don't mean that in a good old boy, back-slapping way. Agencies have to know that the company actually knows what they're talking about and that they can actually deliver what they promise. If they can't, disaster; now they've wasted time and resources and have to start all over. And as huge as OakTree is, as astounding its reputation, we don't have that established relationship. Like Tomas says, missile defense is not a new cell phone."

Ah, the handsome Tomas. "Does Tomas work for Oak-Tree?"

"No, he's with the DOD."

"Defense."

"Yes, Air Force. And he didn't mean to hurt my feelings, with the cell phone comment. He's just being honest. He's the linchpin to the process, literally the most important person in the whole situation."

"Really?" More important than Martin?

"Yes," Dani said, as if she'd heard Ellie's thought. She spoke firmly, the loose bottoms of her shoes slapping against the boardwalk. "The contracting officer is the only one who has the authority to sign the contract. He can't be ordered to by a superior officer or obligated to by a set of standards. So no matter what the generals think, he can say yes or no. Of course, it's a much smoother process if they're happy with his decision—and if he okays a company that fails to deliver it's going to reflect on his judgment. His warrant could be reduced, and so on."

"Warrant?"

"How much money he's authorized to spend. If your product costs two million and he's only warranted for one, then it doesn't matter how much he loves it, it's not going to work. But Tomas has an unlimited one so that's not a problem here."

"Wow."

"Yes, he's good at what he does. And when he's got his twenty with the Air Force he can walk into a lobbying job . . . he'll be a millionaire in six months. Nice work if you can get it."

Ellie waved away a mosquito buzzing around one ear and murmured an agreement. She had learned a lot about lobbying earlier that year.

The tunnel of branches came to an abrupt end, and there was the ocean. A brilliant blue sky and a brilliant blue body of water, only partially blocked by a warehouse that had been painted to match but didn't, quite. As large as an air-

THE DEEPEST KILL   49

port hangar and about as attractive, its long, plain walls had been topped with a few high windows. Good thing the plant life hid most of it from the house—it didn't do much for the view.

"There's the boathouse," Dani said, unnecessarily.

They followed the boardwalk over the sandy ground to the entrance, one door with a simple knob—no lock. Inside, however, Ellie could see why—the building had no wall facing the ocean, only a half-gate-like barrier to keep the waves from knocking into the boats moored there. Locking the door would be pointless if someone really wanted to get in.

One yacht and two motorboats bobbed in the water, secured to individual fingers of docking. The yacht appeared bigger than Paul and Joanna's house, disproportionately huge against the interior attempting to contain it. *Mirrormere* read the script along its stern, a name Ellie recognized from *The Lord of the Rings*. The length ran at least two hundred feet and she could see four levels above the waterline. To her slight disappointment, Dani continued along the back wall and past that mountain of boat, to the other side of the building. Two vessels, dinghies by comparison—identical motorboats, about forty or forty-five feet long. Hardtops, two engines, bow seating. Their sterns read *Wicked* and *Phantom*.

"Your favorite Broadway plays?" Ellie asked without thinking.

"Ashley's," Dani said. Her voice caught a bit when she added, "It was *Phantom*."

She waved a hand at the boat without actually looking at it, the boat from which her stepdaughter had disappeared. Ellie felt some of the air leak from the space. Just a boat, floating gently in its moorings, stubbornly silent about what had taken place aboard its fiberglass.

Ellie approached. The moving water under the wooden decks, the trapped air flow, made her slightly dizzy. Normally she loved the water, any water, which brought back memories of exploring the marsh behind her grandmother's house, swimming in Lake Erie with her cousins and Aunt Rosalie, and canoeing down the New River in West Virginia with Aunt Katey and Uncle Terry, who never seemed to have as much control over the vessels as they should have. But this dimmed interior brought up memories less benign. Ones that went back before summers with her cousins, even before her grandmother's marsh. Ones more primal.

Ellie shook them off. Ashley Post Anderson's unfortunate demise was her first client assignment for the Locard, and she wouldn't blow it. Not for herself, not for Ashley Post Anderson, not for her unborn child.

She could have guessed which boat from the dingy coating of fingerprint powder over nearly every surface. The county techs got an A for Effort . . . the black rubbed off on her fingers when she grabbed the railing for support, but at least she didn't have to worry about touching things. Clearly they would have already gotten any fingerprints, though after a week in the sun and the salt spray and the daily rains—Ellie would bet there hadn't been any, at least not on the upper deck.

The *Phantom* shifted only slightly as she stepped on board. Hardly any current made it into the boathouse and the boat would have good stabilizers. Ashley could easily have handled the vessel by herself, whereas she would have needed a crew to take out the *Mirrormere*.

White vinyl seats lined a small stern area, equipped with plenty of cup holders, footrests, a live well and rigging station, as well as a mini fridge and grill top for cooking up your catch au naturel. "Did Ashley like to fish?"

Dani remained on the dock, checking her phone. "Sometimes, if the rest of us were, but she could take it or leave it. She wouldn't have bothered going out just to fish—she'd go out to be alone, unplug, work on her programs. She said the code really came to her out there, without any distractions."

"And she'd do that often?"

Dani nodded. "Two, three times a week. More if she was having trouble with a program."

Ellie could no more write code than she could write Sanskrit. "What did she work *on*? A—"

"Laptop. It has not been found. Martin tried the Locate feature but it couldn't find a signal, so it's been turned off or is lying on the bottom of the Gulf somewhere. Or destroyed, by—by whoever took her. If someone did." Murder/kidnapping were Martin's theories. Ellie wondered if Dani had any of her own.

Ashley could have somehow dropped the laptop overboard, Ellie thought. Certainly, if it were that vital to her work, she would have gone in after it and been overwhelmed by the waves. Or she and the laptop could have both fallen in. "Did she back it up to the Cloud?" Ellie asked. "Can the project proceed without—"

"Oh yes. I'm sure it uploaded every day when she returned, so it's only whatever she did that day that would be lost. I don't know the details, but I gather from Martin it's not us getting the laptop back that's important. What's important is that no one else gets it."

Competitors. That made sense.

Ellie did another visual survey of the deck, looking for where Ashley could have slipped, or stood on something and overbalanced. The stern had two small jet skis parked on a platform between the stern and the engines, low enough for each to slip into the water without much difficulty. The platform extended out on either side of the outboards for swimmers to climb aboard. The extra area would increase drag, but clearly the ship had been designed for pleasure boating, not racing.

If Ashley had gone overboard with the engines running, to swim or due to a fall, the boat might have gotten away from her until she couldn't stay afloat any more. The Gulf wasn't the ocean but still unthinkably vast. Southwest Florida waters were popular, but a weekday in rainy season would not be their peak time—there could easily be no other boat in sight. Many, many things could have happened, writing a cautionary tale about boating alone. The image made Ellie shudder. "Did she like to swim off the boat?"

Martin had said they were all big swimmers, but this question seemed to stump Dani. "Sometimes. I guess . . . but then her clothes would still be aboard."

"Of course." Unless she decided to jump in with her clothes on—she wouldn't have been wearing much in that heat. And hot flashes were common during pregnancy.

Ellie moved on. The helm had two cushy, swivel seats, a console full of electronics, and a shiny chrome steering wheel. Powder coated each surface there as well, exposing water spots and other dirt, sticky areas on the knobs and console. She examined the electronics, their screens dark. "And the GPS works?"

"Yes. It was checked, but of course only retains stored destinations, and she hadn't programmed in a new location in months. It doesn't record every path the boat takes. We have an antitheft tracker on it, but its battery recharges when the boat's hooked up to power at the dock. Martin thinks it must have worn down and wouldn't hold a charge, and she was out there so long it just died. He blames himself for not checking it sooner instead of just calling her cell over and over." Misery filtered through her voice. She loved Martin, and Martin was enduring the "if onlys" torment of a grieving parent.

"Did the cell have GPS tracking on it?"

"It had an app installed, but apparently she'd turned it off. At least that's what *Greg* said."

Boats came with a host of storage areas, places to keep everything from live fish to paper charts safe from rain, gusts of wind, and a shifting surface. She made sure not to miss any.

Behind a nearly hidden door underneath the steering column she found a collection of laminated maps and two knives. One, an evilly sharp filet knife, had a glossy blue handle, and the other showed spots of rust along the eight-inch blade. Neither seemed particularly clean, but she would collect them anyway. Martin had told her anything she wanted, and it seemed stupid to overlook such an obvious weapon. But with a layer of oily grime on both blades, neither seemed of likely interest.

Technicians had clearly fingerprinted the steering wheel, wanting to know if Ashley had been the only driver that day. The boat had been found drifting—if someone else boarded and overtook the woman, where would they have driven it to, only to turn it loose again? Too bad the GPS didn't record all movement, but of course that wasn't the purpose of a GPS.

Ellie found her attention grabbed by a spot on the wheel where the fingerprint powder had accumulated. Not a print, only a messy pool of something sticky. Residue from a greasy snack? Fish guts?

Ellie opened her kit and rubbed a pair of moistened swabs on the spot. The swabs went into a box and the box went into a manila envelope, which she sealed and labeled. She noted another such spot on the gunwale near a cleat and collected that too. Almost certainly pointless, but she had no better ideas.

The buzz of her phone cut through Dani's expression. "I—they can't be done already—"

She clicked it to speaker, perhaps thinking that Ellie might need information from the autopsy. "Yeah, hon, what—"

Martin Post's voice: "That videoconference today. I forgot."

His wife checked her watch. "Yeah . . . ten minutes . . . I'll get it. What's happening th—"

"Nothing yet. Try to get an extension. I know it's a long shot, but—"

Dani paced a bit along the boards as Ellie climbed over the gunwale to the back platform. "It would be nice, but they'll never go for it. Appropriations has scheduled their bills for voting at the end of this month and of course the whole budget has to be signed by late September or the country doesn't have one. Functions stop, and then the November election could change everything. I'm sorry, honey, but they won't postpone, not even under these circumstances."

The jet skis were still strapped to their berths, unlikely to have been involved. Every buckle seemed in place. Still, Ellie balanced carefully to get a good look at the handles, seats, keys with their curly wires.

Martin said, "The systems they've seen so far won't work. They're just glorified lasers."

"I know. But that's why they have to see yours, and by 'they,' so far, we're up to four Appropriations Committee clerks, counsel and auditor, one senator, two representatives, plus three more from the Armed Services Committee, one general and a colonel . . . and all of them have to be transported, fed, watered, and put up at the Ritz."

"On my dime," Martin griped.

Ellie didn't see a drop of blood, a dent, or even so much as a scratch in the wax. The skis were dirty, certainly, with water spots from the rain and surf, but no sign that they'd been anything but passengers for some time.

"It's your test, hon. That's how it works. We only have a few takers for the overnight, though, probably because it's October and not February. Tomas is guiding them into the bull pen and if the corral breaks down now—" Her gaze fell on Ellie, who wondered if even the FBI security clearance that she didn't have anymore would cover what she was hearing. Probably not.

Dani clicked the phone off speaker, and Ellie took the steps to the left of the helm down to the cabin. She paused at the bottom of the steps, listening, but Dani had lowered her voice.

Glossy teak flooring and table with bench seating, TV, small fridge, stovetop, and even a small oven. Surprisingly kitchsy nautical equipment hung along one wall, old wooden rigging and one of those glass balls encased in netting in a haphazard display that didn't seem to fit the sleek modernism of the estate. A rime of powder dusted every surface, with cleaner patches where the tech had found a print and lifted it with a piece of tape. Taking advantage of the privacy, Ellie quickly opened every cabinet and crawled along the cushions, not caring how her khakis would be covered in black smears. She didn't know what to look for, and therefore looked for everything. Signs of drug use, a struggle, blood, a weapon, a crumpled note or other communications that might shed a light, anything the cops might have missed.

She found nothing.

The small bathroom—"head" in sea talk—had the necessities, but nothing of interest. Seat down, fingerprint powder everywhere, nothing in the trash. A stack of bath towels so thick and fluffy that she couldn't resist squeezing one, feeling the luxury. This left a tiny smear of black powder to underscore the designer's embroidered name and she snatched her fingers back in guilt.

Next she unlatched a door expecting to find a tiny shower area, but instead it opened a shallow case for storing cleaning equipment, a broom, dustpan, long-handled brush. If she used a different latch, beyond *that* was a shower not made for the claustrophobic.

No bedroom, though one could easily flop on the cushy

bench seating if necessary. Clearly the boat had been meant for an afternoon's fishing, while the yacht would be used for longer trips.

The boat shifted abruptly. Dani had stepped on board, probably wondering what was taking Ellie so long. She closed the door on the shower, rotated, and found her way obstructed by a man she did not know—or rather, knew only from the TV news.

Greg Anderson.

Chapter 8

"What are you doing down here?" he demanded, then modulated his voice and question only slightly. "What are you doing on my boat?"

Greg Anderson stood about six-five, maybe two-fifty, in snug blue jeans and a tight black T-shirt that showed his well-developed arms. He had long eyelashes, silky black hair, and even the faint shadow of stubble over his jaw. A tired crinkle to his eyes made him more attractive instead of less, the tiny flaws that make a work of art realistic. He also did not move; they stood separated by perhaps two feet and he blocked the only way out.

"I'm—"

"Martin says you're some kind of doctor."

"Forensic scientist. He wants the Locard Institute to consult on your wife's death."

He tilted his head ever so slightly, the gesture Rachael had said made him relaxed and confident that he had gotten away with something. Ellie saw only perplexity. "What the hell is the Locard Institute?"

She wanted to ask where Dani was, but that might sound

weak, so she began with the employee orientation manual summary. He clearly wasn't listening, and she cut it down to: "We hope to help to answer some questions, but I've only just arrived. I know this is a terrible time, but can you tell me how she'd been doing with the pregnancy?"

He sighed and some of the stiffness left his body, turning away from her into the cabin, and she felt an unreasonable relief. When he faced her again the aggressive concern had faded to a more appropriate sadness ... but he also rested one hip against the doorway to the steps, obstructing, again, the only means of egress. Ellie scooted into the cabin proper to give herself some breathing room.

She wasn't afraid. He'd be crazy to attack her here and now, and she *had* been an FBI agent trained in both offensive and defensive arts. Truthfully, she'd never been that good at either, yet that didn't worry her overmuch now. So not afraid—but definitely uncomfortable.

He answered her question, more or less. "I don't know what you mean. She'd been perfectly healthy. That's what she said the doctor said."

Somebody didn't go with her to checkups.

"I didn't go with her to the checkups. They were always at a bad time, when I'd be tied up with Martin working on the project, and she said she didn't want me to, anyway. Ashley was super independent. She didn't need me holding her hand." His gaze traveled over her pants and gave a snort of suppressed laughter, which exposed matching dimples. "What have you been doing?"

"It's the black powder. It's on everything."

The look turned to disgust and he stopped leaning against the doorway, inspecting his jeans.

"What about the normal parts of pregnancy? Morning sickness?"

"Oh yeah! She puked right and left once she figured out she was pregnant. I kept an empty wastebasket by her side of the bed every night. But it had gotten a lot better after the first, whatdyacallit, trimester. And she had a lot of back pain."

"Really? Where in the back?"

He gestured, placing a palm on his left lower back. "She said the baby sat on a nerve."

Ellie had studied enough about pregnancy to know that four months might be a bit early for that, but it seemed too low for a kidney issue. "Did she have trouble sleeping? Balance problems?"

Something shifted, ever so slightly, across his face, and Ellie wished Rachael could tell her what it might mean. "She'd been sleeping like a rock, but dizzy spells, yeah. We were swimming one night and she went to dive—she loved to dive, Martin had taught her all sorts of fancy ones—and instead, she fell off the side of the board, the high board."

"Did she get hurt?"

"Nah, just fell in the water. I teased her about it and she got mad, said she lost her balance."

"I see. Any other incidents?"

"Not that I saw. But sometimes if she got up too fast, she'd complain about it." A pause to think, and then he visibly decided to pile on. "All the time."

"Any allergic reactions, to food, aerosols, sunlight? Rashes, hives, nausea, throat constriction?"

"No-o." But he didn't sound sure.

She'd exhausted that topic. "Is there any way to tell where this boat went, with the GPS? Or did Ashley have tracking on her phone?" she asked, though she already knew the answer.

Correction: she knew *one* answer.

He looked down, away. "She didn't like phone tracking. She might have been a chip off Martin's block but that didn't mean she wanted him mapping her every move. Or me."

Nor would you want her checking up on yours?

"The signal gets spotty out on the water anyway. The boat GPS *does* show Ashley's last programmed destination, the place she went to and anchored almost every day. The G-men out there already downloaded the info and took a charter out to the area—do you want to see it? We could go."

"Now?"

"Probably your last chance before this tropical storm hits and everything's beached for a week. Sure, half the U.S. government is going to be here the day after tomorrow to watch a missile detection system that probably isn't going to work because Martin still hasn't integrated my video code . . . but, frankly, your tan could use a little help."

The scene of, possibly, the crime? "Yes."

"You're not afraid?" he pressed, a half smile across his lips. "To be alone with me?"

"Is that a dare?"

"Of course it is."

Chapter 9

In the Sierras, during those vacations with Ellie's mother's cousin Roland and his wife Billie, hardly a day went by without dares—simulated scares unheard of at Grandma's or Rosalie's, but those homes hadn't contained three boys under less than stringent supervision. Roland would be at the university, teaching summer session to get all the hours he could with four kids to educate and a fifth mouth to feed for a couple of months every year, and Billie did the meteorology for the Reno television stations. This left the kids with a potentially dangerous amount of unsupervised time. If Jason, the oldest, wasn't leading by example and skateboarding down the empty middle school steps or trying to trap a rattlesnake with an old donut box, he'd be thinking up similar experiments for his brothers to try. Reach the hawk's nest in the hemlock tree. Follow the culvert pipe all the way under I-580. Climb the rungs on the Mt. Rose ski lift tower. A few broken bones had taught the middle boy, Derek, not to rise to the bait. Robin, as the only girl, learned to deflect by pushing Ellie forward as both a sacrifice and a substitute. The youngest, Danny, evolved into the most reckless in his quest to keep up. It had been his idea for her to jump off the roof.

They weren't *bad* children, of course, even fairly obedient in their way, so when Billie had instructed them to rake up all the leaves left over from the previous fall, they did so. Ellie, at eight, did her share—always careful to do her share, not be a burden, not risk any resentment from the others because she was new and different and unbelonging—using a wooden rake missing half its tines. Roland wasn't big on outside chores, so they wound up with a huge pile of mulched sticks and rotting leaf bits, nearly as tall as Ellie herself. So tall, Danny declared, that they could jump from really far and it would act as a giant pillow. The obvious person to go first would be Ellie, the littlest at eight. If she landed safely, the rest could do so as well. Ellie sensed a flaw in this logic but could not articulate it, so up to the second floor of the all-wood split-level she and Danny went.

They tiptoed past Billie's office, where she would be comparing NOAA charts and storms over San Francisco. They stole into the master bedroom, with discarded clothes draped over the vanity stool and matching nightstands overflowing with magazines, reading glasses, hand lotion—the dry mountain air sucked the moisture out of even young skin—and half-empty cans of peanuts. She and Danny worked together to lift the heavy window since the counterweight ropes had broken and propped it with a thick tome titled *Principles of Mathematical Analysis*. Then, Ellie could wriggle out through the open space.

The room sat over the porch, where perhaps six feet of sharply angled shingles provided her a platform. They were rough against her palms, her legs at least covered by hand-me-down jeans dotted with pine needles and dust from the raking job. She took her time to emerge, ignoring Danny's orders to hurry up before his mother heard them. Merely swiveling her feet around and sitting up caused her to slide a few inches toward the edge and she froze, waiting to see if she could stabilize her footing or instead plunge to her death.

While waiting, she let the view distract her.

They lived halfway up Mt. Rose. Outside her room at the back of the house sat only more trees, but from the front of the house she could see over their tops to Washoe Valley and the distant skyline of Reno. She took it in. And it gave her a reason to postpone her leap.

"Get going," Danny said from the window.

On the ground, Jase—who, Ellie reflected years later, really should have known better—backed across the yard until he could see her. "Are you going to do it?"

A cold breeze wafted through her sweater. Temperatures hit the extremes in the mountain—desert hot in the sun, but shifting thirty degrees in an instant once in the shade or near a peak or after dark.

She couldn't sit there forever. With her bottom pasted to the shingles, she shuffled herself closer to the edge and risked a glance down. The leaf pile did not look anywhere near as large as it had from the ground. "It's not big enough."

"It's huge," Robin said, the gleeful look in her eye visible even from a height. Whether she was excited at the activity or excited to have another girl available to her brothers for said activity, Ellie was not sure. She had never been sure about Robin.

"Come on," Jason said. "Piss or get off the pot."

"Don't be a baby," Danny hissed.

Why wasn't *he* out here, if it was so important to be non-babyish? But she didn't bother to ask, knowing it wouldn't do any good. Instead she considered the logistics of getting over the edge without standing up, if she could stay in her snail-like hunch, but every imagined trial resulted in scraping up her back, breaking off the gutter, or landing face-first. No good option. She had to stand.

Her tiny knees trembled as she stretched, convinced that at any moment her feet would slip and shoot her off the edge, clunking her head against the roof and scraping off all her hair and again damaging the gutter, which would surely incur even the easygoing Roland's wrath since home repair ranked with yard work on his "likes" list. But, albeit with agonizing slowness, she straightened. She stood in the open air without a parachute or a magic cape, her only net a pile of dead leaves.

"Go on," Danny called. But he had not even left the window.

"Come on," Jason said, already getting bored.

Robin crossed her arms in disappointment, assuming the experiment a failure.

She was there. She had committed. She had been dared, and any loss of face would have to be borne in grim silence for the entire, interminable three months.

Ellie bent her knees and leapt.

The air felt suddenly warm as she fell through it, and for one breathless, exhilarating moment she knew, with absolute certainty, that she had made the right decision. She *should* fly. She *could* fly. She was *born* to fly.

Then she landed.

The stack that had appeared mostly oak and maple fronds turned out to have a large proportion of sticks and pine needles. Long-dead leaves tended to be less fluffy and much wetter than recently dead leaves, so that they formed more a cushion of piled carpets than a feather mattress, hard enough to knock the air out of her lungs for a moment or two. Plus her body plunged deep into this mess so that when she *did* breathe, bits of dried vegetation came along with the oxygen. The scrapes and at least two punctures on her back would be dressed by Robin that night, inexpertly dabbing with peroxide and Bactine to keep from having to confess to Billie. Billie, at least, remained with her air current charts and only vaguely wondered aloud at dinner why she'd found *Principles of Mathematical Analysis* propping up her window.

But no one else had leapt, and it exempted Ellie from future dares for a whole two weeks. That had been her last summer with Roland and Billie—not because of the roof incident, but because then her grandmother had gotten ill over the winter and Ellie moved permanently to Aunt Rosalie's, who didn't need to farm her out for summer respite.

Greg Anderson didn't propose for her to jump off a roof. Only go for a boat ride with a possible killer. Bravery might not be her forte, but she would not shrink from a dare.

"Well?" he asked. "Do you want to follow in Ashley's last footsteps?"

"Let's go."

Time to jump off another roof.

Chapter 10

Rachael used to love working out of town. She enjoyed researching new locations, what to pack for the weather, scouting unique restaurants and parks, adding to her repertoire of travel experiences. Then came Danton. The scrappy, ebullient little boy had changed her life.

And her vocabulary.

"What was that?" she asked him via her laptop screen.

"Bdsolvin sing!" the two-and-a-half-year-old urchin chortled. "For da balloon."

She didn't know what to say to that.

Her mother's face appeared over Danton's shoulder. "We're in charge of the balloon release for the block party this weekend."

"Balloons are—"

Loretta cut her off. "Bad for the environment, I know. But not these, these are biodegradable. Mrs. Johnson said so, and you know Mrs. Johnson is never wrong. *And* tied with dissolving string—that's the thing. I showed him how the string dissolves in water, and that's all he wants to do now."

"You can't dissolve all the string, baby," Rachael told her son. "The block committee needs that string."

"Bdsolvin!" And he collapsed into giggles once again.

"Are you going to be back in time?" Loretta asked.

"I'd like to be. I'd really, really like to be."

Loretta seemed to regret asking. "I know you're doing your best. So . . . how rich is he? What's the house like? How about that little trophy he married?"

"Mama!" Rachael laughed, summarized the Post estate as succinctly as she could. Then, after exchanging fun but semi-nonsensical conversation with her son, regretfully disconnected and got back to work.

That Martin Post had put his faith in the Locard delighted her. It would raise the institute's profile—they couldn't buy that kind of advertising, and high profiles could lead to increased enrollment and research opportunities. But missing even a minute of time spent with her son sucked. He might be perfectly happy to spend all day with Grammy, and Grammy might be perfectly happy to spend every second with him, but it didn't make Rachael perfectly happy. Not at all.

Yet she loved plunging into a thorny, difficult chaos and coming out with clean and unequivocal answers. Sometimes they brought comfort to the family and justice to the system. Sometimes not. But she had done her job as well as, if she abandoned modesty for a moment, as anyone in the country could. She loved her son, but she loved her job too. The eternal conflict.

It didn't matter that Ashley had been rich. It mattered that she'd been a mother, a woman, a human being. And someone's child.

Rachael had left the medical examiner's office with the victim's blood, hair, one fingernail, a scrap of clothing, numerous photos of injuries, even two milliliters of vitreous fluid, and—the pièce de résistance, a cast of the vertebra-showing the unusual indentation. The medical examiner's staff had provided the dent stone and chatted with her while it hardened enough to remove. She got the impression that the diener had been given instructions not to leave her alone with the body, for fear she might—what, wheel it out a back door and abscond? But she understood—they couldn't afford any screwups on such a high-profile case, and she officially worked for the victim's father, who seemed more and more suspicious of his son-in-law with every passing moment.

Now she spread these items on the kitchen table as carefully as if they were bottles of Château Margaux.

She and Ellie were impromptu roomies for this trip, using the home of Ellie's Uncle Paul and his wife Joanna. Both doctors, they were currently in New Guinea battling Ebola with Doctors Without Borders and were perfectly happy to have someone check the roof and make sure the bills were current in their absence. At least that's what Ellie said. It felt a bit intrusive to look around and see pictures of Ellie's high school graduation, but the house provided all that a hotel room couldn't: space, privacy, and security. Here Rachael could spread out autopsy samples from the most scrutinized family in the country and not have to worry about the housekeeper with a passkey.

She fired up her laptop. Then she let it warm and did another circuit of the living room. A worn leather couch. A pottery vase with a bizarre but colorful structure—she realized it was the shape of a human heart, where the aorta and pulmonary artery were open to receive flower stems, fired in deep tones of red and purple. Beautiful and very strange at once.

That dichotomy seemed to sum up Ellie, the child this household had partly produced. Outwardly professional, warm, confident, a total package . . . someone with her career prestige and fabulous looks should be walking into a room as if they own it. Instead, Ellie seemed quiet without being shy, her movements strangely frozen, as if she hoped to melt into the background where no one would notice her. She stayed too still and approached people too stiffly for someone of her age and status.

This unexpected insecurity, Rachael thought, could have more to do with her past than her present. The background investigation required for hire had been interesting, told of a fractured childhood. Orphaned at a young age, Ellie had been raised by a succession of relatives. This had been her fifth home, here in Florida with the two doctors. Apparently each home had been equally loving, but still, that was a lot of moving around for a little kid.

Exactly what would *not* happen to Rachael's little boy. She wanted stability for Danton almost more than anything, and yet here she was, a thousand miles away from him.

She moved back to her computer, and established a secure link to the Locard.

They had, at least, prevented a fellow parent from viewing the decimated body of his daughter. Martin had insisted, argued, nearly pleaded, but the ME convinced him to remember her as who she had been in life, that it would be a disservice to her for him to think of her as in death. This logic finally worked its magic and he gave up, slumping back onto the waiting room couch like any other average citizen.

Rachael had had many such conversations with many such parents and they were never easy. She understood the need to be sure, the need to prove to their own minds that their child was really gone. They had fought for that child's well-being since the moment of conception, and to decline the final torture of seeing their decomposed, partially skeletonized body felt like rank weakness, abandonment of the one person they had vowed to always protect. From the moment their cells began to split, children—like her son—were both amazing and delicate. The world could seem like one big ball of threat, if you let it.

She didn't intend to let it.

Yet Rachael could never be sure if keeping them from the body might be worse, if their imaginations would end up tormenting them even more than reality would. Impossible to know. A coroner or medical examiner simply had to make the best educated, empathetic guess possible.

Now she downloaded the collection of photos into the institute's computer system and clicked on a video chat with Agnes, the Locard's tech wizard. The young woman answered on the second ring, as if she'd been waiting, though Rachael knew she hadn't. Agnes waited on no one.

She also knew better than to waste time with pleasantries. "Hi, Agnes. I have photos for three-D imaging. I hope they're good enough."

"Let's see." Agnes's face in the video box hovered close enough to see the flare of her nostrils when she breathed in. Behind her, the digital forensics lab appeared as a maze of cords, with laptops and a cadre of cell phones spread around on holders and platforms, charging, downloading, duplicating. "Look okay. You've got all the angles, scales are clear . . . depth as well as width. Excellent."

"I know it's only a tiny nick, but it looks to me like it has some curvature. Can you — "

"Extrapolate to the arc of the object? That's the purpose of the imaging."

A stupid question, in other words, but Rachael had long since gotten over feeling intimidated by Agnes . . . just being Agnes. "Yes."

On the screen, Agnes worked a mouse, gazing at images on her end, and spoke absently. "You think this is from a weapon? Someone killed her?"

"I tried to dance around it as delicately as I could," Rachael confessed as she sat down on a creaking straight chair. "I don't want to tell the guy someone murdered his daughter."

"But that is what you think?"

"I don't know. I keep thinking of an article I read last year about stabbing trauma to the victim's abdomen from being impaled with a beach umbrella caught in a strong wind. In Ashley's case, something must have breached the abdomen—the predator activity there was so acute, while the limbs, fingers, toes, were fairly intact. It makes no sense unless the trauma existed before she went into the water. But we need to make absolutely sure. For her, for the family—a group so important to this nation's security—and him as a father."

"A rich father."

"A very rich father." Rachael could hear keys clicking. "The indentation in her vertebra was made by something approximately two millimeters wide that penetrated the bone by approximately three millimeters deep. But square."

"Square?"

"Yes, the edge that penetrated the bone was not sharp, not beveled in any way. Flat at the bottom—or rather, top."

Rachael pictured this. It didn't necessarily mean the object hadn't been a weapon or boat propeller or some kind of blade, but with a flat two millimeters across it couldn't have been a very sharp one.

"Curvature is approximately .06 millimeter."

Rachael did a quick calculation. "So if that edge forms a circle, it would be a circle of about three centimeters."

"Clearly." A phone rang somewhere in Agnes's lab, sending up a synthesized melody that for some reason made Rachael think of popping soap bubbles. "Is there anything else?"

Rachael thanked her and disconnected, immediately dialing Ellie's number. She needed to catch her while still at the Post's.

The woman sounded a bit breathless, probably distracted by whatever she was doing, outside to judge from the low but consistent roaring of the wind over the microphone.

She summarized the autopsy findings, and Agnes's extrapolation of the indentation. "Of course it's too small of an area to guess at the shape of the thing that caused it."

"I see. Well, I'm on the boat at the moment." The wind sound picked up.

"Good. Also, they found flecks of some dark substance in her hair at the first autopsy and the ME gave me a copy of the results. Some interesting functional groups involving chlorine. It appears to be chloroprene, mixed with some spandex."

"Huh," Ellie said. "Sounds like—"

"Neoprene? Not a surprising thing to find on a boat." She heard what sounded like an engine above the wind roar. "Are you *on* the boat? Like, out in the water?"

The slightest pause. "Yes, so I might lose this signal at any moment. We're going out to see the spot where Ashley would moor every day. It's most likely where she was when she went overboard, but of course we can't be sure."

"Who's *we*?"

"Greg is taking me."

"Greg Anderson. The victim's husband."

"Yes."

Who was clearly within earshot, given Ellie's brief responses. "The father's top suspect."

"Yes."

"Is anyone else with you?"

"No."

Was she *nuts*? Alone on the boat—which could be considered a murder weapon?—with the obvious suspect in any case of a dead wife . . . What happened to Dani? Why wasn't she along? Though it might be that the murderous husband and the very much younger stepmother got together in more ways than one . . . possibilities abounded, all equally dangerous. "Be careful!"

"Yes, of course—"

And the phone became silent. Rachael glanced at the screen, but the call had been lost.

Chapter 11

A few questions about her own sanity also crossed Ellie's mind as Greg started up the engine. He motored the forty-five-foot powerboat out of the opening at more than a no-wake speed, as if escaping before his father-in-law could order them back.

It wasn't as if she was still an FBI agent with a warrant, a sidearm, and a team she could call for backup. This new form of investigating would take some getting used to. But to get a handle on this crime, *if* a crime had even occurred, she needed to see the scene of it. That the scene of it happened to be a mile radius of open water couldn't be helped.

She moved around the center console to the bow of the boat. It had a padded lounging area in the center that could fit three people across and matching benches with narrow tables in the very tip. Under the seats were spaces to store gear and live fish; she lifted each one in turn, but most were empty save for extra life jackets and neatly coiled ropes.

Greg apparently saw no reason to linger and opened the throttle. The boat skimmed over the water, tilting up over each wave and then slamming back down. But the Gulf stayed calm and the boat so well-balanced that it still made for a pleasant ride. The wind cooled even the sun's brutal beams; she could not stay out there long without stronger sunscreen, but a quick touch of vitamin D would be okay.

"What are you doing?" Greg shouted to her as she opened another storage bin.

If he thought the bouncing of the boat would discourage her, he miscalculated. Her sea legs coped easily with the movement. "Examining the area."

"Looking for clues?"

She could hear a touch of derision, but not any real concern. He either didn't expect her to find anything—or he was innocent. Either way, she wasn't about to tell him that she now searched for a two-millimeter-wide blade or possibly a circular item three centimeters in diameter. And something that could cause a compression fracture to a young woman's skull, maybe something coated in neoprene.

But nothing seemed to fit those exact specifications, and anything that might come close did not appear to be out of place or damaged. The poles used to support the hardtop were as they should be and were too large and thick to be the weapon anyway. She wondered if they'd had a speargun on board—it would be heavy enough to cause the head injury and the spear would definitely cause her theoretical abdominal injury, though she didn't think spears were curved or particularly dull.

In the compartment under the next seat cushion, Ellie found a pair of flippers, three sets of goggles, two snorkels, and a single rubber water boot. It looked too small for Greg. "What's this?"

"Water shoe," he shouted. "Ashley liked to wear them when we beached on an island, if she had to walk over rocks or a bunch of seaweed or shells."

"There's only one."

He shrugged, his gaze on the water.

Ellie dropped the single water shoe into a paper bag. It did seem old, dusty, and stiffened around the edges. She then returned the paper bag to her stash of equipment in the cabin to keep the strong wind from snatching it away, and returned to the deck. She paused under the hardtop where Greg stood in front of the wheel looking like a magazine ad for designer cologne.

She finished peeking into every hidden compartment on the deck just as the boat slowed. Then she heard the clanking rumble of a large chain from deep inside the vessel.

Greg walked past her, checked the anchor, turned back, and said, "Well, this is it. This is where Ashley would come every day, according to her GPS."

"How far out are we?"

"About two miles," Greg told her.

"How deep is it here?"

"About thirty feet. Maybe less."

"And this is where she always anchored?"

"About. Say a hundred-foot radius. According to the GPS anyway."

Ellie surveyed the 360 view. To the west, water, horizon, sky, dotted here and there with another boat, a tall sail, a cargo ship. To the east, the shoreline forming a thin line of green.

She had pictured Ashley on her boat, alone, but that had been a grainy, overexposed video clip of imagination. Being there in person, feeling the salty air, the rock of the boat, the silence above the low constant hum of splashes and wind, showed her the truth.

They were, quite literally, in the middle of nowhere. Winds were minimal and the waves followed suit, but still, they were in open water and the boat bobbed without pause.

The odds of someone happening upon Ashley, committing some spur-of-the-moment kidnapping or assault, were nil. Someone either followed her or had been following her long enough to know her habits.

No way someone snuck up on Ashley, either. The endless water span under the bright sky told Ellie that if you wanted to kidnap someone there had to be easier ways to do so.

Though a ship pretending to be in distress could have lowered the girl's defenses—assuming Ashley had been the type of person who would try to help.

Or someone had already been on the boat. The boathouse didn't seem particularly secure, not with one wall open to the air and water. But to get near it they would have to make it past the network of cameras and over the fence installed to prevent someone from doing exactly that.

Unless they came in under the water itself, using a scuba tank. And maybe a wetsuit—made of neoprene. Swim into the boathouse, hide in the boat's cabin, wait until Ashley had driven the boat out to wherever and anchored. But then what? Throw her overboard, drive the boat to another rendezvous and set it adrift? Wrap the laptop in plastic and go back into the water, swim to shore or another craft . . . like what, a submarine?

At this point, all theories seemed equally plausible, and she had no idea how to investigate any one of them.

"So here we are." Greg moved around the center console to join her in the bow, negotiating the shifting deck without much trouble. "All alone."

Chapter 12

Perhaps it was the wind or the speed, but Greg seemed to electrify whatever air he entered, though she couldn't say if it was fear, attraction, or simply the energy that the young and virile inject to the room. He might be an amiable, perhaps mischievous socialite. He might be an opportunist who murdered his pregnant wife.

"Why here?"

Greg still gazed at her instead of the surroundings, so she asked again to let him know the question wasn't rhetorical.

Then he did the same neck-craning sweep she had done, and shrugged. "Dunno. I guess it worked for her. Far enough from land that you wouldn't have other boats dodging around you all the time, but close enough you can still see landmarks. That red roof is the Pirate Cove bar. Well, *was*—the last hurricane took it out and they never reopened."

She squinted. "I don't see the house . . ."

"No, it's just around that corner right there." He pointed to their right, where an outcropping of green blocked the view of the land farther south. "You'd see it if we were a couple thousand feet that way. It glows like a lighthouse with all that mirrored glass. At night we might as well live in a fishbowl."

Did Ashley like this spot because she couldn't see the house? Or because the house couldn't see her? "Was that uncomfortable?"

"Eh," came the erudite reply. "Not really. I'm sure the media floated by to snap pics now and then, but I think the polarization of the windows screwed them up, or something, because no pictures of us having a party or something ever turned up as clickbait. The pool is hidden by the trees, so that's not a problem."

Without the strong wind generated by speed, the sun made her skin ooze sweat and she moved to the command center's bench seat under the hardtop. "She'd just anchor out here and work on a laptop? The glare would give me a headache."

He promptly joined her, too close but not touching. "Didn't bother her. Iron stomach."

But pregnancy changes things. Her death could have been a simple accident—Ashley got seasick or morning sick, was puking over the side, the boat lurched or the sudden inversion made her dizzy and she fell over. Maybe hit her head on the hull or couldn't find the swim platform at the back.

Greg went on, "We used to spend hours out here—well, down in the cabin. Especially when it's this hot."

"Fishing?" Ellie asked.

He blinked. "Fi—no. To have a little private time. Someplace where Deborah wasn't listening. Ashley loved boats. And I loved what boats did to her."

She thought she could pick up the heat of his body, even over the heat of the day. A trickle of sweat snaked between her shoulder blades, as she pointedly ignored his implications. "Ever have guests? Come out here with you?"

"Sure, we'd bring friends . . . but it's been a while, and we'd usually take the *Mirrormere*. This thing is way too small."

Sure, she thought. *Too small.*

"So, what about you?" The boat lurched and he grabbed the steering wheel, noticed he'd done so, and stopped. "Do you love boats?"

"Uh—sure."

"We'd go down to the cabin during this hot part of the day. Temperatures can get in the hundreds out here."

Was he seriously suggesting that they have sex on his dead wife's boat two weeks after she'd been killed?

Or, more likely, screwing with her, punishing her for prolonging the investigation into Ashley's death, which delayed the settlement of her estate, her intellectual property, and any applicable life insurance.

Or, even *more* likely, did he think activating her hormones would simply swirl her up with enough lust and guilt to make her go away?

Good luck with that, dude. Her hormones had long been burned out by injections of gonadotropins and Adam's abandonment.

Another wave, not large, buffeted the ship and Greg couldn't hide a look of distaste. A great many people were okay so long as the ship moved, but sitting and rocking . . . not so much. Yet he summoned the smirk to return. "Want a drink? Lord knows I could use one. And the cabin has A/C."

"Did you and Ashley do any diving?"

"Diving? Like in a pool? Oh—like scuba, underwater. Yeah, we both used to, but not for, I don't know, a couple of years now."

"Do you keep the equipment aboard?" An oxygen tank across the head could easily create a fracture.

"Nah. I think it's piled in the boathouse somewhere. It all

needed to be recertified and I just plumb didn't get to it. Too bad, so sad. Those days are over."

She tried to fit those comments into a context she understood, but they refused to line up. "Over?"

For once, he seemed uncomfortable. "Look . . . don't tell anyone I sounded like a weenie, but when Ashley and I married, everyone seemed thrilled to have me. Total equal. Yay, a son of sorts in the family. But—like this boat. You go out on a boat, it has to be hosed down, the engine flushed, towels gathered up and taken back to the house. Tank gassed up. Scuba equipment serviced. Know whose job that was? Mine. Not Ashley's."

"You don't have—someone for that?"

"Martin doesn't like extra people around, so no, we don't have a guy to flush the boats, unless it's the big one and the cabin crew takes care of it. Landscapers once a week, maids twice a week. No one around more than that except for security and the cook. So I move in, and yeah . . . the car needed an oil change, up to me to take it in. She brought a cat home from college; it was still here when we got together. Who had to take the damn thing to the vet even though it was *her* cat?"

Ellie murmured a *mm-hmm*, to keep him talking.

"That didn't last long. It finally disappeared, gator probably got it. So yeah, maybe I'll be gone by the end of the week, but at least I'll never scoop another litter box."

"Gone? Where are you going?" Ellie asked. Jail? Parents'? Man cave?

"Martin will kick me out the minute the demo's done and he can get someone in to pack my boxes—and as soon as dumping the in-law won't look so bad for him in the press. Then I'll be out on the stoop. I'll lose my house, the Bugatti . . . this stinkin' boat, and, oh yeah, my *job*. And none of it is my fault."

Ellie shifted on the bench, hoping the breeze would pick up—it might be fall in every state north of the Mason-Dixon line, but fall only felt like more summer in Florida. She wouldn't be surprised if Greg's story represented the "poor little lost boy" number in his repertoire of seduction, but she would need Rachael's expertise to suss that out. He seemed sincere, possibly for the first time in her presence. The skin around his eyes sagged, the stubble on his chin had not been perfectly trimmed, and a loose piece of nail hung off one finger. Maybe not defeated, but definitely exhausted.

"I didn't kill her," he told Ellie. "I don't know why she died. I wasn't even here."

Ellie nodded. She couldn't say she knew or that she believed him, because she didn't, not quite. But she didn't *dis*believe him, either.

"And now I'm going to lose everything and it's not my fault."

Not "I've lost everything" as in his wife and child. "Going to lose everything" as in the Olympic swimming pool, French car, and partial maid service.

Greg Anderson might be paper-thin shallow—but that didn't make him guilty.

"Were you happy at all?" she blurted out, only because she often asked herself the same question about her and Adam. When the ending stayed so present in the mind, it could be hard to remember that there had been a beginning. She and Adam had enjoyed each other once, right? It hadn't all been about fulfilling his need for children, or her need for a household to which she actually belonged?

Surprised at the question, Greg gave a blank stare. Then he began to recompose his face. "Are you married?"

Caution alarms popped in her mind. "Not anymore."

"Then you know what it's like. It's not perfect, right? But no matter what happens . . . even this . . . I wouldn't have passed it up." He reached out and put two fingers on her hand, lightly, so lightly that she wouldn't have believed they actually touched if she didn't see it. "Would you?"

Would she? Adam hadn't died. Some eggs inside her, perhaps, an embryo a few times. Adam had *chosen* to leave her. Would she go through that again, given the option?

She wanted to say yes, that she'd brave the pain without hesitation, but it wouldn't be true. If she could have avoided the whole six years, been told up front that she would not conceive and that the relationship hinged on that—hell yeah, she'd opt out. Maybe she was more sensible than most. Or maybe bravery wasn't her forte. "I don't know."

"I would. I would have married Ashley a hundred times." He did not move his hand, and now she felt the warmth of his skin . . . but not his words. They did not match his other speech to date, too slow, without his impulse-driven rhythm. "Even with her family."

Her family. Ellie might not have met any of them before today, but it seemed to her that everyone around Ashley Post Anderson wanted the young woman to fill the roles in their play—as the perfect (obedient) daughter, the perfect (easy) wife—perhaps all the roles except the one she really wanted: mother. Maybe Ashley had been the orphan of her own story, left alone emotionally just as Ellie had been left physically.

Or maybe Ellie had it all wrong.

Abruptly, Greg said, "You can't trust Martin, you know. *Or* Dani. They know a lot more about you than you think."

"Me? Like what?"

He smirked at her surprise. "I'm not sure. Something about your family. That's why he hired you."

"He told me why he hired me. And"—thanks to several profiles of her online and in print—"everyone knows about my . . . unusual upbringing. It's not a secret."

"Every family has secrets."

A good opening. "Including this one? How did Ashley get along with her stepmother?"

His eyebrows stretched up, as if he'd never considered the question before. "Well, she never referred to her as that, for one thing. Just 'Dani.' They . . . were what you would expect: locked in an eternal battle for Daddy's attention that Dani could never win. But I think they were both smart enough to realize that—and they had different roles. Winning wasn't necessary, so long as they both could stay in the race."

"So . . . no arguments, nothing like that."

"Not a thing. I don't think Ashley ever voiced a single complaint about Dani. Other than that she wasn't Deborah, but like I said, they were both smart enough to look past that."

"What about Martin?"

"Did he argue with Dani? Who the hell knows what goes on in their half of the house? Martin isn't big on privacy, except his own."

"No, with Ashley."

"It would be pointless to argue with Martin. She'd whine at him if she didn't get her way, especially about coding design, but it rarely worked. Look, the guy drives me crazy a lot of the time, but there'll never be a smarter guy in the room, and that's just the way it is, so you put up with it."

"Even if he thinks Ashley was murdered?" *Even if he thinks it was by you?*

"I didn't say he was always right." He wiped his forehead and suddenly seemed to tire of the whole experiment. "Are you done? It's horrible out here."

"Yes." Sweat rolled down the middle of her back and her clothes had grown damp. How had Ashley stood this heat, especially while pregnant? Maybe she'd worked in the air-conditioned cabin. Ellie had already gone through it once, but a second look couldn't hurt and the A/C beckoned. So while the anchor clanked its way up and Greg started the engine, she went down the stairs.

The temperature dropped twenty degrees. Ellie felt a twinge of environmentalist guilt at using energy to produce the cooling while the door stood open to the air, but then, it wasn't her boat. She tried to look at the cabin with fresh eyes. Nothing jumped out.

Except her, a moment later when a *bang* startled her. She had not latched the shower door/cleaning instrument compartment sufficiently and it swung loose, slamming back when the boat lurched over a particularly large wave. The door to the shower had been closed, but the door within a door swayed with the waves. As the boat began to pick up speed, it gaped open and crashed into the jamb of the tiny hallway opening.

Ellie leapt to catch it, uttering a mild expletive. Did Martin Post's billions mean that he would overlook scratches and dents in his very slick motorboat? She doubted it. From what she knew of rich people, they usually became rich because they didn't overlook anything. Horribly immature thoughts crowded her head . . . maybe Martin would blame any damage on Greg. Maybe he'd have the whole boat destroyed, for having been the means of his daughter's death. Maybe no one would ever find out.

Then she snapped herself out of the childhood panic and inspected the door. The glossy teak panels had been lined with a rubber edge, which apparently provided just enough cushion to keep her from having to buy Mr. Post a new one. The contents, the cleaning supplies she'd noted earlier, partly spilled out of the opening. Two brooms, a mop, a spray bottle of Mr. Clean. Some Windex.

She picked up a push broom, or a long-handled scrub brush, she couldn't be sure. It had a small head filled with stiff bristles and had clearly been fingerprinted from its bristles to its red rubber tip. Black powder still clung and clean patches with square lines showed where prints had been lifted from the aluminum pole.

An aluminum pole about three centimeters in diameter.

The brush's shaft—as well as those of the mop and the broom, both similar in diameter—showed no signs of having been used as a weapon. No dents, gouges, distortions. No sign of blood—other than powder residue and old fibers in the bristles, the implements seemed as perfect as the rest of the boat.

But she could see that the handles screwed into the items and pulled out a fresh pair of latex gloves. The handle had already been fingerprinted, but still, she grasped only the rubber-covered top and the body of the brush to twist counter-clockwise. Righty-tighty, lefty-loosey.

It unscrewed without hesitation. She didn't have to completely remove it before sighting the dark red stain.

With the brush in one hand, she upended the pole to get a better look. Maybe it was rust. Aluminum wasn't supposed to rust from water, but if they had used it with any bleach-based products, that would do it.

Not rust. A lifetime of staring at blood—fresh, old, diseased, dried, frozen, burnt—had trained her eyes until she felt certain. This was blood, around the threads of a pipe that fit the dimensions of whatever had left a divot in Ashley Post Anderson's vertebra.

The grooves seemed in good shape, not worn or distorted. Only the dried red flakes marred their perfection. More stuck to the corresponding threads in the plastic brush body.

"What are you doing down there?" Greg suddenly called.

"Nothing!" *Great answer, El.* She could have been nine again with an excuse like that. "Just washing my hands."

The boat abruptly slowed. The decorative glass ball clunked against the cabin wall at the shifting tilt and the decorations of antique rigging made scraping sounds that she hoped would cover her movements.

Ellie turned the handle to the right, screwing it almost all the way back in. Then she set it perfectly back into its place and closed the door to the skinny cabinet, moving it slowly but still wincing at the distinct *click* as the latch popped to lock it.

"What are you doing?" Greg called again.

Why had he suddenly gotten so curious? She climbed the steps and said something about organizing her samples.

The Post estate loomed before them. Once again Greg ignored the no-wake sign posted on the rocks of their private little breakwall but did get the *Phantom* back into its berth without hitting the dock. She remembered what he had said before and wondered if he would be flushing the engines and hosing the deck this time—or ever again. Boats were like Christmas trees—taking them out of their box, pure thrill, but putting them back? Pure chore. And why maintain a toy your father-in-law would only take away?

She stayed in the cabin doorway. Had Greg heard the banging? Would he recognize the sound of the shower cabinet door as distinct from other sounds a moving boat might make?

Entering the boathouse from the water felt no different than entering from the grass—shockingly dim before the eyes adjusted from the sun's brilliance, then humid, echoing, and claustrophobic. And this time, with one very pissed-off-looking FBI agent waiting on the deck next to Dani. He caught the rope that Greg tossed him with one hand, and without taking his gaze from them.

Ellie stared, thinking the heat had affected her mind. "What are you doing here?" she asked Michael Tyler, her words oddly loud once the engine had been silenced.

"What are *you* doing here?" Dani asked Greg.

"I live here." His words seemed sharp enough to chip ice. "Just like you." At which she turned and stalked out of the building.

"Working," Michael Tyler answered Ellie, almost as coldly, and she blinked. They'd gotten along so well in their past two encounters . . . Was he annoyed that the Locard had been hired? She had left the bureau, which could be considered slightly traitorous—but since when was this an FBI case?

"I just need to get something—" Greg said, gesturing to the space behind Ellie.

"I think you'd better tie us up," she said quietly. "I don't think Agent Tyler knows what to do."

He hesitated, but the combination of ego stroke and the bow of the *Phantom* drifting ever further from the dock worked against him and he abandoned the cabin to secure the lines. She balanced on the moving deck, staring intently at the FBI agent. When he felt her attention, she nodded in Greg's direction, then twitched her head toward the outer door. She hoped the meaning would be clear: *get him out of here*.

"Where did you guys go?" he demanded of them both.

Greg responded with a grin. Ellie said, "GPS location," paired with another intent stare.

Greg turned to offer her a gentlemanly hand she didn't need. His voice had switched back to a tempo labeled *warm and gracious*. "Thank you for your help. Anything you can tell me about Ashley will be appreciated. I miss her so much already." He squeezed her fingers, firmly but not hard, and pulled—ever-so-gently trying to remove her from the cabin doorway.

"We need to speak to you, Mr. Anderson," Michael said, his voice booming in the large but enclosed space. "It's about your Bugatti."

Brilliant, Ellie thought.

Greg's eyes widened in stark terror, whatever he wanted in the cabin—even if it had been the weapon he'd used to murder his wife—instantly forgotten. "What?"

"If you come with me. My partner is outside, and he needs to confirm—"

The boat shook as he leapt for the deck. Ellie watched the men leave, and waited.

Michael Tyler returned in record time. He didn't even make it to the side dock before demanding, "What was that? Why the hell did you leave with our chief suspect, alone, on the same boat—"

"Technically—"

"—and what the hell was *that* all about, getting rid of him?"

"—Ashley has not officially been the victim of a crime. He couldn't be a suspect because technically there was nothing to suspect him of."

"Yes, but why—"

"And now," she finished, "there is."

Chapter 13

Ellie collected one tiny swab of the blood for the Locard, then helpfully packaged the brush handle for Michael to submit to their lab at Quantico. The local FBI office had sent a team of two technicians to collect it from them at the boathouse and to go over the boat one more time. Now that they knew blood evidence actually existed, looking for it became an easier task than searching for "anything that might mean something." Ellie left them to take apart the drains and the holding tank and the bilge pump.

Luis Alvarez had disappeared with Greg, no doubt scrambling to think up some question about the Bugatti, schmoozing away to keep him occupied. His partner, Michael explained, was really good at that. Dani had not reappeared.

"That handle had been fingerprinted," she said to him. "Any prints identified?"

He pulled out a phone. "I'll find out. So back to you, unarmed, with no backup, going for a sail on a boat with a guy who probably threw his pregnant wife over the side—"

"Nothing points to that. And how did he accomplish that when he left the property before she went out on the boat?"

She turned around in a slow circle, resurveying the area. On the way to the boathouse she had been focused on it, the large building and what it might hold, but now she reoriented herself to the layout of the estate as a whole. "Is that the wall?"

When a gust of sea air lifted the trees, she could just catch a glimpse of the twelve-foot, beige colored concrete block wall. Prisons, she thought, probably have less secure perimeters.

"So?" Michael asked.

"I had no idea it was that close to the boathouse."

"And?"

"And if someone stowed away in the cabin and surprised her on the water, right there would be the logical place to go over the top. Or around the end—it's got to stop at the water. You'd hardly want to come in farther away and risk moving across the property any more than you had to."

"Why not? There's no cameras on the interior."

"But there's people. The family, the maid, a landscaper or two. Maybe not a lot of people, but you could never be sure. And people from OakTree must show up unexpectedly." The line where the trimmed grass ended and the trees and brush began was not uniform, as if the original growth had been left there when the estate was built. Or they had been carefully placed to create that illusion. Ellie moved closer.

Michael Tyler followed her. She had the feeling he still wanted to nag her about putting herself in a vulnerable position with Greg, and didn't want to hear it. Yes, it might not have been wise. But it *had* been productive.

"What are you looking for?"

"I'm not sure. Some sign of how they got in? Have you already had a team canvas this?"

Michael pulled a sand spur from his calf. "Not really. Ouch."

"Lick your fingers first, before you try to pull it off. Not kidding, it helps."

"I thought Florida was supposed to be the land of eternal sunshine and spring break."

"It is. It's also the land of hurricanes, alligators, and Burmese pythons. What do you mean 'not really'?"

He dealt with the needle-sharp burr before answering. "The local office had their team go over the boat, but I doubt they gave the grounds more than a cursory look-see. No one had a reason to believe anyone 'got in.' The crime scene, if we had a crime at all, seemed to be the boat—still seems to be the boat. Either she was attacked on the water, or—" He broke off to squeeze under the twining branches of the pepper trees and his tie got caught in the berries.

Ellie finished for him. "Or Ashley had an accident, fell into the water and couldn't get out again. That still might have happened, and the blood on the brush handle belongs to someone else. Or isn't blood at all."

The small forest wasn't as dense as it appeared from the lawn. Ellie could wind her way through the trunks and shrubs with only a few scratches and a mosquito bite, careful to avoid a few spiderwebs and a red rat snake. She noted a broken seagrape branch, already dried and dangling wildly by a hair, but her knowledge of botany didn't extend to carbon-dating stalk damage. It could have been hanging there for two weeks or two days.

The concrete block wall seemed much taller up close. She turned both ways, saw no person-sized breaches. "This wall stops at the water. I saw it from the boat. A human being might be able to duck under it at that point, where the land ends and slopes down to the water. Even where there's no ground, there's got to be a cluster of mangrove branches to use as handholds. There always is, when there's no seawall or beach."

The FBI agent seemed unexcited about the prospect of following the wall to the water. The heat radiated from the ground and baked them alive while the concrete blocks and tree branches blocked every puff of sea breeze. Only the strongest gusts made it over, as one did now.

"Windy," Michael said.

"Yeah, that's the outer bands of Hazel."

His voice took on a resolutely neutral tone. "I saw that on the news, that it should reach us tomorrow. No one, um . . . seems too concerned."

"It's just a *storm*," she said absently. "What if they went over the top?"

The high wall had the same iron spikes atop it as out by the gate. An intruder could use a ladder or climbing equipment, but they would still need to haul their body over, risking that which men, at least, held most dear. No, the end point would be the easiest to breach—

Then she noticed a live oak—not remarkable in itself, but within five feet of the wall. It had certainly grown wild, as no landscaper would have put it so close to a structure. A live oak could eventually grow to sixty feet and its canopy spread to cover half a football field—a horizontal spread of strong, knurled branches.

And one of those smaller, lower branches had been broken off.

Maybe nothing. Maybe a tree trimmer had misstepped, though she saw no sign that landscaping had been attempted in this area. It looked more like a wild thicket of nondescript forest was exactly what the owner wanted.

Maybe an intrepid paparazzi had shimmied over one of the expansive limbs.

Maybe a bobcat who could benefit from a low-carb diet had pounced.

She grasped one of the lower branches.

"No," Michael said.

"Oh yes." She began to climb.

"You were that kind of kid, weren't you?" he said, but not to be outdone by a mere girl, he pulled himself up its rungs as well. a sturdy growth of perhaps twenty feet and spreading wider than that.

"Isn't everybody?" In Cleveland, West Virginia, Nevada, of course she had climbed trees. By the time she came to Florida she'd been too old, and Florida trees, like much of the rest of its flora and fauna, looked good from a distance. Up close they weren't quite as friendly: now the bark scraped her palms and the branches hid battalions of mosquitos.

Mindful that maybe, just maybe, she had lucked onto the killer's means of egress, she examined the branches before moving along them, watching for caught tufts of fabric or a smear of blood or something really helpful like a dropped driver's license. It also took her mind off the fact that twelve feet appeared a much greater distance from a tree than it had seemed from the ground.

The spikes also looked sharper, and she chose the thickest branch to venture out upon. It rested between two of the spikes, securely wedged, with other branches forming handrails for her to keep her balance. Perhaps she'd let bravado push her too far, as when one cousin had rigged up a rope swing over the river and another talked her into a minidress for the prom. Always trying to catch up, fit in, claim a place at the table required a sometimes reckless commitment. Stop. Breathe. Calm. One step at a time.

"Can you see anything?" Michael asked, only a branch or two behind her.

She could see the Gulf glimmering to her left, over an endless spread of mangroves and Brazilian peppers and the occasional pine. But not a clue left by humans. The trees were no more dense than they were on her side, so an intruder *could* have woven through them to the wall, but where would they have come *from*?

"The closest building seems to be that one." She pointed to a peaked roof at least a mile away and slightly inland.

"It's a library."

Of course the FBI would have already checked out Martin's neighbors. She edged along another foot.

As live oaks were wont to do, its canopy extended far beyond Martin's wall. She had reached the spikes, yet the branches extended much farther, intersecting at points with other growth.

Ellie turned to look behind her. Michael stayed close to the trunk, not trusting the single branch with their combined weight. "I think you should stay there. Someone could have gone from this side over the wall, but we need to know if they could have come from that side and made it over."

"So why should I—"

"In case I get stuck, and can't get back in the tree. I'll need rescuing from this—" She waved at the expanse of tangled green. "It's not like there's a jogging track I can use to get back around."

She could tell he didn't like the idea, either because he was the FBI agent and should be taking the physical risks now that she was an, um, *civilian*, or he dreaded having to explain to superiors how he had lost Martin Post's consultant.

Or because he didn't want to be left alone with the Burmese pythons.

Ellie tried to be observant without looking down, but the trip proved easier than expected. At least until she felt close enough to the ground to drop from the branch, landed on a rock and twisted her ankle just enough to hurt a little and make her collapse, quite ungraciously, on her bottom in the rotting detritus of a moist environment. She stood and brushed herself off, feeling slightly ridiculous.

She rotated through the slight clearing, examining the ground, but saw nothing that couldn't be explained by nature's myriad activities.

There were no clear trails, and no way to know if anyone had been that way, *if* the killer had gone over the wall at that point, *if* the killer had gone over the wall at all, *if* the killer ever entered the Post property. Ashley could have had a regular rendezvous at sea, so the killer knew the murder weapon would be handy.

At least Ellie no longer questioned whether there had been a killer in the first place. That seemed to represent her only useful contribution in two days. "Someone could have come from anywhere."

"Not really." Michael stood on the top of the wall, conversing fairly easily for a man suspended above iron spikes with only a tree branch for balance. "They would have come from the road or the water, and I can't imagine why they would come from the water just to go back out on the water. I don't suppose they came from the library."

"Library patrons," Ellie told him, "would never be involved in a double murder. Plus there's a camera right there."

The wall cameras at the gate had been mounted on poles and could pivot in any direction, tracking movement. But the one she sighted now had been encased in a recess inside the wall, behind a clear shield that bowed out enough to give it the full 180 degree access. That would protect it from rain, falling branches, and animal nesting, but she wondered how often the glass enclosure would be cleaned of salt spray and grime. Who got *that* job?

Okay, enough. The experiment had been to see whether she could get back onto the estate via the same way she had exited and the time had come to find out. She returned to the branch, reached up . . . and couldn't touch it. Stretched. Strained. Gave up.

"Difficulty?" Michael asked. She couldn't tell from his tone if he was screwing with her or if he felt as curious as she about the answer.

A dead cypress log stretched near her feet, and she poked at it with one toe. Still solid, not totally rotten, so she set it on one end and used it as a step stool. From there, if she jumped upward, she could just latch her fingers around the back of the branch. It required gymnastics she hadn't used in twenty-odd years and gave her a temporarily upside-down view of Michael, but she managed to swing her legs up and around the branch.

Congrats, she got off the ground. But now she clung to the underside of the branch instead of the top side.

"You okay?" Michael asked.

She didn't bother to answer, and clearly needed to incorporate more dumbbell work into her daily exercise, but by grabbing another branch, she got herself upright. She scraped both forearms, put a small hole in her tee, and the ivy that had hitched a ride on the oak's foliage left green smears on her elbow, but she flashed a smile of triumph at the FBI agent.

"That was impressive," he said. It might have been sarcasm, but she chose not to take it that way.

"Now we know it's possible, at least."

"Sure, for a rhythmic gymnast."

She threaded her way back to him. "I would assume most hired killers are fairly agile. And I *am* impressed that you're familiar with rhythmic gymnastics. It doesn't get the respect it deserves in this country."

"My daughter started with it this year," he explained, and waited for her on the ground as she climbed down the live oak. "Are you done here?"

She thought. The estate might have a half dozen other breach points, but she wasn't eager to comb the few acres in this oppressive humidity and needed to get her collected samples back to the Locard with an overnight courier. "Yes."

"Good. Because I'm due for a chat with your sailing partner."

Chapter 14

Martin loaned them a conference room, a small one built to hold perhaps six people at a circular table. Floor-to-ceiling windows overlooking the Gulf made it much less claustrophobic, but Michael wondered if the tempting view also made it less productive. It would be too easy for a design team to start thinking about vacations rather than VoIP or varactors. Give him a ratty, closet-like interrogation room any day.

Especially for this guy. Greg Anderson rocked back in the ergonomic desk chair as if enjoying the view after a long day in the office instead of facing two FBI agents about the sudden death of his pregnant wife. He didn't look at either of them, but at the waves.

"Thank you for your time, Mr. Anderson," Luis began. "Let me assure you, right off, that there are not any obvious new findings with this second autopsy."

"Don't know why you had to do it at all," Greg said. "What was wrong with the first one?"

Many people in Greg's position, Michael knew from experience, would add *hasn't she, or haven't we, already been through enough*? The idea of an autopsy, of doctors cutting and prodding a loved one without their permission, seemed a nightmare to most. Greg Anderson sounded truculent and annoyed rather than upset, but to be fair, he'd been living with the situation for over two weeks.

Luis said, "Your father-in-law wants to be sure nothing is missed." The words were chosen deliberately, to needle Greg with the knowledge of who ran the show . . . and it worked. The man's jaw tightened, and the corner of his mouth twisted in what could be disgust, contempt—or fear. He still had the chair angled sideways, facing the water instead of the agents.

Luis got down to it, summarizing the condition of Ashley's body, all the facts Greg already knew. Then he threw in the injury to the inside of her spine. This snapped his body around to face them, but he said nothing.

Luis said, "We've seen the boat, as have you. Is there anything missing from it?"

"Her laptop. Ashley always had her laptop."

"I meant more like boat equipment. Fishing poles, equipment—I'm not much of a boat guy, so I don't know what the terms would be. But did you notice anything missing, or damaged?"

Greg seemed to think about this, but only briefly. "No."

"Everything that should be there was there? Nothing was broken, or bent?"

"No. Why?"

Luis described the small defect in Greg's wife's vertebra. Suddenly they had Greg's full attention as he absorbed this information, face solemn, chin propped on a hand adorned with a three-thousand-dollar watch. He seemed surprised— or was acting surprised. Michael couldn't tell.

"So just supposing your wife suffered some sort of injury—do you have any idea what might have caused it?"

"No."

"There's nothing on her boat—"

"Our boat."

"Your boat that might have caused a—" Words failed him.

"Impaling injury," Michael supplied.

"Not that I know of. And you said this could have occurred after she was in the water? Dead?"

"Possibly," Luis had to admit.

And that seemed to be that.

"If we could go over the timeline again."

Greg snorted and seemed about to protest, but his gaze darted around the room and he straightened up. "Of course. Anything I can do to help. I just miss her so much."

Sure you do, Michael thought, then stopped himself. Most people don't respond well to questioning, because they have all sorts of motives and agendas and warring impulses within them. It doesn't make them guilty.

"On Ashley's—on the day she went missing," Luis began, pretending to check his notes. "You said you both got up about eight?"

"Ashley sets an alarm. Set."

"You dressed, had breakfast in the main house? You mean Martin Post's area of the . . . house?"

"Martin's big on breakfast," Greg confirmed.

Michael asked, as if he were merely curious, "What does that mean?"

"That means you eat breakfast at eight-thirty whether you want it or not."

Hmm. "He's a bit of a control freak, huh?"

"Totally." He hastened to add: "But that's okay. Martin's great—and, more important, he's a great boss. If you've got an idea, he'll give you all the resources you need to get it going."

"That's fine at work. But at home—Ashley just went along with it?"

He glanced at the agents, a child's peek up from under long lashes. He seemed to debate between being appearing harshly truthful or sadly indulgent and took a middle road: "Ashley did whatever made Daddy happy. I don't mean that in a nasty way. I think they both had this mental picture of what a perfect family looked like and tried to be it."

"So whatever he wanted—"

"Pretty much. Ashley drank the Kool-Aid so many years ago that I don't think she ever realized it, that we ate what he wanted to eat and vacationed where he wanted to vacation and contributed to the charities that he wanted and on and on. He'd make her think it was all her idea. It was probably losing her mother or some shit like that, it made them, I don't know, hold on tighter."

Luis asked the tough question. "Why did you agree to live there, then?"

Again, contradictory feelings battled through Greg's expressions. "Why wouldn't I? Don't get me wrong, it's not like I grew up poor. My grandfather founded Gato Lago."

"What's that?" Michael asked. "A restaurant?"

Greg started an eye roll, then thought better of it. "It's a town in Silicon Valley. He was working on AI before anyone else knew the term. Sure, my father broke away to go into real estate, but now he owns acres of Marco Island. I don't want to sound snobby or anything, but my family had money, *real* money, long before the Posts."

No, that didn't sound snobby at all.

"Martin just happens to be a friggin' genius, that's all, but his parents were schoolteachers in some nowhere town in Michigan. So yeah, Ashley and I would live good even if her dad had never written a line of code—but have you seen our wing? Every amenity you could think of and a team of servants you wouldn't even know were there, they're that discreet. So I should get some McMansion in Gateway where

I'd have to do my own laundry and pay a guy to cut the grass? No, thanks." Then he softened his face and added: "And it was what Ashley wanted."

"Did Ashley ever get tired of this—closeness? Rebel a little? Talk about moving out?"

"Never . . . unless he rejected some of her code. She'd always be writing new programs to do this or that, and sometimes he didn't need it or it didn't really improve on what he already used. Those were the only times I'd see her get mad at him. Because, truthfully"—he sighed as if it pained him to say so—"Ashley's work didn't bring anything new to the table. She was good at coding, don't get me wrong, but her real talent was finding bugs in other people's programs. The ones she wrote herself only slightly improved on what already existed. Her stuff was . . . derivative."

"Unlike yours," Michael said, again as if he were merely curious.

"Mine *is* new. That's why I'm working with Martin on this defense contract and not her." He held up a hand as if someone had objected. "I know that sounds mean, but it's the truth. Martin would never admit that Ashley wasn't a genius off the old block, but when it came to business, it was business. Only results matter."

Michael asked, "What exactly was she working on?"

"I can't tell you that."

At first Michael thought he meant he didn't know, but realized his mistake when Greg added, "I'm sure your security clearance doesn't go that high."

"We have clear—"

"Not like this," Greg said. "It took seven months of going through our emails and checking our cavities before we could even submit a proposal to the MDA—Missile Defense Agency. This isn't FBI stuff. It's not even regular Army stuff. Most of Martin's security staff are all ex-military and we can't even tell them a thing about it. This is national interest crap like you wouldn't believe. You'll see when only a few people shy of the president show up tomorrow."

Ego-stroking embellishment? Or plain truth? Michael's job usually consisted of interstate kidnappings and human trafficking rings. Secret Squirrel plots did not pepper his inbox. "I thought you said she wasn't working on the defense contract."

"She . . . I mean, she *was* . . . but not with anything really *important*."

"I understand," Michael said, though he didn't. "We don't need the specifics. Just tell us why you think your wife might have been a target. Especially"—he needled—"if, as you say, her work wasn't truly vital."

Greg thought. Debating how to dumb down the technical information so that it wouldn't violate the National Secrets Act? Or debating how much could be verified for his murder trial? "I'm designing the video graphics interface—basically what will enable the signal receivers to recognize something is a missile and not a Cessna. Ashley had been working the bugs out of the wave filters—not that there were many bugs since Martin wrote all that. We have a demonstration scheduled for the committee that will decide the future of Oak-Tree. It's already been postponed twice."

"But surely now—"

"Oh no. Nothing will hit pause on this process. This project has been in the works since before Ashley and I married, that's how long the approvals and appropriations take. By the time the government actually buys something, the tech is obsolete. One more delay and we're knocked out of the bidding."

"And that's why you think your wife's death—"

"Was to stop Martin. To stop *me*. Do you know how much the U.S. spent on Reagan's Star Wars idea between the mideighties and midnineties? Thirty billion dollars. With a *B*—and it never even worked, really. You think they wouldn't kill for that? During that time period, when that thirty billion dollars got tossed around, *twenty-five different* people working on SDI turned up dead."

Michael had been a schoolkid then, but he had a fairly good grasp of major intrigues of the past fifty years. "What was that?"

"Yeah, not kidding. And the deaths were bizarre; guy crashed his car with cans of gas in the backseat, suicides by people who seemed perfectly happy—"

"Well, that often—"

"It was worth a few assassinations to get your piece of thirty billion—and today's budget would make that seem like pocket change. So if it wasn't the Russian or Chinese military who got Ashley, trying to get Martin to bail on the demo, it'll be Donec or EntreRobotics. They've shot their arrows and those arrows suck, so the only way they'll win the bid is if Martin's fails. Donec . . . I honestly don't think anyone there would have the balls, certainly not their CEO. But EntreRobotics—when they were smaller, gobbling up tech start-ups right and left, ones that held out found their lights turned off and their coders arrested on bullshit drug charges until nuisance lawsuits gutted them entirely. Entre-Robotics is *amazing*. So yeah . . . them, I could see."

Michael said, "Again, you're saying you think these companies would murder your wife over a business deal?"

Greg gazed at him with shock and a touch of pity. "They'd wipe out an entire *state* for a contract this big."

"But Martin Post's daughter?"

Greg shook his head. "Wouldn't even hesitate."

Chapter 15

The sky hurtled toward a deep dusk by the time Ellie pulled in the short driveway of Paul and Joanna's home. The old-style Florida home had pale turquoise stucco trimmed in brilliant white, with Bahama shutters and a privacy fence of fern-like areca palms as high as the roof. A vague light shone from the picture window and she assumed Rachael had gotten a ride from the medical examiner's office. They should have each rented a car, but the Locard, as a nonprofit dedicated to research and training, always operated on a strict budget.

Rachael, clearly, was not the only one at the home.

Aunt Katey had always told her there were two kinds of people in the world, those who like surprises, and those who don't. Be the former, she had advised. Every mistake is a gift of wisdom. Every problem is an opportunity. Every change opens a new world of possibilities.

Ellie had tried, she really had. But change still seemed to bring only stress, and surprises were rarely of the good kind.

Tonight did not make the exception. At least seven of the

news vans that had been parked outside Martin's house were now parked outside hers. Or maybe they were different vans from the same outlets, or different channels, whatever; now she had a group camped on her doorstep and she didn't have a guy in a guard shack at the end of her drive to intimidate them into keeping their distance. They milled about, chatting with each other, the temperature not exactly cool but at least not intolerable after sunset.

She hit the brake and stopped in the middle of the road, staring at the next few minutes of her life like an idiot, afraid to go closer, afraid to turn tail and run in case she attracted their attention.

She debated driving away . . . maybe she could park on the next block and sneak through the backyards to the lanai—until two figures emerged from the backyard and rejoined their colleagues. After that she didn't want to leave the safety of the vehicle and risk encountering the ravenous group on foot.

So, though she would rather have walked into a den of lions wearing Lady Gaga's meat dress, Ellie drove slowly toward her own driveway. *Don't step in front of the car. Don't step in front of the car.*

They stepped in front of the car.

"Doctor Carr! Are you working for Martin Post or the FBI?"

"Doctor Carr! Do you think Martin Post killed his daughter?"

"Doctor Carr! Do you think Greg Anderson killed his wife?"

"Is this just like the case of your cousin's son? Is that why you were chosen?"

Questions she couldn't answer, and which it wouldn't be appropriate even to try.

Ellie took her foot off the gas and let the car roll—surely that should be slow enough to nudge them out of the way without hurting anyone. But instead of nudging, they walked backward just quickly enough to protect their shins, blinding her with camera lights. She had to watch carefully through the bottom corners of the windshield to catch a glimpse of where her driveway began.

She turned the wheel, gently, slowly. It reminded her of *The Birds*, with Tippi Hedron placing her feet caaaarefulllly among the scattered flock on her way to the car. But this flock wouldn't scatter.

She blew the horn. The forms, shapeless blobs behind the light, startled and shifted, and Ellie dared to touch the gas pedal enough to make it up the slight bank that all flood zone homes possessed. When she saw they remained on the sides of the car, she scrabbled for the garage door remote clipped to the visor and pressed it. They wouldn't follow her inside, would they? Surely they wouldn't risk a trespass charge.

It rose with an agonizing lack of haste while she waited, moving an inch every time a reporter tried to get back in front of the car. They hovered around its perimeter but for the most part didn't touch it, to her relief. The damage waiver might not—

"What were Ashley's injuries?"

"Has the baby been found?"

"Was she even really pregnant? No one's seen photos!"

A man with shaggy, dirty-blond hair knocked on her window. "Hey! Have you missed your time in the spotlight? Is that what this is about?"

Ellie pushed the gas more firmly this time, and shot into the garage at more than recommended speed, pressing the remote furiously before she'd even stopped. It plodded downward at the same agonizing crawl, but at least she had gotten inside the familiar, secure home.

She turned off the engine, letting weariness flood her for one moment. What a day.

She picked up her purse and her envelopes of various swabs, climbed out.

And collided with a body.

"Hey!" she screamed, scuttling back, feeling the heat from the car's engine as she steadied herself on the bumper.

Then she ran for the door, mercifully unlocked, and whipped through it, shut it, locked it, jumped away as though the metal could burn her skin.

The house seemed silent at first. Then she heard the hum of falling water. Rachael was in the shower. No other sounds reached her ears, not even from behind the door she now faced.

Oddly, it had been in a garage where she'd first realized that a man could be something to be feared. She had been twelve, and the man had been her Uncle Wayne.

Chapter 16

Sure, in all the books she read and television shows she watched, men were always threatening some beautiful woman, but then another man, handsome and nice, would show up to rescue her, so it all sort of canceled out in Ellie's mind. But Uncle Wayne made her realize that humans couldn't be figured out like an equation or characters in a script. Sometimes, they couldn't be figured out at all.

She had moved in with him and Aunt Rosalie after her ninth birthday. It had seemed an ideal solution at the time— they lived only a few blocks from her grandmother's and she'd been playing with their two daughters and one son since birth. She remembered Uncle Wayne as a handsome man in a crisp uniform, hugging his children fiercely before driving off to a deployment in some foreign land. The first Gulf War had officially ended, but the morass in the Middle East had not, and Aunt Rosalie would be left largely alone for the next two and a half years. Rosalie would fill that gap as she always had: with religion.

During her time at Rosalie's house, Ellie spent more time in church, in prayer, volunteering at soup kitchens, and painting homes for humanity than she would during the rest of her life combined. Rosalie was strict: mentally—the children did their homework as faithfully as they prayed; physically—there were never a lot of sweets or dinners out at Rosalie's house, not that she could afford it on a soldier's salary and her own part-time work; and spiritually—the devotion and good works were never about control but a caring, genuine commitment to the common good. If Ellie learned from the hippie-ish Aunt Katey to nurture herself, she had first learned from Rosalie to nurture others. A good lesson, and sometimes she thought much of the world could benefit from being raised at Aunt Rosalie's.

Then Uncle Wayne came home.

At first he seemed merely tired, the uniform now worn and frayed at the cuffs. He still hugged his kids fiercely, included Ellie, kissed Rosalie long and hard. He raved about the simple meals, saying how sick he'd been of eating out of cans. He smiled at his two girls as they chattered about school friends and playing soccer with someone's battered ball on the patchy grass that passed for a park on the next block, and at Ellie when she spoke of Halloween costumes. He tried to circumvent his eight-year-old when the boy demanded typical boy stories of pitched battles, blood and guts. But the smiles were always strained. The corners of the lips couldn't hold them for long, and his mouth would slip back into a straight line, the gaze back to a spot on the wall behind them, a spot so far away that his eyes could never quite focus on it. The dust of the desert would not quit his pores no matter how long he spent in the home's single bathroom, and the children were told, in Rosalie's stern tone, not to complain if they had to hold it.

Ellie saw all this, and clearly, Rosalie did as well. The other kids soon got over the excitement of having their father back and slowly they too came to wonder if they'd really gotten him back at all. The household settled into a subdued, uncertain hum of caution.

Uncle Wayne didn't seem to remember what to do with himself in his own house. It didn't occur to him to take out the garbage or cut the grass or seek a new job, so Rosalie continued doing all those things as she had before. He would wander into a room where Ellie and her cousins might be doing their homework or watching a stupid sitcom; he might hover, glance around at a picture or the window, then wander out again. Once her little cousin asked what was wrong with his father, and the girls, upset without knowing why, because everyone in the house had become upset without knowing why, told him to shut up. Ellie felt for him and wished she could explain, but she felt equally clueless. She and the older of the two girls, Maureen, had heard of post-traumatic stress disorder, but had no idea what to do about it. They were too young and too shy to suggest mental health care to Aunt Rosalie, who surely had figured that out herself, but if she discussed that with Wayne, they did it quietly. In front of the kids, after those first few weeks, they stopped speaking at all.

Halloween came. Uncle Wayne took one look at the trick-or-treaters swarming his street, ghosts and pirates and ninja warriors and zombies, and fled up the worn steps. For the first time Rosalie let the kids go out alone, with uberstrict, I-mean-it instructions to stay within arm's length of each other and not move away for any reason and especially you, Glennie, or all your candy will be taken away. Then she went upstairs as well, and they didn't see her for the rest of the night.

A week later, Ellie and Maureen had been playing Barbies with Margery on the nailed-down planks of wood that passed for a tree house in the maple next to the garage. At nearly twelve they felt too old for dolls, but it kept Margery quiet and that had become their primary goal every night after school. Noise needed to be kept away from the house. No one had said so, but the only thing a child can do to help the adults around them is to stay out of the way. They were children, so they stayed out of the way, not even knowing what it was they were helping. This had become their new normal.

Margery, at nine, still loved her dolls, and spent hours poring over the Barbie Magical Mansion she'd talked her mother into buying at a garage sale. She maintained it with her future real estate agent's care, using stickers to fix the curling wallpaper and flooring, cleaning the miniature light fixtures with Windex as though they really were crystal. But that night she'd gotten too enthusiastic about adding sprigs of evergreen needles to the window boxes and snapped one off. Nine might be too old to cry about such things, but Ellie could see the lower lip tremble.

"I'll get some glue." Ellie ran off to the house before Margery could burst in to demand her mother's attention, because they all knew her mother had her hands full, with some unknown, invisible, increasing source of weight that had filled the house and would eventually crush them all.

The detached garage barely held one car, but that one car almost always rested in the driveway among the snow and leaves. It might have been safer there, in truth, since the garage appeared ready to blow over in a strong wind. But with six people in a small house every precarious space had to be utilized, so tools, bins of holiday decorations, and other supplies were kept on its haphazard wooden shelves. Glue was a tool, so Ellie headed straight in to the already-open cavern. A switch on the wall lit the single bulb.

As it flickered to life she saw Uncle Wayne, standing not four feet away. He'd been facing the back of the garage as if gazing at shovels and rakes and old paint cans, which he couldn't have seen in the pitch darkness.

Her heart immediately began to pound, so hard it should have broken a few ribs, and white noise filled her ears. It wasn't that he had startled her in a dark room. It wasn't that she was afraid to be alone with him. It wasn't that he didn't even turn around to see who had turned on the light. It was that what he was doing made no sense at all.

It seemed incomprehensible, and since it was incomprehensible it was also paralyzing. She had no idea what to do.

Should she run? Say "Hi, Uncle Wayne"? Turn the light back out?

He didn't move. He didn't even appear to be breathing. Maybe Wayne was perfectly sane and she was the one who now hallucinated. Maybe if she moved forward and touched him, he would disappear like fog.

And while she debated, he shifted.

He began to rotate, slowly turning around, and she decided on an option without thinking.

Run.

Except she couldn't. Her feet had frozen to the floor, quite literally. They'd even grown so cold she couldn't feel them. She couldn't feel anything, not her hands or her back or her stomach, only the pounding against the inside of her rib cage, pounding and pounding.

His eyes held no recognition. He didn't know who she was and somehow she knew he didn't care—it mattered only that she lived and breathed, and that had to stop. He had to stop it.

He stepped closer and reached for her, so fast it seemed like a jump cut in a horror film, too fast for her even to gasp.

But she could move fast too, it turned out. She pivoted and went into motion so quickly that, looking back, it seemed impossible she hadn't fallen. She felt the air behind her move as he reached out a large hand, could swear she heard the swish of his arm nearly touch her hair—she could see how narrow her escape was as if she had eyes in the back of her head. She turned the corner and flew to the tree.

She made herself pause at the three nailed rungs that rose up its trunk, waiting to see if Wayne would follow, waiting to compose her face to keep from scaring the other girls. She watched the driveway.

He didn't appear. His shadow did not stretch across the cracked concrete. No sound followed her.

She forced her facial muscles to relax into nothingness, then climbed up.

"Couldn't find it. Let's go inside, there's probably some in the basement. It's too dark out here to fix it anyway." Without waiting for the inevitable protests, she picked up the Magical Mansion—gently, moving with care, not risking more damage that might set Margery into a wail or require more supplies—and backed down the tree trunk.

No one else in the yard. The lights in the house glowed, illuminating the grass nearly as bright as day. Aunt Rosalie's thriftiness did not extend to the electric bill, or perhaps she didn't care for the dark. Not when Uncle Wayne was away. Not now that he was back.

Carrying the Barbie house, Ellie padded over the green to the narrow strip that ran between the house and the fence—not the obvious choice, not the driveway leading to the side door. But Maureen had caught her tone and didn't question, and Margery followed where the Barbie house went.

Ellie circled around to the front door, open and unlocked at that relatively early hour, and up the stairs to the girls' room. There she set the house down and went to find her aunt Rosalie, telling her in a quiet, adult way how she'd found Uncle Wayne standing in a dark garage staring at the back wall. Ellie had delivered the message and left, not asking for an explanation or a plan. Ellie was not quite twelve years old and knew enough to know that she knew nothing, not what her uncle had endured or how Rosalie should handle it. Nor did she ask.

Weeks later, after the kids returned from school one day to find the living room looking as if a bomb had gone off, every piece of furniture awry, pictures off the walls, lamps knocked over, Rosalie handled it. All four children were packed off to Rosalie's cousin Billie's house in the Nevada desert, and Wayne began seeing a therapist at the Veterans Administration.

Billie and her husband Roland's house at the foot of a mountain had been Ellie's summer home while living with her grandmother, so it felt familiar to her, but Rosalie's children had not been too happy about the arrangement. When Aunt Rosalie took them to the airport, she pulled each away from the others, one by one, for a quick heart-to-heart. Ellie had never asked what the others had been told, and to her, Aunt Rosalie said Ellie had to leave temporarily because Uncle Wayne did not feel well. He needed to heal, and they only had a few weeks of school left anyway, and they would all be back together for Christmas. Ellie should not feel worried or scared and if she did, to say her prayers and the Lord would protect her. But she did not have to worry about Uncle Wayne. Uncle Wayne would never hurt her, could never be a danger to her, or Maureen, or Margery, or Glennie. He *loved* them. Did she understand?

Yes, Ellie had said, though she didn't, not with the strong feeling that love had nothing to do with it, that Uncle Wayne was very much a danger, and that now Rosalie would be alone with him with only the Lord to protect her. That might not be enough, but she and Maureen and the two younger ones certainly wouldn't be, either. Rosalie was doing what she should do. She was being a good mother.

And she'd been right, in the end. Something did help Uncle Wayne. In the new year the three cousins moved back home to start the spring semester at their old school, and over the years Uncle Wayne had returned to being a husband, a father, a wage earner. He never quite lost the tinge of sadness around the mouth, but Ellie could chat easily with him now at reunions. He took an interest in her work and told her about the challenges of his security company. Aunt Rosalie had said he would be fine, and fine he was, and she had never doubted Aunt Rosalie again.

But Ellie had not gone back to their home. They had enough to handle with their own three, and Aunt Katey and Uncle Terry had stepped up. She'd started the second half of the seventh grade in Ansted, West Virginia.

For a moment now, her heart thudded just as it had then. Ellie was no longer eleven, but the man now in her garage could be every bit as dangerous as Uncle Wayne.

Chapter 17

He must have ducked under the door as it closed. Was he the only one? It had happened so fast and in the dim light of the garage, she couldn't be sure. Would this basic door lock work? Should she barricade it with something?

Stop. Think. He had already entered, surely he wouldn't add "breaking" to the crime. A legitimate news agency would never condone such aggression. But what if he was freelance or an unpaid blogger—or not a reporter at all?

She put an ear to the door. Had he left through the side door? The garage had nothing to steal other than some rakes and potting soil and a twenty-year-old bicycle. He could go through her car, which she kept scrupulously clean, but there would be her rental form and a GPS in the glove box . . . though what use that would be to anyone . . . She could set off the car's alarm with the remote in her hand, blast his tender eardrums. The house also had an alarm with an ear-splitting shriek, but she didn't know how loud it would be in the garage, and likely it would hurt her more than him.

At least she could picture him sweating in the hot environment with no breeze.

"Dr. Carr," came a voice. He sounded almost patient, as if she were a spoiled child refusing to come out of her room.

Should she call the police? That sounded embarrassing, that she couldn't handle kicking out a reporter by herself. Wouldn't the guy leave once the sweat soaked his shirt? Or would others join him? They wouldn't want to let him get a scoop, might trickle in until they once again surrounded her car. The one with the possibly substandard damage waiver.

She threw open the door.

It was the blond reporter, lounging against the rental's bumper, a miniature camera in one hand and a microphone in the other. At least none of his colleagues had joined him. "Dr.—"

"Get off that car!"

He straightened, taking his time to step to the side. "What is your capacity in this case? What did you see at the Post bunker today?"

"What the hell are you doing in my garage?" If she opened the overhead to shoo him out like a pesky fly, would more rush in?

He smirked. "Bruce Dunning, Forester News Service. And don't you mean your aunt and uncle's garage?"

She walked up to him, knowing that she fumed, knowing his camera rolled. "Fine. My aunt and uncle's garage. The point is, *not* yours. Get out."

"Why is that, anyway? I would think the prestigious Locard could afford an Airbnb." The sandy blond hair fell into his tan face, putting her in mind of a surfer. "Has it fallen on hard times since the murders? Are you hoping Martin Post can refill your coffers?"

She wanted to grab him by the ear and drag him to the door, but had more sense than to push, or touch, or do anything that could be later characterized as "attacking." So from a foot away from his face she spoke, clipping off her words. "No comment. Now leave."

"Hey, I get it. The Locard is a class place and you can't help that your cousin was a psycho. This is a chance to repair your reputation. I can help you do that. We have outlets in all fifty states."

She pulled out her cell phone, and dialed 911 with pointed concentration.

"This is the third-richest guy in the country, and he called you. There's got to be a reason."

Ellie gave the dispatcher her name, then: "I'd like to report an occupied burglary in progress at one-eighty-two Oleander Drive."

The reporter's eyes widened slightly. "Burglary? I'm not taking anything."

"Doesn't matter. You're inside the property. Yes, he's inside my garage and refusing to leave."

He spoke more quickly. "You're going to have to talk to someone. It might as well be me. I'll be sure to paint you in a good light."

Into the phone she said, "I don't *know* if he's armed."

"Let's face it, you need all the positive publicity in the world to get your life back. We could work together." But his face lost its veneer of sneer.

"I suppose he *could* be," she told the dispatcher.

Bruce Dunning took a step back, both literally and figuratively. The garage didn't have a lot of extra space and she didn't move out of his way. He gave her one narrow-eyed glare to save face, then turned and walked all the way around the rented car with exaggerated measure. He reached the side door, looked back at her with the same pointed calm, and exited.

With no one else in the room and no need to save face, she ran to the door and locked it, flipping the dead bolt. "Okay," she told the dispatcher, "he's gone."

"Are you safe?"

Ellie went inside and did a quick scan of the house, but other than water running in the hallway bath, the rooms appeared empty. She asked the operator to cancel the call and disconnected.

Halfway through a deep breath, in through the nose, out through the mouth, it rang again. Unfamiliar number. *"What?"*

"Dr. Carr?" The voice rang a bell, but she didn't know which bell.

"Yes?"

"This is Tyler." When she didn't respond, he added with a touch of asperity, "From the FBI?"

"Yes. Yes, got it. Sorry."

"Are—are you all right?"

In through the nose . . . She explained about the reporter in her garage.

Michael Tyler sounded utterly unsurprised, and asked the same question the dispatcher had. "Are you safe now?"

"Yes. I think so. I was safe the whole time, he just wanted a story, but that's so bloody obnoxious to barge in like that . . ."

"Is your home secure?"

"Uh . . . I think so." She did another quick scan of the rooms, aware that the lights flicking on and off made her actions clear to the crowd outside, no doubt to their amusement, but she didn't care. At least she didn't find any climbing through her windows like a bad remake of *Night of the Living Dead.* The water had stopped in the bathroom and Rachael called a hello as Ellie went by. In the living room, she went to the front window, leaving those lights off and staying well to the side of the glass before peeking cautiously through the miniblind.

She watched as Bruce Dunning regaled his colleagues with his tale of brief captivity at the hands of the humorless and slightly crazy forensic expert. The rest of them had apparently remained in the street instead of attempting a breach—unlike Dunning, his fellow reporters had the professional standards and the spark of integrity he lacked. "Yes. It's secure."

"Do you need protection?"

She hesitated. She'd *love* protection. She'd love to know that this would not be a repeat of several past cases, that someone would come and chase all those vans away and tell everyone to leave her alone. Paul and Joanna's neighbors would probably like that as well.

But the reporters were within their rights and doing their jobs, and a camera and a microphone were hardly weapons to fear. "No. I'm fine. Sorry if I sounded freaked out. What—what can I do for you?"

"It's Ashley's blood. On the brush handle."

"Wow, that was fast. Your lab must have really fired up the Rapid DNA and—oh."

"Yes," he said. "Oh."

Next stop, they would have to compare the edge of the pole to the indentation in the victim's vertebra. Neither she nor Rachael were qualified to do that; they would need a bone expert—or rather the FBI would need a bone expert—

"And the prints lifted from the handle all belonged to Greg."

"Oh," she repeated.

"Exactly. We're getting a search warrant for all of Greg's areas, including his man cave storage unit, to be executed tomorrow. Mr. Post wants the Locard to be present. So I'm delivering the message."

"Sorry."

He made a low sound that might have been a chuckle. "Don't be, it's okay. You found the pole our people missed, so maybe that lu—maybe you'll . . . find more. And Mr. Post insists."

And when Mr. Post insists . . .

"If you don't mind my asking," he went on, "how long have you known Martin Post?"

"Since about one o'clock this afternoon."

"No offense, but if it's nothing personal, why did he hire you?"

"He hired the Locard. I don't need to point out their reputation."

"Of course not. But he asked me to make sure you arrive at his house tomorrow at ten. Not you and Rachael, just you. He seems . . . focused."

She explained the connection to her uncle, but added: "I don't understand it, either. Maybe he figured that since I'd turn in my own cousin—"

"That you'd tell the truth, no matter what. Even if it's not what he wants to hear."

"I guess. But I'm not sure that quite makes sense."

"Nothing about this case quite makes sense," Michael said, and hung up.

Rachael walked into the kitchen, dressed to relax in a fresh tracksuit. "I have unabashedly gone through your aunt and uncle's cabinets. For dinner options we have canned soup, frozen vegetables, or dry cereal."

Ellie cast a vote for "all of the above."

Chapter 18

They passed around stale crackers and equally stale soft drinks, taking care not to spill any on the pages now covering the dining room table. Ellie gave her boss a condensed recap of her encounter with the reporter, and they both cast a nervous glance at the door leading to the garage. A courier had already collected the samples from the boat to get to the Locard so that the scientists there could work their magic. Rachael had arranged to work with the FBI bone expert to compare the brush handle threads to the bone indentation.

Ellie said, "Though we already know whom the blood and the prints on the weapon—if we can call it a weapon yet without confirmation—belong to."

"For the sake of argument, yes, it's the weapon. Which means things aren't looking good for the cute young husband. With whom you spent the afternoon alone on a boat."

"Don't you start. Michael already bitched me out about that."

"*The* boat, in fact, which could also be considered a murder weapon because without it, Ashley Post Anderson might not be dead. What do you think of him?"

"Michael?"

"No! The delectable Greg Anderson."

Ellie almost spit Diet Coke across the table. "I thought you thought he was guilty!"

"I do. I also think he's delectable."

Ellie rose to dig through the pantry for some peanut butter, belatedly hoping that Rachael's deception detection wouldn't peg that as evasive. "Not *quite* the word I'd use. Young. Strong. Maybe hiding a bit of insecurity."

"Insecure about his place in the Post world, or insecure because he's not sure he can get away with murder?"

"I'd guess the former. It can't be easy living in the orbit of a billionaire genius." She emerged from the pantry, jar in hand. "And that house."

"That house. Gorgeous."

"Cold. This should still be good, right? Peanut butter never goes bad."

Rachael inspected the contents of the jar. "Looks okay to me. Do you mean the temperature or the overall aura?"

Ellie regained her seat, armed with the jar and a butter knife, the silverware still in the same drawer it had been when she lived there. "The temperature was perfect. The furniture is perfect, the pictures are hung in a perfectly straight line, the windows sparkle, the bedrooms play music as soon as you walk in, whatever kind you like. Apparently Ashley liked Beethoven. Or Greg, can't be sure."

"I wouldn't guess Greg for a classical fan. He doesn't get a choice in the music playlist?"

"Who knows? Maybe it knows one person from the other and it was Martin's playlist. It seems to me a little weird that they live there at all, but then, I wouldn't let pride keep me from that kind of luxury."

"You didn't even like the place!" Rachael laughed.

"Just the decor. Minimalist isn't my cup of tea," Ellie

went on. "It was *too* minimal—you couldn't tell, from looking at the place, that real human beings lived there. But
everything else was appropriately fabulous." Ellie wondered
if the words were true even as she said them. Something
about living under Martin Post's eye did not appeal to her.

But to Ashley, of course, it would feel like home. Or it
didn't, and Ashley lived there because Martin wanted her to,
and it never occurred to her to do anything other than what
Martin wanted. When we're discouraged from questioning
as a child, Ellie knew, sometimes we never pick up the habit
again. The narrative gets cemented into the young mind and
heals over, never to be fully exposed again.

Rachael said, "But with all the technology, there's no
video surveillance?"

"Nope."

"Do you believe him?"

"I'm not sure. Not sure at all." She told Rachael about the
electronic house assistant Deborah, and Rachael reacted just
as Ellie had.

"His dead *wife*? How does the second wife feel?"

"I didn't ask. But I thought she was sweet, didn't you?
Very caring."

"Maybe." Rachael built a cracker sandwich to chew as she
thought. "Thanks for the protein. I did a quick survey of the
supplies but I didn't want to be searching through your aunt
and uncle's things."

"Nonsense! Search through anything you like if you need
something. Paul and Joanna won't care. They're pretty minimalist themselves, and aren't here more than they are." Ellie
wondered if that was why Martin Post had been Paul's patient. Kindred spirits. Both craving for more meaning in life
than possessions. Difference was, Martin could afford the
possessions as well. "If we stay here much longer we're going to have to stop somewhere and get some real food."

She noticed Rachael frown, peanut-buttering another cracker with a great disinterest, and said, "I hope you're comfortable enough here. If you aren't we could—"

"No, no. This house is great. I just . . . hate being away from my kid."

Ellie didn't know what that would feel like, so she gave her boss a moment or two of silence to deal with it. Then she asked, "What did *you* think of Dani?"

"She seems pretty straightforward. Her man's in pain and she wants to do whatever she can to help, whether that's managing his schedule or waiting quietly on standby. Maybe she's a trophy who knows what side her bread is buttered on. Maybe she's the evil stepmother who's slipping it to that cute Tomas from the garage, killed her rival, and plans to stay under the radar for the duration."

"Is that possible? Do we have a timeline?"

Rachael wrapped up the remaining crackers. "Martin seemed to think I'd already know it, since the media has printed so much about the case. The family of four had breakfast together. From there, Martin spoke at a luncheon of tech company start-ups at the Naples Ritz. Dani toiled at researching and distributing over two million dollars in charitable funds from their foundation, breaking only when their cook brought her lunch. Greg left the property to go to his workshop—apparently, it's a rented office-slash-man cave. So okay, maybe the unrelenting luxury of his father-in-law's place does get to him from time to time."

"The warrant covers that." Ellie told her the plans for serving a search warrant the next morning.

"You'll have to tell me about it. I'll be with the FBI's anthropologist. Want to bet this man cave is more about porn and video games than writing code?"

"I only make bets I'm sure will win."

"Where's the challenge in that?"

"There isn't one. That's the point."

"Anyway, the security guy let Greg out of the gate just before nine. And Deborah said Ashley went out the front toward the boathouse at nine-fifty. Martin came back about two-thirty and found Dani still working. About four, Martin went to ask Ashley something, couldn't find her, asked Deborah, and realized she was still out on the boat. Called her cell, nothing, but they'd been working balls to the wall on this satellite defense system and sometimes she turns her phone off so she can concentrate. Greg returned after five, they all got more concerned, called her cell, still nothing, checked the boat tracker, no signal. The boat tracker's battery has gone coincidentally dead. Don't like that, but turns out the other boat—"

"*Wicked*—the sister boat is the *Wicked*."

"Okay, well, Miss *Wicked*'s tracker also had a dying battery. The two boats are identical, built at the same time, fitted out with the same equipment."

"And her phone?"

"Found on the boat, sloshing around in the daily rainstorm pond that had formed on the deck. After the cell phone had been soaking for two weeks they couldn't get anything from it. They had tried the phone locater app, right away that afternoon, but it must have been too far off shore to get a signal. So from there—the agony began. The Coast Guard searched, but it's a big Gulf."

The two women were silent for a moment, as if in remembrance of a woman they'd never met.

Rachael went on. "So everyone's got an alibi, of sorts, but not a great one. Martin was gone for hours at an event that's only five miles from home. Dani was home but seen by the staff, and Greg left before Ashley did and there's no way back onto the property without tripping a camera."

"Ashley goes out on a boat into the open Gulf, where

anyone could have approached her. Another boat, someone on a jet ski, a Navy Seal who can swim twenty miles without breaking a sweat."

"Someone could have pretended to be in distress. She seems like the kind of person who would rush to help—of course I'm getting that impression from her clearly biased father. It could also be a simple accident. She had a dizzy spell and fell overboard, the damage to her abdomen is due to predators or even a propeller strike."

"Could that have caused the cut to the vertebra?"

"I don't see how, without hitting a few ribs. It's too far up in the cage."

"I've seen a lot of murders," Ellie said, a sudden weariness threatening to overtake her. "But this may be the weirdest."

Chapter 19

Thursday
Day Two

The reporters were mostly gone the next morning, only one battered sedan with an indecipherable magnetic sign sticking to its door left at the curb. Ellie checked, staying to the side of the windows, peering through the miniblinds without touching them, as careful as if four trained snipers waited outside for a clear shot. Then she berated herself for being a wimpy idiot. And then she kept doing it anyway, until she felt satisfied that no others remained—other than the sedan, and she couldn't even tell if anyone sat inside. At any rate, after a quick breakfast with Rachael she felt brave enough to back the rental out of the garage and into the street, alert to any movement, terrified that she might accidentally hit someone with a camera. Ellie had seen enough traffic deaths during her early career to consider automobiles the most deadly weapon, and the general driving habits of the American populace had not improved since then.

But no humans appeared in the quiet street, no head popped up in the sedan. Either it had been disabled and abandoned, or its occupant slumbered on.

Ellie wished she could. After her usual one hour to fall asleep had stretched into two, then to two and a half, she'd thrown off the covers and stomped back to her office ... correction, her aunt and uncle's office. She'd made her movements as silent as possible to avoid waking Rachael. In her own house, for the first time in her life, she could make all the noise she wanted in the middle of the night. At least insomnia seemed easier to manage when one lived alone.

"At least" ... the series of essentially optimistic people who had raised her had drilled the phrase into her head. At least we made it home before the rain hit. At least the car runs. At least you don't have to live with strangers. One could always—always—find one good thing about any given moment.

In the office she'd pulled out the photos she'd taken of Ashley Post Anderson's abdomen, reduced to a gaping hole where a baby bump should have been. But she couldn't come up with a single good thing.

Now she pulled up, again, to the dead woman's home. If one could call this a home.

Without Dani in an open garage to distract her, Ellie traveled farther into the compound and discovered a beautiful entranceway with a curved portico and tidy, sustainable landscaping. The angles were still square and boxy, modern and plain, but it had a space to park the rental under the portico, behind someone's SUV. Dani Post emerged from the automatic doors to usher her into what looked like the lobby of a very expensive hotel with towering ceilings and leather couches.

Dani appeared no less stunning than the day before, the skin creamy, the hair engagingly awry, yet her body language spoke of both weariness and agitation. She grabbed two water bottles from inside a wine fridge that served as an end table and handed one to Ellie without asking. "Martin will be here in a minute. We just got the weather report for tomorrow and it's a nightmare—tropical depression Hazel is going to hit just as we have sixteen people here watching Martin's system work."

She collapsed onto the couch and Ellie idly wondered if it were leather or vinyl or made by monks in Nepal. She didn't know what to say, with not even a vague idea of what this "test" entailed. "That must be very difficult at such a time."

"I know it must seem strange that we don't cancel, in light of—what happened to Ashley. But it truly isn't an option. It has to get to Ways and Means to be included in the defense budget. Two of the senators are up for reelection and one has ticked off his party enough that he may get yanked from the committee, and those changes could shift the committee's attitude. Tomas worked his Air Force contacts until they found a location for the East Coast base—Highland County—but if that governor loses his election—and he probably will—the environmentalists will have the ear of his replacement and nix the deal."

"How do you keep track of all those factors?"

"It isn't easy." Dani fluttered a hand, clearly working to force her face back into its usual mask of calm. "It has to be done—both for the country's sake, and for Martin's. Having something to focus on may be all that's keeping him together. He's not eating, not sleeping." After a moment, she added, "And for Ashley's sake. She worked so hard on it."

Speaking of Ashley, while she had the stepmom to herself . . . Ellie sat down on an opposite couch. High-grade vinyl, she decided. "How was Ashley doing with the pregnancy? Did she have any issues . . . that maybe she didn't want to talk to her dad about?" *Like, the baby wasn't Greg's, or she actually hated coding?*

Dani blinked at the change in topics, but then left missile defense behind with apparent relief. "No, really. First of all, she seemed the quintessential glowing mother-to-be. Second, there's *nothing* she wouldn't tell her dad."

"They were very close." A statement, not a question. And yet a question, which Dani heard, understood, and answered with a slight smile.

"Was I jealous? Yes and no. Martin doted on her, but he had high expectations as well. I watched her work so hard to live up to what she thought he expected, and I'd think, I'm so glad I don't have to do that. It's a reprieve to be the only nongenius in the house. I could sympathize about their stress but didn't have to partake." She drank from her bottle, her expression softening. "And we were so excited about the baby. I never had much interest in having children—Ashley was a grown woman when Martin and I met—so I was totally down with being the adoring grandma without having to go through the mommy marathon." Her smile faded. "Ashley was the only other person who understood Martin, could make him happy. She was my *ally*. And now . . ." Her voice trailed into silence.

"How do you feel about Deborah?" Ellie burst out. Then she squirmed and thought, for the first time, that maybe some questions *should* be discouraged.

"How do I feel about my husband talking to an electronic version of his dead wife all the time?" Dani laughed and tucked an errant strand behind one ear. "I couldn't care less, if it makes him and Ashley feel better. I love that he loves so deeply. I love that he doesn't leave people behind—because that means he won't leave me behind either."

Dani Post, Ellie concluded, was either very secure or very intelligent, and most likely both.

Martin Post walked in, dressed much as he had been the day before, loose but not baggy jeans and a long-sleeved T-shirt. "Good, you're here."

"Sorry if I'm late," Ellie said. "I was—"

"Not at all," Martin said. "Your uncle was the same way, would keep me waiting if he had a patient with greater needs. One of the reasons I always trusted his diagnoses. You even look like him—and your mother."

"I . . . how—"

To Dani, he said, "Is Tomas here?"

"Not yet."

"Okay, take care of him. And don't forget that Greg is around . . . somewhere."

To Ellie, he said, "Let's go."

Chapter 20

About half a mile down a sparsely populated road sat the SecuritySite U Store It office, a small building inside a wall nearly as substantial as Martin Post's estate. Ellie wasn't concerned about the wall. Her current worry drove two car lengths behind her.

Five minutes after she left the Locard, a small blue sedan popped up in the rearview mirror, with duct tape flapping from one cracked headlight—so, not the one that had been parked across the street that morning. She mentally dismissed it, made the light onto 41 north, and heard the squeal of tires as it followed her through the intersection under what had to be a now-red light. Still, she didn't think much of it. Stoplight periods in Florida were notoriously long; local wisdom had it that even young drivers forgot where they were going by the time one changed, and having to wait through another cycle could throw your whole schedule off.

It stayed two lengths behind her. An SUV pulled into the space, decided she wasn't driving fast enough, and pulled back out. The blue sedan stayed there, not speeding up, not slowing down.

Still, not remarkable. Another characteristic of Florida road-ways: because so many routes were cut off by canals, lakes, marshes, there were few shortcuts from one place to another. The main thoroughfares stayed crowded because drivers had no other options. But when she moved into the center lane, the sedan moved. She caught a glimpse of the driver.

Shaggy hair to the top of his loosened collar. Head not turning to the side mirrors, not texting, not changing the radio stations, only focused straight ahead—on her.

Using voice command, she got the phone to redial the last number, Martin's. He answered by asking where the hell she was.

"I'm sorry, but I think I'm being followed by a reporter, and I didn't want to let him trail me right to your door."

A snort that would have sounded like a laugh if she hadn't known better. "Let him. He can join the club—I had six right behind me."

"Oh. Okay. I—"

"Leonard will let you in. Just get here."

He hung up. The possibility that she might not *want* to wade into the media pool either did not occur to him or didn't meet his standards for consideration. He knew her history, so she bet the latter. Martin Post might have been the son of schoolteachers long ago but he had grown accustomed to his place in the world now—and his place was to be obeyed without question.

She allowed herself the brief, uncharitable thought that there was only so much behavior to be excused by grief, then pressed the accelerator. As long as Bruce Dunning of For-ester News Service didn't plow into her rear bumper, he could do whatever he damn well pleased.

You can't trust him, you know, Greg had said. But Greg's prints, and his alone, had turned up on the murder weapon, so his credibility could be considered questionable.

Nor did his choice of hangout inspire her. Water views

and landscaped areas of Florida could be beautiful, stunning against the backdrop of a sunset. But the rest of it looked like this—flat, dusty land crowded with haphazard, scrawny greenery not chosen by anyone, even Nature, for its appeal. And off this long back row sat the SecuritySite U Store It facility.

The office building hardly made her think it would live up to its name. It needed fresh paint, of the mold-resistant kind. Any green areas grew wild. Without neighbors to complain, appearance had taken a backseat to practicality.

The facility had a solid wall, yes, and a hefty gate that opened for her after she threaded into the rental past the news vans lining the shoulderless country road. Foxtail and other tall grasses grew out of standing water in its side ditches. If the top heavy news vans slid into a trench, they wouldn't get back out again. Ellie smiled to think of leaving Dunning behind in the precarious landscape while she could stay on the solid pavement.

Then she drove through the gate and forgot all about him.

There were two men overseeing the entrance. One, a too-thin teenager with pockmarked skin, wore a stained gray SecuritySite polo. The other guy, presumably the aforementioned Leonard, appeared to be a twin of the one in the guard shack at the Post estate. He pointed toward the center aisle and she drove into an alley of endless overhead doors. Surely Greg must use his unit for exactly what he should—storage—because why would someone who lived in such luxury at home choose to spend his free time in a place like this?

Martin waited alone outside one of the regular doors, not an overhead. His Tesla sat parked in the narrow aisle of pavement. The sun turned it to a griddle and the heat radiating in miserable waves made her short on social graces. "Where's everyone else?"

"The agents? Getting their search warrant ready, I suppose. It's this way."

"But—"

He led her through an interior hallway to a heavy door. It opened to an interior apartment. Despite the low-key look of the exterior, Greg's crash pad turned out to be more than a storage garage—more a small warehouse with four different workbenches, one eighty-inch flatscreen TV, and two smaller ones facing a leather pit couch with accompanying end tables, humidor, two oversized refrigerators, a full kitchen, and excellent air-conditioning. It might be the average man's dream garage, but it didn't come close to the standards of the Post estate.

Still, it was certainly private—the very opposite of the "fishbowl."

She wandered through the kitchen area. Dust coated the range burners, and she doubted he did any real cooking there, simply intended to have a meal his father-in-law hadn't dictated. One of the refrigerators had a glass door like an oversized wine fridge; it had been packed with cases of IPAs and even more bottles of plain water. Game controllers littered the coffee table.

The television area had been made cozy, in a very masculine sort of way. Shelving units flanked the screen, stuffed with magazines (about high tech, not scantily clad women, Ellie noticed), several trophies from high school and college, one of those motion-activated singing fish (now unresponsive), shot glasses from different cities, and a plush stuffed frog. It all fit overgrown frat boy Greg to a *T* in a way that almost charmed.

Ellie looked around for any sign that Ashley had ever set foot in the place—a framed photo, a hoodie that would fit her slight frame, a bag of Cheez-Its. Nothing. Either she didn't visit the workshop often, or she felt no need to leave her own imprint.

Video games aside, Greg did real work there as well.

"What is all this?" she asked, moving toward the workbenches.

"Greg's projects." Martin spoke grudgingly, as if reluctant to give his son-in-law any more legitimacy than honesty required. The workbenches had been designed with a tower of drawers at each end, and he opened one. "He does graphic interface design."

She saw only a bunch of computers, monitors, wires, and keyboards. The pervasive quiet of the place probably made it easy to concentrate—or throw raucous Super Bowl parties without the neighbors complaining. "He worked on stuff for your company and the new defense contract *here*? Weren't you worried about security? I mean your house has so much—"

Martin shrugged. "Hiding in plain sight. Corporate thieves would never think to look for him here, and this place is a lot more secure than it appears. No windows, and he reinforced the walls and door. A bazooka couldn't get through that thing once it's locked. Wi-fi is triple encrypted, and all his devices will reformat without the proper passwords."

If it seemed secure enough for Martin Post, she thought, it must be. "Where *is* Greg? And why are we looking through his stuff without him?"

"Technically it's *my* stuff, and he's probably being arrested by the FBI agents. And we're here to find out what he did with my daughter." He shut one drawer, moved on to the next, moving quickly but without haste. Methodical, focused. The way, she realized, he did everything.

"So you want to search the place before the warrant gets here? Martin, wait. You can't do that."

"Of course we can."

Oh no, no. Ellie had written hundreds of search warrants

during her time at the bureau. "Nothing we found would be admissible—chain of custody will be worthless without the warrant in place. And there's no need for it. Just wait for the agents."

He didn't even pause. "I don't need a warrant. Start at that end."

"Martin, listen to me—"

He stopped then and fixed her with a look of impatient patience. "I pay the rent on this unit."

"Because you pay Greg's salary? That will not fly in court—"

"No, I literally pay the rent. This is company property— we did it this way so Greg could work on the CurrentSDI project outside the development offices. He insisted that this place, no one would pay attention to—he'd be hiding the project in plain sight."

"That still might not protect you in court. Employees' desks, lockers, they can be legal gray areas. And I can't help you with digital evidence, anyway, I have no idea what I'm—"

He had moved on to another drawer. "Don't worry about the tech. I'll take care of that."

If he wouldn't listen to the law, maybe he'd listen to logic. "Martin, you hired the Locard for our expertise, so take advantage of it and listen to me. You're only ruining the chances of your son-in-law's conviction if you contaminate any evidence of her murder."

"I'm not looking for evidence of *murder*—the feds can do that. *I'm* looking for evidence of espionage, and I want *you* to look for evidence of Greg's mistress."

She blinked. That was not where she had expected this to go. "*What?*"

He slammed the last drawer shut, moved to the next bench. "You're a woman. If a woman is meeting him here, you must know what she'd leave behind."

"Martin, what are you talking about?"

"Just this: Greg is having an affair. As soon as he's arrested, he's going to lawyer up and she's going to see him on the news. Then she's going to disappear, and he'll never have to admit it. We have to find her before that happens."

"Isn't that the agents—"

"The feds are going to come here and look for blood and payments to hired killers, not lipstick left by some piece on the side."

"They will definitely be interested in a motive."

"But it won't be in the scope of the warrant. So if we find evidence of her it won't make any difference to their search anyway, will it?"

Well, that *was* logical. "What makes you think he's having an affair?"

Martin's eyes narrowed. "I heard him talking to her. I even know her name—Kayla."

"When? Where? He was on the phone with her in your house? That was careless of him."

"Tell me about it."

"What else did he say?"

"That he'd see her later, but nothing more specific."

"That could be anything. A coworker, a meeting with a lawyer—" The look on Martin Post's face reminded her of Uncle Wayne in his bad moments. She changed the subject. "What did you mean about espionage?"

He had reached one of the several laptops and touched its nearby mouse. The screen glowed to life. "Greg isn't just a cheat and a killer. He's also a spy."

Chapter 21

Ellie had grown tired of saying *"What?"* She crossed her arms, and waited.

Martin Post visibly forced himself to stop and explain, standing uncomfortably still and speaking as rapidly as he could and still be intelligible. "CurrentSDI—our 'Star Wars' plan—will be under the purview of half a dozen different concerns—the Missile Defense Agency, Northern Command, Strategic Command, the Army National Guard—and all of them have to be happy with our product. We have a test scheduled tomorrow with the Hundredth Missile Defense Brigade in Alaska, and if it isn't a complete success we might as well not even bother going to the congressional hearing on the fourteenth. On top of that the White House and Congress haven't reached a deal on the deficit reduction, so they're going to have to slash fifty or a hundred billion from the budget. Part of that is military, and part of *that* is Missile Defense."

"How does that affect—"

"The quickest, easiest way to reduce costs is to cut your

contractors. Or take the cheapest one. The bottom line is going to be all that matters. It won't even matter if the system works or not because the representatives usually don't know what the hell we're talking about anyway. But they can all read a number. And this morning Deborah told me EntreRobotics is going to have a lower number than Oak-Tree."

Ellie uncrossed her arms. "You mean Deborah, your . . . house assistant?" *Please tell me he's not communicating with his dead wife.*

A smile played across his lips, one brief mirage. "Deborah isn't there just to help you order stuff from Amazon or remind you of your doctor's appointment. She monitors every news channel, every online post, every talk radio podcast, every cryptocurrency exchange, then sorts, picks out, interprets. She can tell you whether it's likely to rain in Abuja next month or the date of the last reported Bigfoot sighting. She's like Alexa with a hundred times the analysis power. Why do you think my stocks do so well?"

"Okay," Ellie said, stock prices the least of her interests right now. "What does all that have to do with Greg?"

"I've seen a memo that went around their executive board, that some stupid board member accidentally forwarded to his rebellious teenager. They knew exactly what number they had to beat and Greg was the only other one who knew. I'd been keeping the total picture from my own developers for precisely that reason. So just him, and me."

"Not even Ashley? Or Dani?"

He shook his head with impatience. "Dani's not involved in the business. And of course Ashley knew. I'm not worried about *her*."

"But her laptop was never found."

"The memo was dated three days after she disappeared. Her killer didn't get the bid amount from her laptop. That *only* leaves Greg."

"So you think your son-in-law purposely passed vital information to your competitor?"

"I don't see what else the evidence could mean."

That, she had to admit, seemed a valid point.

"What about cameras? I saw them on the way in. Has anyone checked whether Greg was here on the day Ashley . . . went out on her boat?"

"Yes, of course. The police let me know—without actually giving me information on an open investigation—"

Of course. Money opened doors, and it also loosened lips.

"—that the surveillance video here shows Greg arriving just about the time he said he did."

She waited for the "but."

"And leaving—by the front door, as he usually did. But the back door camera is glitchy, goes offline for periods of time. There are some dead spots in the camera positioning. If he had taken the back door, hugged the building—where he parks his car is not visible. He could have done it. Could you check the bathroom? Please?"

Counting on a glitching camera sounded risky, but since she wasn't familiar with the layout of all the buildings and parking areas, she couldn't be sure. She also wasn't sure his legal argument regarding proper chain of custody would hold water, but seeing as neither of them were designated law enforcement personnel anyway, it might not apply. Her head swam with images of mistresses and white-collar payoffs.

The bathroom lights came on automatically. The room resembled the Post estate more than the living area, but minus the stunning views of the Gulf. Shower stall with marble tile and glass enclosure, three sinks, and two closeted toilets. High-end quality but no maid service, and water stains coated the glass and lower mirrors. That was the problem with restricted access areas like cutting-edge technology or forensic labs—you had to do your own cleaning.

Donning latex gloves, she started at one side and began opening drawers. The lack of cleaning staff—or Ashley, perhaps—became even more apparent as random accoutrements had collected in each one without any sense of organization. Small bottles of shampoo, aftershave, liquid soap, aspirin, vodka existed in a jumble with expensive razors, combs, unwrapped toothbrushes, and the operating manual for the flat-screen in the next room.

Then she found the drawer.

Everything a girl might need to have on hand. Toothbrush, mint-flavored paste, Lancôme eyeshadow, Bare Minerals powder, Clinique skin cream. Two shades of Ulta lip gloss and floral scent body spray. All neatly arranged in what appeared to be alphabetical order by manufacturer.

Ellie examined each item, but the owner hadn't been helpful enough to write her name on any of them. At the back, however, a pastel container rattled when she picked it up, and inside lay a ring and necklace with a heart pendant. The gold wire inside the heart shape spelled out *Kayla*.

Ellie hesitated. She didn't feel comfortable spying on some unknown woman at the behest of Martin Post, who, for such a logical man, seemed to be running on pure emotion in this.

She stood for so long that the lights went out. *"Hey—"*

They came on again as she shifted, and Martin appeared in the doorway. "Find anything?"

She held up the necklace. "Looks like you were right about the name. What else did you overhear of Greg's conversation?"

"He said 'it can't be much longer now.' I have no idea what that meant . . . and, 'what hours are you on today?' so obviously she works."

"Someplace with flexible hours. Anything else?"

He screwed up his face in thought, and for one moment she could see the boy he had been, nerdy and focused. "Something about inventory. He said 'something-inventory,' like it was a question."

This still seemed careless of a man living in Martin Post's house, but then it had been trying times—whether guilty or innocent—for the young man. "How did you happen to overhear all that?"

"I—he was in the kitchen. He didn't know I was there."

"Which kitchen? The main one, the one off that living area where we first talked—or the one in Greg and Ashley's wing?"

He tried to school his face, but he'd grown used to questions always traveling one way, from him to others. Never vice versa. Like most people who didn't need to lie often, he wasn't very good at it.

Maybe, Ellie thought, *with Ashley gone Greg had let his guard down, had stopped covering his tracks. And maybe—*
"You said Deborah works throughout the house."

"What, the smart assistant? Yeah."

The storage unit/man cave remained utterly silent, isolated so completely from the outside. She could hear only a clock ticking somewhere in the main room . . . otherwise she might think time had stopped. What had Greg said about taking the boat out with Ashley? *To be somewhere Deborah wasn't listening.* "But if you told her—it—to activate the microphones in Greg's apartment, it would do that. Wouldn't it?"

He said nothing.

"Martin! Seriously? That's a complete violation of privacy, of wiretapping laws, and now any evidence found as a result is poisoned! It won't be admissible."

Had she really just scolded the third-richest man in the country?

Yes. Because she was right on all counts, and according to Grandma, those were the times to "stick to your guns."

But Martin Post didn't care. "I told you, admissible doesn't matter. Greg having a mistress isn't a crime, except in the court of public opinion. I need to wake up that court so I don't have to face boycotts for turning against my poor, handsome son-in-law."

So was this about justice? Revenge? Or keeping the stock price strong?

"We have to find this woman, first to prove she exists, second because she has to know something about Ashley's death. She might have *planned* Ashley's death. What if she has a boat and drove Greg out to the water, then away after he did it?"

Ellie took a breath. "I get that—material witness, possible coconspirator. This facility has cameras. If she came here a lot, we should be able to get her photo."

"That would take too long! They might have an escape clause—he could have socked away millions for her to spend the rest of her life in Aruba rather than testify against him."

"Okay," Ellie said. "But it's not going to do much for your sales when it comes out that you bugged your own house."

"It's not going to come out." He took her silence for granted with such assurance that it chilled her. It wasn't even a threat. Just an observation. Ellie was, after all, merely a temporarily engaged consultant.

As if to soften the implication, he furthered his appeal: "It's my *daughter*. What wouldn't you do to find out the truth about your mother?"

Chapter 22

She felt the open drawer poking into her spine because she had backed into it. "What—what do you mean, the truth? My mother died in a car accident." Or had she? Ellie had run across some data during the chaos at the Locard in the previous month that seemed to suggest otherwise. She had found her mother's case listed as a homicide—no information other than that stark term. She'd been trying to look into it long-distance for years, and that tidbit had renewed her interest—not that she'd gotten very far.

She told Martin Post none of this, not in light of his disregard for other people's privacy.

He said, "Yes. But do you know the circumstances?"

"How do *you* know the circumstances?" Why did he keep mentioning her family? She had thought it was some sort of emotional appeal, using family to tug at her heartstrings, to make her work harder. For all his straightforward, blunt, nerd image, Ellie had begun to think he might be as good at manipulation as any slick politician.

"I'd met her once, at your uncle's office, so he told me about it when she died. And as I said, I learned a lot about you in a short time before I asked you to investigate my only child's death. I know you've been lobbying the Cleveland PD to release the accident files, but they keep saying they can't be located."

This was true. The files at the police department had been shifted around more than once in the past twenty-six years and locating one that might not even involve a crime would take time that no one wanted to spare. It stayed on their to-do list. She had also reached out to professional contacts at the Cuyahoga County Medical Examiner, where her mother's body would have wound up, but they had gently deflected. *You want to remember your mother the way she was, not how she looked on a steel gurney.* She had heard pathologists give so many family members the same speech over the years, and they were right. Not helpful, though.

But her efforts had been sporadic. Between getting divorced and moving, starting a new job and moving again, the challenges of her work at the Locard and the recent events there, the facts of her personal history had slid down the priority list. "Yes . . . only because it's something I felt I should do. When I divorced—but why are *you* talking about—"

"Ellie, I'm not trying to use your pain against you."

That's exactly *what you're trying to do.*

"I'm just trying to give you my perspective. We break boundaries in tech to move forward. Personal reticence isn't going to hold me back from doing *everything* I can to find out how and why my daughter died, and if I become the most hated man in the world to do it, I don't care."

Another message? *I'm not afraid to get my hands dirty on Greg—or you.* Was she supposed to be afraid? "Okay, back up. What circumstances?"

"Her car went off the road into the river. Technically, she drowned."

"I know that."

"But you survived."

This last statement made no sense. "Of course I—"

"You were there. You were in the rear passenger seat when the car went into the river."

She stared so hard that pinpricks of light exploded at the edge of her vision.

He asked, "How did you get out? Do you remember?"

She remembered many things, vague impressions of sights and smells, of her mother in their backyard picking mealy apples and laughing, of being carried by her father into the doctor's office with a thin blanket over her head to keep out the winter air, a set of colored plastic blocks on the living room rug. Nothing about a car crash into an icy river. "That can't be right. I wasn't in the car, and even if I was, how could you possibly know that?"

"Your uncle was still my regular doctor then, when he had an office here. I'd even met her once. I guess the two of you were visiting. You were just an infant. I'll be honest, she left an impression. Your mother was a very beautiful woman. You look like her."

If he thought flattery would help, it didn't. Ellie could only stare, with no idea at all what she was supposed to do with this information, why he was telling her, whether it was even true.

She said, "I lived with him for over four years and he never mentioned you. Or me being in the car." But, of course, the subject never came up. Don't ask about your mother, it's too painful. You can ask about your geometry homework, why the neighbor kid has a brace on his leg, and the pharmacological effects of statins, but about your own personal history—we'd really rather you didn't.

Martin went on. "I had insomnia, chronic colitis, other issues after Deborah—my wife—died. She had also drowned after an accident, so he told me about his sister. I think he wanted to cite an example of not letting grief overwhelm you, about having to care for a young girl, I don't know, but . . . that's how I know. My *point* is," he added with a return to his earlier urgency, "that I'm going to make you a cold, hard deal. Help me find out what happened to Ashley, and I promise I will get for you every single scrap of paper that exists regarding your mother's death."

He was waving a carrot she hadn't even known she wanted. Could he be lying, improving his technique after she made him 'fess up about the smart assistant?

But now that she *did* know—

How could she have been in the car? How could she not remember that, even at four? But four was so little, so very tiny . . . even if she had been in the car . . . but in the water?

Had she watched her mother die?

How did she get out, then? She didn't learn to swim until she lived in West Virginia and spent summers in the New River with her cousins.

Perhaps the car hadn't been fully submerged and some Good Samaritan pulled her out. But then why had her mother drowned, and why couldn't she remember? She'd been very young, yes, but she certainly remembered her father leaving two weeks later. *That* she could recall as large and clear as an IMAX movie.

Her father had always been lanky, with wiry arms and fingernails bitten to the quick, but stubble had papered his cheeks and jaw and he smelled sour, as if he'd ignored his body for too many days. He had crouched down to look her in the eyes, but then put one hand on her shoulder as if she were forty instead of four. He gave his only child no reasons or thought process for this abandonment. He did not assure her of continued safety or love or a bed to sleep in or that she would eventually find a way to deal with life's blows. Even his last words were self-serving: "No matter what they say, this isn't my fault."

Then he walked away. She had no idea, then or now, what

he'd been talking about. As she got older she refused to think of him at all.

But some car crash into an icy river? Maybe, even at four, she had trained her mind not to go there.

Or, someone—like Martin Post—had their stories seriously crossed.

Martin interrupted her thoughts. "Help me find this woman before the media does, and I'll help you, but either way, I'm going forward. Let the courts work out proper search procedures and chain of custody. There's nothing you can do about that."

True. She couldn't keep the man from spying on his son-in-law, and if said son-in-law would shortly be taken into custody, Martin would have no more opportunity anyway. She said, "If this woman exists, and we find her, you'll have to tell the FBI agents what you did. It would sabotage their case if it came out later."

"Fine. As soon as he's arrested and they search his phone—whichever burner he's using to talk to her—they'll find her anyway. But that may take too long—before they started talking about her work schedule, Greg said something about bags. Like, 'Bags packed?' I'm not sure. He mumbles sometimes."

Well, that *did* put a slightly different cast on things. Maybe he should have led with that. "Anything else? Are you sure? In the past? Had Deborah listened in . . . to . . . your daughter and her husband? Your guests? Business colleagues?

"What? No! I'm not some kind of *voyeur*. I was desperate, that's all. And I still think I was within my rights."

I'm not so sure of the former, Ellie thought, *and regarding the latter, you weren't.* But the law would figure that out.

She began looking at the back of the cosmetics again. Kayla kept herself well-stocked; in addition to the half-used items, she had two new lipsticks, a facial buff, and acne cream still in the packaging.

"Think we can track her down with nothing but a first name and an eyeshadow palette?" Martin chuckled, with the kind of rattle one breathed on the way to the gallows.

"Maybe." She turned over the unwrapped items, the ones still in their plastic packages. Martin watched over her shoulder, his breath moving a few strands of her hair. She usually didn't like men—anyone, really—getting that close to her, but there was something strangely sexless about Martin. The power he wielded, that of wealth, influence, and unimaginable access, could be terrifying, *was* terrifying . . . but it wasn't physical. She didn't fear what he would do in her presence. She feared what he would do when alone with his electronics.

But right now, she focused on Kayla's cosmetic supply.

"The same SKU numbers," Martin said.

Well, he *was* the smartest guy in the room.

Unlike UPC bar codes, which were assigned by the manufacturer, SKU were designed by the companies selling the products to mark inventory and price. The first six SKU numbers of the four unopened items were the same.

Martin said, "So she's a loyal shopper to someplace."

"I'd say Ulta."

He stared at her, really and truly surprised, a look she hadn't seen before. Had she actually both scolded *and* impressed the third-richest man in the country in the same afternoon? *You're on a roll, Ellie.* "This new mascara, the bronzer, the purple eyeshadow are Ulta brand. They wouldn't be sold anywhere except at Ulta stores."

Martin made another leap. "She works there."

"Or it's her favorite store."

He pulled out his phone. "She was talking about inventory. Yes, that could involve thousands of professions, but it's worth a try. Deborah, where's the closest Ulta store?"

Even his phone assistant has his dead wife's name?

The tinny voice reported an address on 41, the main drag through all of southwest Florida. "Would you like me to call it?" Yes. Yes, he did.

A woman answered, the squeak in her voice making Ellie wonder if she could be old enough to wear makeup, much less sell it. It was a beautiful day at Ulta and how could she help them?

Martin said, "Can I talk to Kayla?"

Ellie held her breath, not sure what to wish for. If Kayla existed, what would Martin do next? Insist on driving over to the Ulta store, drag Kayla out to his Tesla, and take her to the FBI field office? Or to his own black ops site? At this point nothing would surprise her. Martin Post was the wildest of wild cards.

"She's not in yet."

Ellie breathed out, unsure whether she felt relief or new apprehension. Or pride. Her deductions had yielded fruit— maybe. Kayla was not an uncommon name.

"Oh. When will she be in?"

"Let me see—I know she's on today. Chantel, when is Kayla gonna get here? T—two? She starts at two. But anyone here can help you. Were you calling about a specific product or—"

"Thank you," Martin said, and disconnected. An expression of triumph straightened his lips, what passed for him, in this new stage of his life, as a smile. "Let's go."

"Martin! What are you going to do?" She followed— chased, more accurately—him out of the bathroom.

Where she ran straight into Agent Tyler.

Chapter 23

To Ellie's great relief, Martin realized the difficulties of locating and apprehending the home-wrecking Kayla by himself and brought the agents into his confidence. Either that or he feared Ellie would promptly betray his plans. A preemptive strike instead would put him on the right side of the two agents. He emphasized how vital Greg's mistress would be to their case and how she had to be collected immediately and with care.

This conversation also had to be done with care. Greg himself stood ten feet away, and not yet under arrest.

Michael Tyler gave them a quick recap. He and Luis had gently informed Greg of the search to be undertaken. Greg had not argued too strenuously but insisted that he be present. His consent was not needed since they had a warrant, but in his desire to appear cooperative he also did not summon a lawyer. Investigators never knew how long the non-lawyer stage would last; it was like trying to estimate how long you could play ball under cloudy skies before they opened and rained you out. You had to keep swinging while you could.

Greg seemed more nervous than Ellie had seen him thus far. With no female in sight—other than her—he let the cool bad boy image slip and bounced on the balls of his feet, chewing at a cuticle. He watched with alarm over the shoulder of a young man in a shirt and tie as the guy typed on one of his, Greg's, laptops. "The future of our country is in this room . . . and hey, you can't look at that. It's proprietary."

When the man completely ignored him, he appealed to his father-in-law. "Martin. Do you really want to give them access to that? What if one of them's a plant for EntreRobotics? Or the Chinese?"

"Mr. Anderson—" Michael began.

Martin Post looked at his daughter's husband as if he had never seen him before. Ellie thought he might forfeit the missile defense system a hundred times over if it got him to who killed Ashley . . . but his intellect gave protest. "They're not seizing or copying the hard drives. Only examining for anything relevant to Ashley."

"Why would there be info in my stuff relevant to Ashley? I came here to get *away* from—" He stopped, but too late. Martin glared.

Michael Tyler made a diplomatic suggestion. "Let's wait outside. We can discuss—that other matter."

He expertly herded the irate father-in-law out into the hallway, leaving his partner inside with Greg and the other agents. Ellie followed, hoping that they would stay in the overwarm but at least shaded passageway rather than emerge on to the blistering pavement. The heat remained brutal. Ellie had considered throwing a lab coat over her tee to give a slightly more professional appearance, but it was just too bloody hot. The FBI agents had no such leeway, she supposed, and their faces showed a slick sheen above the knotted ties and suit jackets. She only felt sorry for men and their fashion requirements on such hot days . . . and that they couldn't wear high-heeled pumps.

Then a new arrival interrupted her thoughts.

A woman entered the hallway, from the opposite entrance than Ellie had used. Amazing hair in glossy black, well past her shoulders. Huge blue eyes topped expertly contoured cheekbones. She wore a black skirt and jacket with a white blouse over stylishly comfortable shoes. Her left lapel bore a pink name tag. It did not surprise Ellie to read *Kayla*.

She did not seem concerned at the people in the hallway, only tossed a smile at Michael and Ellie and made to walk around them. But then, behind Michael's towering form, she saw Martin Post.

And stopped dead. Her face slackened in shock, and recognition.

She tried to recover. "Excuse me." She moved to slip by Ellie, ignoring the door to Greg's unit, no doubt planning to stop at a different door. There she would pretend to have forgotten her key, and make a discreet exit with no intention of returning.

Martin said, "Kayla?"

Michael said, "Ma'am—we're going to need to talk to you."

Just then the other outside door opened and a man entered. Even with most of his form lost to the flash of blinding sunlight, Ellie caught the swing of the shaggy hair.

"Mi—Agent Tyler," she hissed. "That's the reporter who came into my garage last night. Bruce Dunning."

The door clanged again, and two more entered the long but narrow hallway behind Dunning. The FBI agent's head swung left, then right, then settled on Kayla. "Miss—"

"Parker," she supplied.

"You came here to see Greg Anderson, didn't you?"

She had been expecting the question, of course . . . that didn't mean she knew how to answer it. "Um—"

He kept his voice low. "If I could beg your indulgence, ma'am, all of us should leave right now and that includes

you. Unless you want your picture on every newscast tonight."

Ellie would guess the woman's age at about twenty-two,
but right then she could have been a scared high schooler.
She took one look at the approaching reporters, Dunning already lifting a camera to his face, turned her back, and fled
down the hallway. The three people behind her would shield
her figure from photos, Ellie reflected as she followed,
Michael's hand lightly on the center of her back. In his other
hand he held his phone, whispering an update to Luis, warning him not to open the unit's door. It locked automatically,
Ellie remembered. The search warrant domain would remain intact.

But what on earth was going to happen once they reached
that door at the end of the hall?

The reporters were shouting questions, reasonable in-
quiries but not ones Martin would answer.

"Mr. Post! What are you doing here?"

"Dr. Carr! Was Ashley murdered? How does the ME feel
about the Locard consulting?"

"Agent Tyler! Is a storage unit related to her death? Are
you arresting Post? Are you arresting Anderson?"

"What's it going to take to tell us the truth about Ashley's
death?"

Kayla Parker burst though the exterior door as if the
hounds of hell were at her heels, but wearing wedge sandals
she couldn't outrun her boyfriend's father-in-law. Martin,
one step behind her, grabbed her arm, but she leapt into the
driver's seat of a sky-blue, four-door Kia. He had to snatch
his hand back before she could slam it in the door, and instead jumped into the backseat.

Ellie slowed enough to turn to Michael.

"Get in." He gestured toward the passenger seat, and
folded himself into the backseat with surprising agility for
such a large man.

She hesitated.

"You always hesitate," Esteban told her once. She heard his voice now as if he were in the room. "That's what cripples you."

Her shuffling between extended family did not end on her eighteenth birthday. Loving, well-meaning aunts and uncles refused to abandon her. During college breaks she caught a bus south to Los Angeles to bunk with her mother's cousin Tommy and his wife Valeria and their sons. It worked out. Valeria loved having another female in the house, and taught Ellie conversational Spanish and how to make flan. Mateo and Esteban brought her along to all their favorite spots, touristy and locals-only alike. But any spot with Esteban became her immediate favorite.

Dark eyes that saw far too much, hair that always seemed just-so-appealingly tousled. Slender but wiry. Intelligent but cool. A measured tone to a calm voice that both soothed and irritated. Trying to figure out the exact biological relationship between second cousins, whether any sort of pairing would be problematic, helped her to pass genetics but created many sleepless nights.

She had finally concluded that pairing would be biologically permissible but emotionally inadvisable.

Perhaps she had just been too hesitant.

He had said this in the course of a poker game, but as always with Esteban, his words had a deeper meaning beyond her waffling over a two-chip ante while holding a pair of fours. Esteban and Mateo played poker as if it were a blood sport, a fight to the death in a theoretical realm where you could die as many times as you wanted and still be reborn with the next deal. "Life is short," he told her. "Take chances."

Ellie yanked on the car's handle.

Kayla hit the accelerator before Ellie was fully inside . . .

uncomfortably, since she'd dropped down onto the rhine-
stone letters of Kayla's Balenciaga handbag, a pink hard-
bound notebook, two pens, an industrial-sized insulated
water bottle, and a pair of sunglasses, mercifully unbroken.
As she tried to adjust all this to one side, Michael asked
Kayla how she'd gotten into the facility.

"Through the back entrance. Why are you people in my
car?" Kayla sped through the uniform rows of storage units,
each one looking exactly like the other, without hesitation.
She had obviously been there many times.

"Could you go through that entrance now? I realize this is
not our standard operating procedure, Miss Parker, but this
is not a standard moment."

"But why are you in my *car*?"

Michael kept his voice calm because no one was. Ellie had
had the same training. When the victim/witness/suspect is
uptight, keep the voice steady, focus on specifics, and take
your time. "I assumed you would not care to speak to the
media at this point in time, and frankly we would prefer you
did not as well. But that is, of course, up to you."

"But why—"

"You wouldn't want us talking to them either," Martin
interjected. "Or I'd have to tell them that you're the piece on
the side my son-in-law was cheating on my pregnant daughter with."

"Mr. Post—" Michael began.

"Just stating a fact."

Ellie turned to look at the driver. She had a grim set to her
jaw and her knuckles had turned white on the steering
wheel. She was so very young.

Kayla braked hard at the gate that led to a back street, and
they waited in silence for the electric eye to activate it.
"Where am I going? Am I dropping you some—"

Michael spoke. "Could you take us to Riverside Drive
and Fourth, please?"

Kayla leapt through the gate but stopped at the road, nonplussed.

Ellie said, "Go to Goodlette-Frank Road."

The car moved again. Michael was undoubtedly directing the woman to the Naples Police Department. He and Luis had been working out of it since the FBI did not have a field office in Naples—only an hour plus up 75 to Fort Myers, or two hours east to Miami.

But she didn't say so. He'd been right, these were *extremely* nonstandard operating procedures, and she had no idea what Michael would do with either Kayla or Martin Post and did not want to interfere.

Kayla burst out, "Where *is* Greg?"

"He's with my partner," Michael said, "going over some things."

"He's inside your little love nest," Martin said, "while the feds search everything he's got."

Kayla tapped the brakes for a stop sign and glanced over at Ellie, her face a mask of appeal, either for confirmation or moral support. Ellie couldn't give much of either.

"Mr. Post—" Michael began. "Miss Parker is being kind enough to provide limo service for us—"

Martin grasped the driver's seat back, fingers digging into the upholstery, shaking it in agitation. "Did you help him? Did you help him murder my daughter?"

"No!"

"Mr. Post!"

Kayla's face screwed up and her voice seemed to disintegrate into shards of pain. "He didn't! He couldn't have. I *know* he couldn't have!"

Michael said, "It's probably best if you don't say anything more, Miss Parker, until—"

She stopped at a red light and let out a sob. "I know he didn't, because he was with me!"

Chapter 24

"It wasn't my fault, I swear! I had no idea he was married!" Kayla told them the whole story between choking cries and the usual stop-and-go traffic between the too-numerous traffic lights on 41. The strengthening wind whined softly as it skimmed along the windshield, adding to the noise. Ellie buckled up, not at all confident that the driver could see the road properly through her tears.

Michael said, "Miss Parker, it would really be better if you waited until I read you your—"

"It was a party. An OakTree party, actually."

Martin let go of the seat back but leaned forward, as far as the seat belt would let him, as if he wanted to catch every word, every detail, every nuance.

"At the Ritz-Carlton. You were unveiling a new phone or something, and my girlfriend dragged me there because somehow she thought you might give away some free or at least a coupon. I went along for the appetizers and champagne." She sniffed, and looked even more acutely miserable than she already had. "So we dressed up real cute and—I guess we sort of crashed it. Sorry."

Ellie saw Martin Post blink. Even he didn't know what to say to that.

"Anyway I started talking to this guy about the sushi, and he said his name was Greg, and he worked at OakTree. He didn't say anything about being married, didn't wear a ring—I had *no* idea he was related to you." She checked the rearview mirror to see the fuming billionaire. "I don't pay a lot of attention to high-tech stuff. I can't afford it, and don't know how to use it anyway. And it's not like his picture was all over BuzzFeed or something."

Ellie found herself nodding. Martin valued peace and privacy, and of course what he valued, the household valued. Ellie hadn't had any idea what his daughter had looked like or that she was married or that she was pregnant until the disappearance. So it didn't seem odd that Kayla wouldn't recognize the son-in-law of the third-richest man in the country.

But surely once Ashley disappeared—

"My girlfriend didn't have any idea who he was either, and the three of us wound up hanging out in the hotel bar until all hours. He asked if he could see me again, really polite. So of course I said sure."

She stole another guilty glance at Ashley's father. Martin said nothing, and the FBI agent didn't either. He had advised her *not* to speak, and because she chose to anyway this speech counted as "spontaneous statements." Therefore it should be admissible in court, if it came to that. Ellie figured Michael must be scrambling back and forth in his mind— was he blowing the case by not terminating this impromptu interview, or would it be okay? They formed three witnesses to say the statements were spontaneous, but three witnesses for the prosecution who would easily be portrayed by defense as biased. Would "the Kia interrogation" go down in FBI history as brilliant or a brilliantly effed-up blot on his career? She felt for the agent, but there wasn't much she could do about it. In the enclosed space of the small car it felt as if Kayla had burst like a geyser and turned the air to steam. Ellie wiped beads of sweat from the back of her neck.

"So we started going out, but—God, I should have known something was up!" A change came over her voice, a note of regret mixed with annoyance. "It was almost always during the day. Maisie at Ulta told me, *that's a red flag, you sure he ain't two-timing?* But he said he worked evenings at OakTree, that he was on a project with another guy who was kinda eccentric and wouldn't come in until late—that was probably all a lie, wasn't it?" she suddenly demanded of Ellie, without giving her a chance to respond even if she could think of something to say. "How could I have been so stupid? *Everything* was there. I never met his friends. He could come over to my teeny little apartment but I never went to his, *nooo*—he said he roomed with two other coders and had no privacy." She reconsidered this in light of the new information. "Does he even *have* an apartment?" she asked, again of Ellie.

"In—a way." If you could consider a wing of the Post estate as an "apartment."

"I figured he was sleeping"—Kayla gulped—"at the unit even though you're not supposed to do that there, but it's not as if they're going to check. I felt *sorry* for him. Seriously? He drove a Bugatti but he had to share a crappy apartment? He said he won the car in a poker game. And I *believed* him!"

She wound down for another stop sign.

Martin spoke, calmly now. "I think I remember you."

Kayla's head whirled around, bones audibly cracking, then faced front again just as abruptly. "You do?"

"At the Ritz, yes. It was the GS12 phone. Who let you in? It was a closed event."

The smooth voice didn't fool her—the head of whichever security guard she and her friend had finessed would roll if she gave them up, and she spoke firmly to say she didn't remember. "I wasn't paying attention to the party, only the free food . . . eat a little, flirt a little, go home. But then I met Greg."

Despite her agitation, her face softened at the memory.

"He was so *nice*. I wore my pink Donna Karan A-line dress, the one with the ruffles, though . . . it's not *really* Donna Karan, and it was kinda a mistake because it's too low-cut on me and those tech guys act like they're still in college at a toga party, but Greg didn't stare at my boobs once. He *listened*. I talked more than he did. On our first date he came to my door with three-dozen pink roses, he said because I'd been wearing a pink dress and because red would be too presumptuous. But that time I was wearing a red dress and we both laughed and laughed."

Ellie watched her losing herself in the memory until the pickup behind them blew its horn, long and hard. The light had changed to green.

Kayla drove on. "He really was respectful. We didn't have sex until—"

"Miss Parker," Michael interrupted again. "It would be best if this could wait for a more formal setting."

"I know, I know—and it *is Miss*, you know. *I'm* not married."

She stole another look at the face in her rearview mirror as if seeking confirmation that she had been a victim, not a player. She didn't get it from Greg's father-in-law, so she doubled down: "I just want to make it clear, I didn't know he was married. I *swear* I didn't know."

Ellie wanted to pat the girl's hand and make soothing noises, assure her that of course she hadn't. But that might encourage her to talk more when she should stop, and besides, Ellie didn't feel entirely sure of Kayla. The quaver had left her voice and in its place, a sort of definite quality made the words feel slightly rehearsed.

But of course they should have been—in the two weeks since Ashley's disappearance, Kayla must have realized the world would find her. Not if, only when.

As if she could hear Ellie's thoughts, Kayla continued. "I'd seen the news about Ashley, right away. I thought it was really sad, but I never connected Greg to it, other than working at OakTree. I never saw him on the news, not at first."

"He didn't want to talk to the media," Martin said, "until I made him."

Ellie glanced round at him. His face could have been carved from granite, unmoving and cold.

"It was almost a week later . . . my day off, I was puttering around, washing some dishes, and had the TV on. A news break came on about Ashley still being lost at sea. I thought that's such an old-fashioned way to put it—and then Greg was on the screen, making a statement, asking for help!" Here Kayla gave a gasping sob, put her hand to her mouth, then made a sharp turn onto Goodlette, pulling in too tightly behind a dump truck. Despite its tattered fabric covering, its load of sand blew steadily out of its dump box. Ellie couldn't see it but could hear the nonstop rain of hard, tiny grains. "I thought, okay, maybe that's Greg's sister, but then I thought no, he's an only child, well, maybe it's a neighbor—I couldn't believe it when it said he was the *husband*!" The word came out as a slight wail, and then the geyser pulsed again as tears flowed anew. "That has *never* happened to me! I've dated guys who were jerks, who had arrest records, who lied and said they didn't live with their parents, who lied and said they were executives when they worked in the mail room, but I've never had one lie about being *married*!

"And oh, we had such a fight! I called him immediately, he didn't answer. I called for two hours and then finally I went to the storage unit. I knew he'd have to come back there eventually and I would damn well wait until he did. I'd call in sick to work for a week if I had to, but he was going to see me."

"How did you get in?" Martin suddenly thought to ask.

"I have the code. And a key to the unit."

Ellie glanced at him again. So much for his triple encryption and door that could bear up under a bazooka. Greg had simply lowered the drawbridge and let a major security risk walk right in.

"About five that afternoon he walked in, pretending like he knew I'd figure out to meet him there. He didn't try to deny it, I'll give him that—he immediately said he couldn't answer my calls because he'd had to destroy the phone we used, there were too many people around him all the time."

Martin jumped on this. "What did he do with the phone?"

"Miss Parker—" Michael tried again.

"Do you have a lawyer?" Ellie asked her.

Martin burst out "Carr!"—to remind her who she worked for and how that was *not* Kayla Parker.

Ellie didn't care. Kayla's rights had to be protected, or else the considerable mountain of information she possessed might be tossed right out on the courthouse steps.

Kayla said, "Me? Like, my own lawyer? Of course not. No! Anyway Greg said he soaked the phone in his fish tank, and then tossed it out his window on the way to the unit. And . . . he said he hadn't meant to lie to me."

From the very first moment? Ellie thought. When he'd taken off his wedding ring at a company function? She wondered where Ashley had been that night. She wouldn't have been pregnant at that time, close to a year ago.

"I was *so* angry. But he said . . . he just . . . he and Ashley . . ."

Don't, Ellie silently warned, *tell Ashley's father how Greg described his child as an overbearing harpy who "didn't understand him."*

She didn't. "But I know he didn't do anything to her. He

really cared about her. He couldn't leave her alone during the pregnancy, that's why he hadn't told me about her or her about me. He wanted to wait at least until the baby came, to get her through that."

What a prince, Ellie thought.

"And he was with me that day. The whole day!"

"Which day?" Michael asked, probably unable to help himself.

"The day she disappeared. We were at his unit. I had that day off too, and I wasn't feeling that great—my cold was beginning then—so usually we'd go to the beach or Tin City or the casino, get dinner on Fifth or something, but I wanted to curl up and drink coffee and binge-watch *The Haunting of Hill House*. I love scary movies," she confided to Ellie. "So we were there from, like, early, before lunch, until—I don't know, dinnertime; he was starving but I had no appetite. I just wanted to cuddle. That was the last time we— well, never mind."

A convenient little alibi, Ellie thought. *If* it was true. Kayla and Greg had had two weeks to work on it.

But the young woman seemed genuinely outraged that Greg had lied to her, that he had betrayed her so. She had nothing to gain from Ashley's death that Ellie could see . . . surely Martin had the real money tied up in an airtight prenup, so even if Kayla walked down the aisle with Greg in the future, it wouldn't net her anything close to Ashley's assets.

So, no reason to invent an alibi for a killer—other than love. And a girl who wore earrings in the shape of butterflies might believe in love.

Mercifully, the trip had ended. "Pull in here," Michael instructed.

"The *police department*?" Kayla squeaked, and Ellie wondered where she'd thought they'd been heading—Starbucks?

Too bad. She really *could* use some coffee.

Chapter 25

By the time Ellie had been returned to the SecuritySite U Store It to retrieve the rental, mercifully unmolested in the fracas, heavy clouds made the sky unnaturally dim. And by the time she made the drive through rush hour traffic back to the temporary Locard headquarters—i.e., Paul and Joanna's house—people in Seoul were waking up to find out that Greg Anderson had a mistress, and that mistress had provided an alibi for the day of Ashley's murder.

"Toldja so," Rachael said, stirring something in a pot on the stove.

"No, you said he was lying. You didn't specify it was about a mistress."

"Oldest story in the book. There's probably a blurb about it written in cuneiform on a stone tablet somewhere. New love, but still chained to the ball and an in-law who wielded so much power that losing your job would be the easiest part of the divorce."

Ellie rushed to clarify what had become, to her, the more pressing topic: "Are you *cooking*?"

"Woman does not live by stale crackers alone. At least not this woman."

"You are my new best friend."

"You mean I wasn't already? I stopped at a grocery on my way back from the ME's office—we're positive that pole made the indentation in the vertebra. All characteristics match. The blow was more or less straight on, and angled slightly upward."

"But the food."

"Did you hear what—"

"Yes, the right pole. Great job. But I can't focus when my stomach wants to somersault over to the stove and dive in."

"Can't." Rachael replaced the lid on the pot, turned the burner's temperature down, and turned around to lean her back against the counter. "It's just some beef with okra, but it needs to simmer a good forty-five minutes."

"Agony."

"You'll survive."

Just then a bolt of lightning lit up the dim sky, so bright it seemed a camera flash had gone off in the breakfast nook.

"*Dayam!*" Rachael burst out. "What—was that lightning? Or have the media mounted a frontal assault?"

"Lightning."

"And . . . it does that *every day*?"

"No. Only in the rainy season."

Ellie's boss squinted at her, as if scanning for sarcasm and not entirely sure of her results. But she said only, "What about the money? Is there a huge life insurance policy? Does Greg get a share of the Post estate in the event of Ashley's death?"

"No. Martin confirmed that for me on the way back to the storage unit," Ellie told her. The brilliant man had seemed to be thinking things through aloud, and not caring if she or the nice patrol officer who chauffeured them overheard. "Greg doesn't benefit financially from Ashley's death, period. Martin had insisted on a prenup—and if there's one thing I think we've learned from this family, it's that if Martin insists, then that's what happens—and Ashley didn't even have life insurance. Martin thought it was a waste of money, which I guess makes sense. It's hardly as if the Posts wouldn't be able to afford a funeral or the baby's college tuition."

"Huh. So why kill her? Not to mention your own child . . . that's pretty damn cold. Though if he *is* that cold, he might have figured once the baby was born he'd never get away from the Posts. He'd be tied up with them forever."

"I don't know." Ellie heard a note of hopelessness in her own voice. "It's a marriage, so who knows. Maybe Ashley was not the sweet girl she seemed. Maybe he's not the overgrown frat boy he seems. Maybe he was a Chinese plant the whole time."

"A what?"

Ellie slumped into a chair. "There's a lot of high tech here that any company in the world would kill to get their hands on. Maybe Greg secretly worked for EntreRobotics and told them where to find her. They tried to snatch the laptop, she struggled, they killed her."

"Maybe Ashley secretly worked for EntreRobotics, and *Martin* killed her."

Ellie protested: "Uh-uh, no way. In a fit of anger, maybe, but a premeditated plan, no. Ashley was the most important thing in his life, hands down. More than his wife, more than his company."

"So a betrayal would be that much more—"

"Maybe. But I doubt it. It would really help to know what was on Ashley's laptop, but there's no trace of it, and even if someone could tell me, I wouldn't know what they were talking about."

Rachael took a seat as well, and told her that the Locard

THE DEEPEST KILL 171

secretary, Carrie, had called to give the results of the swabs they had overnighted.

"They're done already?"

"The chem prof let his students do a cage match between the GC-mass spec and the FTIR on that sticky stuff you found on the boat."

"Who won?"

A gas chromatograph-mass spectrometer worked by "volatizing" the sample, turning it to a gas, and then using a second, inert gas to inject the sample through a capillary column filled with a solid substance. Different compounds became separated as each type took a longer or shorter period to get through this column. As the compounds exited, the mass spectrometer took over, ionizing them and separating these ions further by their mass-to-charge ratios. The end result became a series of peaks showing the quantities of the different compounds.

The Fourier Transform Infrared Spectrometer, on the other hand, didn't need to destroy the sample and only measured the way different chemical bonds in the sample absorbed or transmitted infrared light. From this it could show the presence of different and common "functional groups" such as a carbon-oxygen double bond or a cyclic ketone.

The GC-MS was better at showing the small components of the substance while the FTIR illustrated more how the components worked together. Results from the first resembled more a series of skinny bar graphs and the second, an EKG. Either result would be compared to a library of spectra to identify the substance.

Real-life results, of course, weren't as they appeared on television shows. The spectra might tell them that their sample was latex paint. It wouldn't tell them that this particular paint was Behr Marquee One-Coat in Heirloom Rose. They also didn't have a handy hack into Behr's sales database to tell them how many gallons had been sold in Naples, Florida, through which stores, and to whom.

But Ellie would take what she could get.

"I'd say the FTIR won by a nose." Rachael turned her tablet screen toward Ellie to show her the results. "Your sticky stuff seems to be polyvinyl alcohol. Nothing exotic."

"Sutures?" PVA had long been used for surgical stitches. The water-soluble strings would eventually be absorbed by the body after incisions had healed.

"Dissolving sutures—or dissolving balloon strings."

"Balloons?"

Rachael ignored this. "That's one of the uses, but there are so many. PVA strengthens textile yarns or makes paper more resistant to oils. Apparently the students got a kick out of it, insisted that Carrie tell us they used it to make slime in middle school science class."

"Slime."

"Yep."

"Never saw the attraction of that stuff, myself."

"Danton *loves* it. Mama says if she has to clean it out of the carpet one more time she's going to have me banned from Target."

Ellie stared at the screen, as if the jagged rise and fall of the spectra could tell her what, if anything, this meant. "The boat floated around for a week; any sort of debris could have blown in or out. Ashley had probably brought snacks—"

"How could anyone work without snacks?"

"—so food and its packaging would be around."

"Or," Rachael said, "someone used dissolving string to tie the steering wheel in place, knowing that this daily deluge you say is normal would wash it away."

"Huh. They come aboard, kill Ashley, take the laptop, rig the steering wheel to send the boat out into the Gulf, and with luck, sink in a storm and disappear. Though if they wanted to sink it they should have just pulled the drain plug. Eventually the bilge pump would burn out. Boats are designed *not* to sink, even in storms."

"Maybe they aimed it toward land."

"Why?" Ellie asked.

"They wanted it to be found."

"The boat, but not Ashley. Interesting. Of course, if they really didn't want Ashley to be found, they would have weighted her down with something." She rubbed her jaw, using her fingers to stretch it out.

"TMJ?" Rachael asked, setting her tablet down.

Temporomandibular joint dysfunction could be a common cause of mouth pain, Ellie knew, but that wasn't her problem. "No, it—" She hesitated, but in a burst of honesty went on: "I know it sounds dumb, but sometimes I walk around with this calm, pleasant smile pasted on my face because I know calm and pleasant is what I'm supposed to be and it's what puts other people at ease . . . then suddenly I realize that my jaw is sore from grinning like a happy idiot for hours."

"It's not dumb," Rachael said. "It's what society teaches us a woman should do. Everyone else's comfort is more important than our own."

Ellie slumped against the table, abruptly feeling the long day in her bones. "Yeah. But you know, I like that about us. I wouldn't want to change it. I just get tired of it sometimes."

They stood in silence for a few moments, contemplating polyvinyl alcohol and society's gender demands. Then Rachael said, "Buddha said that a gentle smile, a *sita*, is the point at which we approach the transcendent, the spiritual, the sublime. Keeping one on our lips brings a feeling of peace to our day."

Ellie considered this. "That does seem a much better way

of looking at it. More like a relaxation technique than pur-posely suppressing one's personality just to fit in. Forty-five minutes?"

"At least."

"I'm going to go for a run, then. Maybe that will line up all these facts in my head so they start making sense."

"It's going to rain. And the humidity is, like, ninety-five percent."

"I won't go far. And this heat is nothing compared to summer."

"Fine, but don't come crying to me when you have a heart attack. What's the mistress like?"

"Young."

Rachael made a face. "Aren't they always?"

Chapter 26

"Dude, you *didn't*."

"I wasn't given much of a choice." Michael handed his partner a coffee cup, courtesy of the Naples Police Department break room. "Things happened kind of fast. I couldn't get her to shut up."

"But an interview in motion! And she was driving. And you weren't even in the front seat!"

"I *know*." It had been, Michael reflected, about the worst possible situation for interviewing a witness.

Cops had reasons to talk to people in small, empty rooms, across a blank table—no distractions, nothing for the person to do or comment on or attend to. Nothing to keep their hands busy to disguise nervously tapping fingers or cause their eyes to dart from side to side or push around with their feet. Feet could be the body's lie detectors. We learn young to school our faces, but that discipline lessens on its way down the body. Hands aren't as controlled as eyebrows, and toes aren't as controlled as shoulders.

Cops also had reasons to start out with small talk, calm, nonconfrontational. This helped to establish the interviewee's baseline behaviors—how they looked and acted when they answered easy questions with obviously true answers: their names, their addresses, where they work. Yes, they wouldn't be *completely* relaxed, because who would be completely relaxed in a small room at a police department being questioned about something bad that happened? But they'd be a lot more relaxed than later, when asked about their role in that thing and perhaps needing to lie about it. Constant, steady surroundings also helped to differentiate between behavior of discomfort from lying about the crime at hand, or because the room was too cold, or because, in Kayla's case, the light turned yellow at the last minute.

Agents also had reasons to videotape or record or at least scribble a note or two of what the person actually said. Relying on one's memory had never been a good idea, and an investigator's "contemporaneous notes" always counted for much more in a courtroom than a report written hours or even days later.

So, yes, getting Kayla's statement during their very own version of Mr. Toad's Wild Ride, when she had been majorly distracted by Florida drivers, traffic laws, three possibly hostile total strangers who had thrown themselves inside her vehicle, all while escaping the following sea of ravenous media hounds, when Michael could only see one side of her face and her eyes reversed in a rearview mirror and very little of her body—it had not been, he had to admit, ideal.

And not at all proper FBI standard procedure. They had tried to fix it by having her repeat it all in a small, plain room and with the video and the note-taking.

Her story hadn't changed. Greg had been with her since right after he left the Post estate—at which time Ashley had not yet gone out on her boat—until five when he left to go back—at which point Ashley had already been declared, at least by her father, to be missing. She was certain of the times, even adamant.

Michael finished his coffee. They had the break room to themselves, the regular officers going on or off their shifts or busy writing reports, and the admin staff had gone home.

Luis said, "It kind of makes sense, as she explains it. The day stuck in her mind because she had a cold and felt crappy, which is a little awkward when you're only there to have sex. I can picture that, he's trying to be the understanding guy while she's watching the clock, secretly hoping the date ends sooner rather than later. But when she was blurting all this out in the car, did you believe her?"

"Yes." Drawing out the syllable just a little.

A little was enough, because Luis knew his partner. "But you're not sure."

"It's been a week since she found out about Greg, and his connection to Ashley. She had to figure we'd catch up with her at some point."

"Not necessarily. My wife's brother has been painting houses for two years and her mother still insists he's just on a break from med school. Human beings are really, really good at magical thinking."

"Yeah, but past the glitter eyeshadow and the neon stars on her fingernails, she seems sharp enough to me. They had seven days to get her story straight."

"Frosted."

"What?"

"Frosted eyeshadow. Not glitter."

"What's the difference?"

"Glitter is metal flake, dude. It would slice up your cornea." Luis drained his own cup. "Okay, then. We check her details. Stores are usually open until nine or ten. Then we could drop in at her apartment, make sure she isn't packing her bags for Aruba."

Michael stood up. "Frosted. Got it."

Chapter 27

Ellie took off from the driveway and ran along the empty sidewalks, keeping a slow, steady pace to warm up her muscles, the same route she had taken all through high school. Spanish moss drooped from the oaks and sycamores, and the humidity—she hadn't missed that. DC could get incredibly humid at times, but not for ten months out of the twelve.

As usual, running helped focus her mind. What was the deal with that storage unit, anyway? Greg stays married to Ashley when he clearly isn't happy, keeps living in her father's house—wants to *keep* living in her father's house with its outstanding luxury—but then talks his father-in-law into renting a windowless tin box for him, purely to have *one* space to himself?

Maybe it wasn't Ashley or the luxury that he couldn't part from. Maybe access to the inner circle of the brilliant Martin Post, the apex of the biggest, best tech company in the world, was what Greg didn't want to let go of.

Or maybe, like so many people, what Greg thought he wanted hadn't been what he really wanted at all.

Or again, like so many people, he wanted everything. The

inclusion. The prestige. The fame and attention that came from being one of the Posts, even if by marriage, to have breakfast with the same people every morning. Maybe he even wanted a baby, provided all he had to do was hand out cigars and maybe bounce it on his knee once in a while. But at the same time he also wanted to hang out and play video games instead of working, wanted to have a string of interchangeable young beauties who would hop into the Bugatti without question.

Maybe he had been dazzled by the glamour of the Post family, only to find his soul mate in Kayla. Though having met Greg, she felt this to be the least likely theory.

Who knew? Who ever knew what they really, truly wanted?

Ellie had always thought that all she wanted was to have her mom and dad back. But then she would be a different person now, maybe a weaker person, or maybe a stronger one.

A fertile one. One who hadn't moved through five states before college. Would she want that?

Hell, yeah.

After circling the block once, her muscles had adjusted, become looser. She barely paid attention to what her body did, other than watching the concrete squares for uneven edges . . . she'd scraped too many knees that way. With windows tightly closed to maintain the air-conditioning, little sound could be heard along the street, though the hum from a main road floated in and another jogger pounded up the sidewalk somewhere behind her.

The hum reminded her of that afternoon's commute. How could there be a rush hour in a place where most people were retired, and those who weren't likely worked in the irregular hours of hospitality, retail, or food service? But then there still must be plenty of nine-to-five type concerns . . . schools, doctor's offices, banks —

"Dr. Carr?"

"Oh *hell*." She stopped, in order to turn and give the man a proper glare. "I suppose I should be grateful that you're not trying to break into my house this time. Excuse me, my aunt and uncle's house."

"I never tried to break in. I simply wanted to interview you."

"Well, you can't." She began running again. He kept pace, dressed in khaki pants and a T-shirt already spotted with sweat.

"Bruce Dunning, Forester News Service. In case you forgot."

"I had." He wore sandals closed with Velcro straps; she could easily outrun him, but wasn't about to try. That would be undignified. Besides, they were on a public sidewalk and he *was* doing a legitimate job, so she tried to forget how much he'd startled her the night before. "Mr. Post asked me to consult on something that is not only his family's personal business but an open police investigation as well. I am legally and ethically constrained from blabbing about it. Sorry."

"Who was that girl you ran off with? Was that the mistress?"

"No comment."

"Kayla Parker? She already gave a statement to the press."

"Then you don't need me, do you?"

"What was Ashley working on?"

"No comment."

"Was it the CurrentSDI project?"

"No comment."

"Does Martin Post think Greg killed his daughter?"

"No comment."

"Have you heard of the Star Wars Deaths?"

Ellie took a moment to sort those words into some sequence that would make sense, and couldn't. She opened her mouth to ask him what he meant, remembered that she was not supposed to be commenting, shut it again, and picked up her pace.

"From your expression I'll take that as a *no*." He seemed to find this greatly encouraging even as his breath grew short and the sweat circles in his shirt widened. "Way back in the dark ages before personal computers on every desk and watching TV on your smartphone, in 1983, Ronald Reagan talked about starting the Strategic Defense Initiative, a bunch of satellites to float around in space and shoot down any missiles incoming from Russia and China. Everyone promptly named it Star Wars. It never came into being, but that was okay because it freaked out the Soviet Union enough that it collapsed."

"That probably wasn't—"

"The only reason, yeah." His language stayed leisurely, as if he had nothing better to do on a hot night than jog in inappropriate attire while delivering a history lesson. "It never came into being because A, detecting and tracking missiles from outer space so that they can be picked off in the sky like a game of Asteroids is not as easy as it sounds, and B, the cost was astronomical. No pun intended."

"Wasn't it?"

"But for a while, defense research and technology was hot and heavy. Scientists all over the place worked on it or pieces of it, university types, military subcontractors, guys at GE. Computer guys. Not Martin, he was a kid developing Oak-Tree at the time. But his rival, EntreRobotics—they were EntreComp then—were the tech half of McCann. McCann diagnostic programs were used in most ICBMs at that time and still are. An ICBM is a—"

"Intercontinental ballistic missile, yes, I know. When do we get to the part about deaths?"

"It's munitions, Dr. Carr. They're always about deaths."

He puffed this out so solemnly that she began to wonder

if he had some antiwar agenda to push with the story. Or he wanted to make her feel guilty enough to keep listening. They had come back around to her starting point, but she had several laps to go and she didn't pause.

"So everyone's working on Star Wars, right? And they start dying. They fell out of windows, jumped off bridges, one put a bunch of gas cans in his car and crashed into an empty building. Another tied one end of a rope around his neck, one end around a tree, got in his car and drove—who *does* that? One overdosed. Two died of apparent autoerotic asphyxiation, though they didn't call it that then."

"And this was all in 1983?"

"Between '82 and '88."

Ellie didn't keep the skepticism from her voice. "If there's one thing I can assure you of, it's that people do die—"

"Twenty-plus. Some reports say twenty-five, and most in a two-year period. They worked for different companies, defense contractors, research, like that, but all in some way connected with SDI. There were four guys from a subsidiary of GE, called Marconi, like the guy who invented the radio, four guys from Marconi died in *one month*! Two of them in the same day. That time a guy fell"—his fingers made air quotes, the hands swaying as he ran—"from a bridge near the same property where a woman supposedly put a rope around her neck, tied her own hands behind her back *and* her feet, then hobbled on her high heels over to a lake to drown herself. Can we slow down?"

"No."

"All these people had, usually, either just left a company or were just about to get promoted. Somebody was covering their tracks, that's for sure. They were all British too . . . I guess the Americans weren't much of a threat at the time." He glanced sideways at her. "Unless you guys did it. The FBI."

"Not to my knowledge," she said.

He did not seem reassured. "People assumed it was the Russians, and the Russians implied it was MI6, but it could have been other SDI companies. So either someone wanted to knock off all of the competition, or working on SDI makes you crazily suicidal."

"And which do you think it is?"

"I don't think it's the latter."

They had come round again. He stopped, so she paused without thinking, which gave him time to look pointedly from her to the house and back again. "Got coffee?"

"Not a chance."

"Water?"

"Two more laps."

"*Two?*"

She took off. She thought he might wait there for her return, but then the slapping of his loose soles on the sidewalk pounded up beside her. "Maybe working on SDI doesn't make you crazy, but makes your coworkers crazily competitive. *Maybe* it was the Russians, or maybe it was someone at Marconi determined to claw their way to the top. Or EntreRobotics, determined to keep the U.S. market to themselves."

"That's a leap."

His pants were lengthening into gasps. "It's a jeté worthy of Nijinsky, I know that. But here's the thing: work on SDI largely petered out when the Soviet bloc collapsed. No need to worry about shooting the things down when nobody's lobbing them at us. Bush the first scaled back the program, and Clinton slashed it even more by agreeing to outsource the management and development. Contractors are a huge chunk of the federal budget, of course. Not even defense contractors—the biggest campaign contributors to our representatives? AT and T, FedEx, SBC. I did a story on—"

He paused to breathe as they began the last lap, and apparently decided she didn't need to hear about his body of work right then and they ran for a while in silence. She had to admit that he did a pretty good job of keeping up with her, even in sandals. His arches would pay for it later.

When his wind caught up with him, he went on: "So Star Wars faded over the years but it never really went away. The stream of money to R and D became part of the steady stream of defense spending without anyone paying too much attention. The cost of putting all those satellites in space kept it unrealistic—but then 9/11 happened, and suddenly no cost was too high again. The threats like Russia and China might have faded but now morphed into Iran and then Iraq and now North Korea."

They were rounding the corner back to Paul and Joanna's house, and she felt she'd waited long enough for him to get to the point. "So—"

"Two things. Post has figured out how to bounce signals off enough space junk so that we won't need a whole fleet of satellites, and our old buddies Russia and China are working really hard on hypersonic missiles."

"Uh-huh."

"SDI is suddenly hot and heavy again. And maybe a new host of scientists are going to start dying—starting with Ashley Anderson."

She said nothing. That seemed like one heck of a "maybe." She had been so focused on the Post family dynamics that theories about rival companies had been background art to round out the scene. Now this reporter's angle . . . "Your theory is what, exactly? That some long-standing, shadowy group of Bilderbergers is keeping SDI technology from developing?"

"Oh, everyone wants it developed—but by them, and only them. If Donec gets it working first, then EntreRobotics and Martin Post have spent millions in development for nothing. The country doesn't need *two* systems, right?"

So, corporate espionage. But of a much more deadly type

than usual. She slowed in front of Paul and Joanna's house, started a cool-down walk.

"Are we done?" Bruce Dunning puffed.

"We're done."

"Then why are we still moving?"

She didn't bother to answer, searching for a reason not to dismiss his breathless commentary as a typical wacko conspiracy theory.

He sensed her fading interest and went on, his shirt now quite damp. "I've been combing through the EntreRobotics staff directory going back forty years. The same three guys have held the reins all that time, started out like Jobs and Wozniak in somebody's garage. Gyles, Milligan, and Johnson. Their staff at the Gato Lago HQ call them the Three Witches—doesn't quite make sense, gender-wise, but there you are."

"Okay—"

"Know who Peter Gyles is?"

"No, I don't. Mr. Dunning—"

"He's Greg Anderson's uncle."

She blinked. That *was* interesting. At least on the surface.

"He's Greg's mother's brother. Lives in Big Sur, so it's not like he comes for dinner every holiday—in fact Gyles hasn't been known to visit here, ever."

"So they're not close." But surely Martin Post would have known everything about his son-in-law even before he officially became his son-in-law. She had gotten familiar with how the man operated . . . especially when it concerned Ashley. Martin would have known whom Greg played in the second-grade Christmas pageant.

"But they're still blood. And Gyles has no children of his own, no wife, no personal life at all. So I figure he gets up in years, starts to think about legacies, maybe reaches out to the closest thing to a blood heir he's likely to have."

She finished the circuit and stopped again, determined to

end the interview or chat or lecture or whatever. She hadn't washed her face in fourteen hours, nor had she eaten in nearly that time. Her stomach ached for Rachael's beef with okra and she could smell her own drying sweat. "So maybe he has Greg go deep undercover as Ashley Post's husband?"

"If this is the same guy who assassinated over twenty scientists just to corner the market? Absolutely."

"That's a great deal of speculation, but if you think it's a viable theory, you should tell the police. Good luck, and have a nice evening."

"Wait!" he said as she turned away.

"Yes?"

"You sure you don't have any coffee?" He gave her a wry grin, or what was supposed to be a wry grin, boyishly charming, appealingly naughty. It did absolutely nothing for her.

She said good night and went into the house.

Where she planned to fix herself a large bowl of their dinner and eat it in front of her laptop where she would Google "Marconi" "Star Wars Deaths" and "EntreRobotics."

Except that as soon as she entered, Rachael greeted her with two words: "Something happened."

Chapter 28

Michael Tyler, uninterrupted by eager news reporters, had finally gotten something to eat—a personal first, cheese grits with shrimp, followed by wondering where the dish had been all his life. But he too longed for a shower. "How do people stand this humidity?" he asked Luis.

"I guess they acclimate. Probably keeps your skin young, all the moisture."

"I'd rather get old."

"Hate to be the one to tell you this—"

"Then don't." They were back in the rental car, having spent an interesting hour before dinner with the manager of the local Ulta store. It had been the most comfortable hour of the day, that spent in the large, bright store that had the air-conditioning set at subzero and smelled great. Michael had even bought a bottle of aftershave that Luis said made him think of "something Taylor Swift would wear." He meant this as a compliment to Taylor Swift. To Michael, not so much.

But the visit had produced more than olfactory success, and because of it they were on their way to Kayla's apartment to ask why she had lied to them about every single tiny thing.

She had *not* been hanging out in Greg's man cave storage unit all day when Ashley and her boat went missing. She had been at work since before Greg left the Post estate until after he returned—a very long day during which her attendance had been vital. She'd been training three new employees, caught lunch at the Moe's in the same plaza with two co-workers to celebrate one's birthday, helped out in the salon when a hairdresser called in sick, and then worked with her manager to sort out a shipment of Redken products that had arrived at the Ulta store in south Naples instead of theirs. The manager recalled the day quite clearly because of that snafu and so would the regional manager in Tampa since they had exchanged rather heated words over the matter to the point that, frankly, she was lucky she still had a job. The local manager, not the regional one, hierarchies being what they were. Not to mention the three new employees who would certainly remember their first day on the floor. Oh, *and* the store had time-stamped video of the entire day, which the FBI agents had viewed and which clearly showed Kayla with her glossy black locks, working her very tight buns off.

And no one remembered her having a cold.

Put bluntly, Greg couldn't have come up with a *worse* day to need an alibi from Kayla, even if he had tried.

Coworker Chantel—the one with the recent birthday—also said she had long suspected Kayla's "Greg" of being married, and what's more, so had Kayla. A girlfriend's job is to inspect a GF's BF for red flags, and they flew thick and fast with Greg. "I told her the guy had to be shady, almost always seeing him during the day, never going to his place or meeting his fam? She said yeah, she knew it, but it was okay. I said it's *not* okay if some irate wife shows up on your doorstep!" Chantel had shrugged her muscled shoulders. "She said she knew what she was doing."

A girl with pink-tipped hair had also shared with the agents, in between working her register. "I asked if she would break up with him if he turned out to be married. She just laughed and shook her head. I expected her to say that it wasn't serious and she only wanted a little fun with no strings, you know, but she said 'I know what I'm doing.' I asked what that meant and she said that meant he had serious funds. I said, 'You mean you're only into him for his money?' and she said 'Well, it sure as hell ain't his personality.'"

Her fellow cashier agreed. "Look, I like Kayla, she's a sweet girl. Give her a sob story she'll take your shift in a heartbeat. Remembers everyone's birthdays, that sort of thing. But she is *all* about the money. Every two weeks when we get our checks, she always—"

At this point the first cashier grinned and nodded. "*Always.*"

"—opens it up, looks at it like it's covered in shit, and says, 'Well, I'm never gonna get anywhere like *this.*'"

"Every time," the first one said.

Yet Kayla had said she assumed Greg to be a low-paid tech coder. The agents had thanked the ladies of Ulta and left the nice-smelling place behind because, long story short, Kayla had some explaining to do.

"Told you they had two weeks to come up with something," Luis said.

"Actually, I said that."

"But I agreed. You know . . . she had to figure we'd check with her boss. And what about the storage unit video? Greg showed up there on the day in question . . ."

"No one looked for Kayla on it, didn't know who she was then."

Luis spoke with some satisfaction. "But we do now. Her

not appearing will be one more overlooked nail in Greg's designer coffin."

"As you *did* say, magical thinking. She probably just hoped we'd go away, and besides, what choice did they have? It was worth a try."

"We need to put a tail on her and Greg both. What if she really *is* packing for Aruba?"

Kayla's apartment building would be considered small and cozy in DC, only three stories with open landings and hallways. Florida didn't do skyscrapers, other than a few towering hotels near the beach. This might be due, Michael reflected, to a foundation of sand and crushed shells and too little bedrock, or the availability of cheap land, but in any event they didn't need to bother with an elevator. He and Luis climbed the concrete steps, still damp from the requisite afternoon rain, and knocked on the door of 2-C.

Michael then noticed two things: no one answered, and the door hadn't been fully shut. The knock pushed it enough that a sliver of light appeared between the door and the jamb.

Luis swore, clearly thinking that their witness/suspect really *had* lit out for Aruba.

Michael knocked again, jarring the door another inch. He called out his name, who he worked for, and that they were looking for Kayla Parker, even though Kayla Parker would know all that already.

Still no response. Without thinking, Michael put his hand on the gun at his belt and he and Luis took up positions on either side of the door, clear of the opening. One thing he had to say for Florida, Michael thought—the concrete block walls would stop a bullet much more effectively than drywall and siding.

From this position he shoved the door open with one hand.

Kayla's description of her apartment as "teeny" seemed

accurate, with the kitchen, dining, and living areas all immediately within view. A single hallway led to other doors.
Michael guessed you could fit the whole floor plan inside the
main area of Greg Anderson's storage unit.

The kitchen light shone, as did a lamp on the end table
next to the couch. Flickering colors told them a television
played on mute. At first all seemed normal, if empty. No
suitcases or clothing scattered in a haste to leave. Then they
saw the blood.

On the far side of the couch, which faced away from them
into the room, large red drops had pooled on the beige-and-
sage patterned bamboo carpet. They led up to a limp, white
hand, the fingers adorned with glittered—or frosted—nail
polish.

Now Michael did pull out his gun. They entered, silently.

Over the top of the couch they could see the living area.
Kayla stretched along the floor, partly on her left side. She
had changed from earlier in the day and wore very small,
stretchy shorts and a white tank top. She faced away from
them, but the blood caught in her hair did not bode well.

Michael strode over and pressed two fingers to her carotid. Nothing. Her cool flesh gave not the slightest tremor,
her eyes were open and staring. A marble statue of Nike,
covered in red stains, lay next to her right shoulder.

He stood and turned, and realized Kayla had not been
alone.

Greg Anderson lounged on the couch, unmoving, his
hands stained with blood but his temple and perfectly
coiffed hair blotted with it as well.

Michael didn't know whether he should cuff him or check
him for a pulse, the man lay so still. He moved over to do the
latter, but suddenly Greg gave a sigh and a tiny snore. No
more blood oozed from any place Michael could see. The
beige couch underneath him appeared clean. Greg had no
apparent injuries.

He and Luis exchanged a look. Then Luis closed the apartment door without making a sound, circled the couch and stood over Greg. Michael walked quickly but lightly up the hallway, finding two bedrooms and a bath. The lights were helpfully lit in every room so he could quickly assess their status: empty.

No one else was there. Only the dead Kayla Parker and the live Greg Anderson.

Then Michael did check Greg's carotid just in case the sigh had been gasses settling in a decomposing body.

But then the man stirred, gave a startled twitch, and opened his eyes. They widened almost comically to see Michael and Luis staring down at him. "What the hell?"

"That's what we'd like to know," Michael told him.

Chapter 29

"Thanks for coming," Michael said, as Ellie and Rachael mounted the steps to the second-floor landing.

"Wouldn't miss it for the world," Ellie joked, then surveyed the landing to see if any bystanders had overheard her gallows humor.

The FBI agent told them what a canvas had established. A neighbor had seen Kayla, alone, pull into her usual parking space about six but had not remained outside to see her enter the apartment. No one had seen someone *other* than Kayla enter her apartment, though her unit sat on the corner, first one reached from the stairs. There were three other sets of stairs, as well, one at each corner of the building, leaving a visitor a selection of routes to take. No one had heard an argument or the sounds of a fight.

Greg had left the storage unit at about the same time, according to the agents still working there; apparently he'd also had the sense to use the back entrance to avoid the phalanx of media still corralled outside the front gate. No one they'd found had seen Greg arrive at the apartment complex or, when shown a photo of the man, could say they'd ever seen him there before. But though Kayla had been pleasant, she hadn't gotten particularly close to anyone interviewed so far, and all residents said they didn't know much about her beyond her name.

"Video?" Rachael asked.

Michael gestured at the wall, encompassing the entire campus as one entity. "None, anywhere in the complex. This isn't the low rent district but it isn't the highest, either."

"And Greg was here too?"

Michael showed them the quick photos he'd snapped before Greg Anderson had been arrested and removed. The young man had been found with blood on his hands, clothing, and head; he had no injuries and had been, apparently, asleep.

Michael noticed their raised eyebrows. "Yes, asleep. Said he came over to, quote, talk about the day's events, unquote."

"To find out what she told you," Rachael translated, "and get their story hammered out."

"Surely, though that would take a mallet at this point. According to him, they did not argue. He tried to comfort Kayla after the day's stresses but was so worn out himself that he stretched out on the couch, and that's all he could tell us. Then he asked if Kayla was dead, I said yes, and he burst into tears." The FBI agent appeared less than moved when describing this show of emotion. "Luis took him to the station to nail down his statement."

"You're taking blood and urine, right?" Rachael asked, adding, "Never mind, of course you are."

Ellie didn't think too many killers took a nap at their crime scenes, though it had been known to happen. Greg had been under great stress for two solid weeks. If he had killed his wife, he would have spent every minute wondering if or when some unforeseen detail would catch him up. If he thought Kayla wouldn't stand by him, might want to leave him, it might have thrown him into a frenzy only for him to realize too late that he couldn't conceal his guilt here, whether this was his first *or* second murder. The chase had ended, and he had no more hope of escaping his fate. This might bring about the same kind of peace that allowed criminals to sleep soundly in a holding cell at the jail—the body's relief that, though they have lost, at least there is nothing more to be done.

Or he could be under the influence of some narcotic. She hadn't seen any signs of substance abuse in Greg—red eyes, lack of coordination, slurred speech, or flickering eye movements—but if ever there were a day when he could have used a Xanax, today would be it.

"Yes, all body samples. And that, ladies, brings us to now."

"Jurisdiction?" Rachael asked.

"Since this obviously relates to Ashley's death, Naples PD is happy to let us handle it, and the ME is fine if we use you instead of their investigator. They still get the body, of course, but you can attend."

"Good," Rachael said.

Ellie felt slightly dazed by the fact that a girl she'd been sharing a wild car ride with only hours earlier had been killed. She had never had to work the crime scene of someone she knew, at least not knew well. There had been an ambushed agent, and then of course the mess at her cousin's house. She hadn't known Kayla well either, but she couldn't forget how Kayla turned to her in the car, seeking guidance and moral support from the other female there, even if a total stranger. The girl had been beautiful, and young, and dating someone fabulously rich—and so *alone*.

And now, in death, she would stay that way.

Ellie and Rachael entered the apartment together, both pausing in the doorway to take in their first impressions.

A small place, kitchen on left with a nook for a table and chairs to barely seat four. Living area on right so that the back of the couch created a border and sort of an entryway. The couch faced a wall of bookshelves: the television played silently across from a love seat placed at a right angle to the couch. Clean and scrupulously tidy—no piles of old mail on the table, no sweatshirts strewn across the furniture, no collection of flip-flops tangled by the door. No dishes on the floor for pets. The couch set seemed in good repair; the end tables didn't match but were real wood and polished to a soft gleam.

The color scheme seemed to be the same as in Greg and Ashley's bedroom, cream and sage green with the occasional bamboo leaves motif. It made Ellie wonder if Greg had chosen the decor in both places, but then she dismissed that thought. He certainly hadn't shown any flair for design in his man cave, the one area that had been entirely his.

Still, interesting. Perhaps Kayla and Ashley had had numerous tastes in common. Perhaps those similarities had attracted Greg to his mistress in the first place.

Donning paper booties, masks and gloves, the two women entered and circled around the couch and love seat to the body on the floor.

Kayla's figure, so perfect in life, remained largely perfect in death, marred only by the injuries to her skull. From chest down Ellie saw no marks or stains on her save a few spots on the bleached white of her tank top. The fingers of her right hand had smears of blood but no defensive wounds.

Rachael spoke without, at first, touching the body. "Looks like at least the first strike occurred when she still stood upright. She probably put a hand to her head. Then the next couple of hits and she went down."

"Died quickly," Ellie concurred.

"Relatively little blood for decent-sized wounds. I see three. Almost sure it will be compression to the brain, the actual cause of death."

"Certainly not exsanguination. Bet he used the base."

Ellie used a pencil flash to examine the marble statue of Nike without touching it. The headless, armless replica of the winged figure looked heavy. "Goddess of victory. But whose victory?"

"Not hers. And Greg is now even more sunk than he was before."

"Tip broke off." Ellie pointed to a small, separated piece. The area rug with its pattern of bamboo fronds ended just past the coffee table and the marble statue had fallen onto the ceramic tile, breaking one wing and chipping the tile. "That had to make quite a *clunk*. Maybe people in the apartment below heard it."

"Be nice to have a timeline," Rachael agreed, crouching by the body. "Her jaw is starting to stiffen, though she keeps it pretty cool in here. I'd say at least two hours."

In general unison they stood and looked at the blood pattern as a whole. But as a whole, there didn't seem to be one. Two single drops led back to the couch where Greg had been laying. He had left smears on the middle seat and back cushions, where his hands would be positioned while stretched out.

They did a quick canvas of the rest of the apartment, checked the kitchen and bathroom sinks, towels, and garbage cans. No blood. No sign that Kayla had fled someone through the short list of rooms or engaged in a drawn-out struggle. No lamps knocked awry or overturned chairs.

Kayla's Balenciaga purse sat on the bistro table, her Oak-Tree cell phone tucked into its gaping side pocket as it gave a soft chime of notification. The electronic device would, no doubt, be a treasure trove of information—but that would come later, when either FBI or Locard digital techs could download it all properly. For now, given the highly techy cast of characters, Rachael used Kayla's lifeless finger to unlock the screen, then put it in airplane mode. That should prevent any remote wiping. *Should* being the operative word—Ellie felt they could assume nothing when it came to that highly techy cast. The Posts and their satellites made her feel like an elderly Luddite clinging to his flip phone.

It appeared that Greg had hit his mistress several times with a marble statue, dropped it, then staggered over to the couch, collapsed, and did not move again until the FBI agents woke him. He made no attempt to clean his hands or the murder weapon, or flee the scene, making him about the most brain-dead murderer she'd ever investigated. He had either suffered a complete mental break, or—

Or what?

Michael hovered in the doorway, watching and listening, occasionally turning away for a short telephone conference with his partner.

Ellie guessed that Kayla had been standing in the living room, between the bookshelves and the coffee table. "Possibly watching the television? Maybe watching herself running from reporters?"

"And he came up, pulled the statue off these shelves or the coffee table, and clocked her with it," Rachael said.

Ellie dropped to her knees, using her own flashlight to skim along the tiles of the floor. "Tiny spatter, mostly at ninety degrees."

"Decent velocity, drops straight down."

"I doubt she went down with the first blow. Maybe to her knees, maybe a crouch. She put her hands to her head."

"Then he hit her again on the back center of the skull . . . missed her hands, didn't damage them, or maybe she took them away to look at the blood. She goes down then, and this third blow"—Rachael pointed to the ragged tear in the scalp, the dried blood forming a crust on the black hair— "causes this impact pattern along the edge of the rug, here. Low angle, low velocity. And that was it."

"Lividity is consistent."

The cherry flush had formed under Kayla's skin along the

left side of her shoulders, face, legs, as the blood settled according to gravity.

Kayla had not moved again. Her bloodied fingers left no smears on the tile, the spattered drops remained intact. The statue had been dropped. Three blows, and the young woman's life came to an abrupt and unexpected end.

Why?

"Why would he kill Kayla?" Ellie asked of no one in particular. "She was his alibi."

"About that," Michael said, still in the entryway. He told them how they had completely dismantled Kayla's statement. "She had to know that in the long run, it wouldn't hold up."

"Wouldn't they have figured that out at the time? They'd have had two weeks—well, a week since Kayla learned who Greg was—to invent something better."

Michael shrugged. "People who don't make a career of crime don't come up with the most plausible explanations. Maybe she did point it out and they still put their heads in the sand and hoped it would blow over. When it didn't, he blamed her. Who knows?"

Ellie said, "They could have argued about anything—it had been an incredibly stressful day for both of them. You had breached his man cave and begun to check every single thing about him. She had been thrust onto the world stage as a gold-digging home wrecker—which, yes, she should have been prepared for that exposure—but, as you said, thinking about a possibility and actually experiencing it are two different things. Especially as roughly as she got thrust into it today. Maybe she told him she couldn't take it."

"Maybe anything," Rachael summarized. "It will be interesting to see what Greg says." She wondered aloud where the statue/murder weapon had come from, and they examined the end tables and shelves. Kayla had been too good a housekeeper for there to be a handy gap in the dust that matched the statue's base, but they concluded Nike had formed one partner in a set of bookends. Bast, in all her Egyptian feline glory and cast in similar marble, propped up a collection of books on various topics. Two on the open end had fallen over, not to look decoratively casual but most likely because Winged Victory had been removed.

Ellie brushed fingerprint powder over the shelf without much enthusiasm. "This wood's too porous, barely finished. The powder's going to sink down in the pores like the finger oils probably did, and be a pain in the butt to clean off as well."

Rachael said, "Nike—"

"Oh, I have high hopes for that. The only thing better than polished marble is glossy porcelain . . . plus I think Greggie left his fingerprint in blood. But that can wait for the more ideal conditions at a lab. I just wish he would have grabbed it by the solid, square base instead of the top where there's wings and shoulders and folds of robe to break up the print pattern."

Rachael faced the shelves as well, studying the books. "Greek history, the architecture of the Parthenon, pyramids, and who killed King Tut? A biography of Margaret Bourke-White. Two books about the 2008 financial crisis. An insider's guide to Dublin. Girlfriend wanted to go places."

"Don't we all?"

Chapter 30

Now, Ellie thought, Kayla would never see the pyramids, or the Acropolis, or where James Joyce hung out as he wrote *Ulysses*. She brushed powder across the rest of the shelves, which held framed photos: Kayla with various unfamiliar people and groups of unfamiliar people, Kayla on a beach, Kayla with Greg—a selfie, taken on the couch of the now-familiar man cave. More knickknacks, a stuffed cat, plenty of books ranging from world history to Harlequin Romances.

She and Rachael moved on to the kitchen. Ellie finger-printed the sink edges and counter while Rachael poked in cabinets for clues to Kayla's health and eating style. Her death had—clearly—not been due to any medical issue or a mystery like Ashley's, but they still wanted a complete picture of Kayla's life. She had eaten to maintain her figure, a lot of low-fat, low-carb, no-sugar items, fresh fruits and vegetables. To drink, calorie-free lemonade in a two-liter bottle and three bottles of IPA beer.

Ellie thought the smell of hops lingered in the air, and sure enough, a single glass bottle rested on the top of a granola bar wrapper in the kitchen garbage can. A few drops of liquid still swirled at its bottom. Ellie plucked it out to swab the mouth of it for saliva, curious whether Greg drank it or Kayla. She couldn't see why it would matter, but no one knew what details might become important as the investigation progressed. Better to collect a useless piece of evidence than to not collect it and wish later that she had.

Kayla's pantry contained almond flour and brown rice and two large cases of bottled water that probably weighed as much as she did, a not unusual stock item for hurricane territory.

A basket labeled *First Aid* held the usual: bandages, Tylenol, antibiotic ointment, aspirin, Cold-Eeze tablets, eyedrops, stomach remedies, and a three-year-old bottle of prescription hydroxycodone, still half full.

Water drops remained in the bottom of the sink and an empty water glass sat on the table, which she and Rachael collected for prints. The dishwasher had not been run, only half full.

The bathroom held a prodigious and unsurprising amount of cosmetics, hair products, and bath fizzies, but no drops of blood or suspicious drugs. Skin care products stuffed the medicine cabinet, leaving few gaps on its shelves.

The medical examiner's team arrived. Rachael bagged the dead woman's hands to preserve any hairs or skin under the fingernails, and they ushered Kayla's stiffening body into a body bag.

Ellie and Rachael moved on to the bedroom. With the body gone, Michael locked the exterior door and joined them.

The apartment had two small bedrooms, both as neat as the living area, one serving as a bedroom and the other, an office. If a friend wanted to flop there, he or she would have to use the couch.

The bedroom held no more surprises than the bathroom—more skin care products, books, reasonably priced but good quality jewelry, and a wardrobe carefully designed to flatter and complement.

"She knew what colors suited her," Rachael murmured.

"I needed this girl to come to my place and give me a makeover," Ellie found herself saying, and Rachael laughed. The end of it faded into something more melancholy, noting that Kayla would never wear any of her pretty dresses again, never brush on a swipe of bronzer, never spend a lazy afternoon giving herself a mani-pedi.

Ellie turned away and did a quick sweep of the rest of the room. It all seemed ordinary and expected, with nothing that appeared to relate to Greg or Ashley.

Function ruled form in Kayla's spare room, used for both storage and for the everyday housekeeping that comes with human life—paying bills, sending birthday cards, accumulating change for the laundromat machines, and cataloging one's DVD collection. Kayla preferred animated Pixar films and epic romances.

A laptop with a blank screen sat at the center of a desk, its power cord snaking from a tidy charging station as did the cords for a Kindle, a wireless earbud, and two other currently absent electronics. Rachael checked the ends. "Looks like one for the OakTree phone in her purse and, this one . . . the cord is Android."

The women and the FBI agent looked around, checked the drawers. No Android.

Also on the desk, Kayla had piled more guidebooks: Hong Kong. Sydney. Prague. Fodor's *Essential France*.

Rachael said, "So girlfriend didn't just dream about going places. She planned on it."

"But up until two weeks ago she thought Greg was a penniless coder. And she certainly didn't make enough at Ulta for this kind of travel budget."

"Then it turns out that not only did Greg have a piece of

the Post fortune, but that they might be needing it to post his bail."

Michael said, "She might have known all along, according to her coworkers. She at least seemed to know he had a wife."

"She could have guessed that," Rachael said. "It's not hard to figure out, once you look for the red flags. Don't look at me like that—I'm not speaking from personal experience!"

Ellie laughed, then studied the dog-eared pages, the worn edges. "These are older than two weeks . . . a long-term plan or wishful thinking?" Ellie knew all about that, having fixated on Athens after reading Helen MacInnes's *Decision at Delphi*, carefully checked out of the Haven, West Virginia, public library. But she hadn't gotten to the Acropolis yet. And now, neither would Kayla.

Rachael went on. "What if Kayla was playing the long game? She'd have more motive to kill Ashley than Greg would."

Michael said, "But without Ashley, Greg *didn't* have a piece of the Post fortune. Only a prenup cast in iron."

"Unless it was actually about love and not money," Ellie said.

Rachael and Michael both seemed to consider that. Then each said, in unison: "Nah."

Ellie studied a bill she had picked up. "This is an apartment, and Paul and Joanna are in a three-bedroom house. Apparently Kayla had to pay utilities here, and . . . her electric is less than theirs, not surprising, but her water is nearly three times more."

"They're not there," Rachael said. "I mean—you know what I mean."

"They were home all last month, and it was still much less than this."

"Her toilet runs?" Michael guessed.

Rachael said, "I haven't heard it. The sinks aren't dripping. She's on the second floor—surely someone would have noticed a leak by now. Landlord gouging?"

"Seems a weird thing to gouge on. It's so disproportionate. Maybe she just peed a lot." Ellie nodded at the towering stack of toilet paper bundles reaching more than halfway up the wall, next to no less than five gallons of laundry detergent.

"I'll bet she shops at Costco," Rachael said. She read aloud from the next item, a letter signed *Mom*, chatty and heartbreaking, talking of Kayla's father's dog winning a ribbon in some unnamed event, Kayla's brother coming home from some unspecified trip, and that she looked forward to the family reunion on its future, unspoken date, and how she hoped to see "them."

"Had she planned to take Greg?" Ellie wondered.

"He'd have had to come up with an excuse to skip that one. All it would take is for one of her fam to read *Technical Wizardry* magazine or, hell, check some obscure Instagram feeds and Greg's cover would be blown. There'd be a Kayla-sized meltdown right over the potato salad."

Unfortunately Kayla had discarded the envelope, so they had no idea who Mom was or where she might live. Ellie had gotten pretty good over the years at parsing a person's home to find names and numbers of the closest family members, the next of kin who needed to be informed of the death. But Kayla's office didn't leave any obvious clues. There were other cards, photos of people, but without last names they had no way to know who might be a close relative and who might be an old school pal. With luck the contact list in her phone would have an entry for *Mom*, *Dad*, or *Sis*. Or the apartment manager or Ulta would have an emergency contact.

Michael slid the computer's mouse one inch across its pad. The screen thought about it for a moment and then lit up.

"Not a good idea," Rachael warned. "If you want our digital lab to take this thing apart, download her emails, documents, photos, browsing history, the best thing to do is to do nothing. Unplug, close, and bag. Every time you open a file or a photo, you're changing things."

He scowled at the keyboard in frustration. "You're right, I know."

But the screen had glowed to life without a password, illuminating the last thing Kayla had been reading—a *New York Times* article about Martin Post's wife's fatal accident. Despite Rachael's warning, all three heads bent over the small screen and read in silence.

> *AP—Naples, Florida: Deborah DuPont Post died on Tuesday at her home in Marco Island after a poolside accident in which Mrs. Post apparently slipped and hit her head on the diving board, after which she fell into the pool. Residents of San Diego, the Posts were vacationing at their second home over the Thanksgiving holiday.*
>
> *Deborah DuPont Post was forty-eight years of age. Born in New York as one of the many heirs to the DuPont diversified fortune—*

"That would have been just before their merger with Dow," Rachael said.

Somehow it did not surprise Ellie at all that Rachael could pull that factoid from her neocortex. Even the FBI agent glanced up, impressed.

The article continued with details of Deborah DuPont Post's education, work as a fund manager, and extensive list of charities and philanthropic endeavors, such as founding a scholarship for girls seeking STEM majors and improving the water filtration in the towns around their rubber plantations in Cameroon. It was at a dinner to benefit that project that she met Martin Post. They were married the following year.

> *She invested heavily in her husband's company, even more so in recent years as OakTree flirted with bankruptcy in the wake of the global financial crash.*

"That seems like kind of a snotty thing to put in the woman's obituary," Ellie said.

"Money brings out the catty in people," Rachael said. "Especially people who don't have it."

> *Other family members temporarily suspended her activity on the board until OakTree righted on its own.*
>
> *Mrs. Post is survived by her husband, Martin Post, and child, Ashley DuPont Post.*
>
> *The official cause of death is drowning. Her attending physician, Dr. Paul Beck, testified before the brief inquest that Mrs. Post had been complaining of bouts of dizziness, which may have contributed to her accident. These were likely due to an aneurysm-induced compression to the middle cranial fossa, thus injury to the cranial nerves that caused her to become unbalanced and fall into the pool.*

Ellie and Michael both turned to Rachael for a translation from the medical. "What does that mean?"

"An aneurysm caused swelling on the brain that made her dizzy. At least that's what your uncle thought."

A short pause ensued.

Then Michael said, "Whose uncle?"

Chapter 31

Michael Tyler caught up with his partner at the police department, where Greg had been ensconced in an interview room after the long process to inform him of his arrest, swabbing the dried apparent blood from his fingers, collecting his fingerprints, taking his mug shot, taking more photographs of every inch of his body both clothed and unclothed, collecting his clothes in separate paper bags sealed with labels, providing him new clothes in the form of a prison jumpsuit, drawing blood and having him contribute a urine sample, then kindly settling him down with a blanket and a cup of coffee. By the time all that had been done, Michael had returned from the crime scene.

"Any surprises?" Luis asked.

"Not really. Any from him?"

"Nope. He's been playing dazed and confused. Keeps saying things like he doesn't know what happened, and is Kayla really dead, and he can't believe it, but we've been cutting him off until we're in the room with the video rolling. Ready?"

"I guess." Michael rubbed one eye. He felt the fatigue

crowd in and wished they could wait until after even a few hours of sleep. He knew his partner must be feeling it too, since he didn't even make one joke about how at least this time they wouldn't be careening through the streets of Naples with Greg at the wheel.

But if Greg were still willing to talk, and without a lawyer, they wouldn't make him wait until the agents grabbed a snack and a nap. Maybe he would confess to killing both women, and Michael and Luis could go back to their respective homes in DC and shut off their phones and get some rest and maybe a decent pizza—

"In here," Luis said. A Naples PD detective joined them, a taciturn man who seemed perfectly happy to let the agents do the work. Jurisdiction remained slightly up in the air; technically Kayla's death seemed to be simply a murder that took place within the city, a local crime. But the feds had the related case of Ashley Anderson and it seemed both logical and convenient for Naples to sign off on Kayla's as well. Arguments demanding jurisdiction only happened on TV—in real life, departments were only too happy to hand off a sticky case. The local officer even took his chair and sat against the wall, dumping the entire proceeding squarely in the bureau's lap.

As with every other indoor facility in the Sunshine State, the A/C seemed to have been set lower than necessary and Greg used the blanket with which he'd been provided. He first wrapped himself up to his chin, a clear self-soothing mechanism, but once the agents entered, the need to be manly asserted itself and he flung his arms out to shed the hunk of material . . . then promptly changed his mind and gathered it in again. Going for the beleaguered, pathetic look—playing dazed and confused, as Michael's partner had so succinctly described. Michael hoped everything Greg said and did in the interview would be as easy to interpret.

They took care of the preliminaries—made sure the recorder and the video system functioned, informed Greg of his rights, reiterated his right to an attorney and endured that split second when he thought about it before saying no. They asked if he were comfortable or under the influence of any drugs.

Greg said only: "What happened to Kayla?"

"We're going to need your help with that," Michael said, in the mildest of tones. "Obviously, you know her. She was your girlfriend?"

The young man made a show of looking down and letting his shoulders slump. "Yes. We dated."

"When did you meet Kayla?"

Now he made a show of thinking hard, screwing up his eyes, the better for brain-wracking. "About eight months ago."

"Before Ashley's pregnancy, then."

Greg blinked, as if wondering what *that* had to do with anything. "Yeah."

"Where did you meet?"

"At a party. A work party, a product release."

Luis took over, his warm voice equally mild. "Where was Ashley?"

"When I went to that party? Out of town . . . cutting the ribbon for a library, I think, some university her father endowed in a flyover state. Something like that."

"Okay, so you met her at this party—"

"Yeah. And she was hot, so I asked her out—"

"Did you tell her you were married?"

"Of course not." He stole a glance at the video camera in the corner by the ceiling and possibly recalibrated. "Look, you don't know what it was like, living with them."

"Ashley and Martin?"

Greg leaned forward. "It's his universe, man. His world, his rules. He's the benevolent genius who knows what's best for all of us. He's the reason we're all there."

" 'We,' who? You and Ashley?"

"And Dani. Ashley, of course, was special, being his kid, his flesh and blood, his chip off the old block." The words were sharply bitter, but the tone seemed resigned, almost as if he felt more pity than resentment for his dead, pregnant, cheated-on wife. "But even her—she could step onto the dais, but there wasn't a throne chair for her to sit in, you know what I mean?"

"Tell us about it."

Greg squinted at Luis, recognizing this solicitous inquiry for the trap it was—to keep him talking until he'd spun enough web to get stuck in—and yet kept spinning. "You think it was easy living in that house? He tells us what to wear to events. He tells us what we're going to eat for dinner most nights—and you don't want to *not* show up, because then suddenly your code has flaws and your API is junk and you have to start over."

"Did you and Ashley discuss moving out?"

"Ashley leave Martin? Never. She was breast-fed the Kool-Aid from birth, so what the hell was she supposed to do?"

"Did you discuss divorce?" Luis didn't ask if Greg had *considered* it, Michael noticed. Don't hand him the out of a simple yes or no answer, easier lies to tell.

"No!" He expressed shock at the idea, and added piously: "I couldn't leave Ashley. And certainly not my own child."

"But she wasn't pregnant then. When you met Kayla."

"I know, but . . . I loved Ashley, and she loved me. Besides, I couldn't leave her there by herself."

Michael pointed out, acting as the very subtle heavy: "But you said she was happy in her father's house."

"Not happy. Institutionalized. Look, I'm not pretending it was torture . . . only a constant, low-level foundation of stress. I never intended to leave Ashley for Kayla."

Michael heard: *Let's eliminate that motive right now, shall we?*

"I guess with Kayla, I just wanted something that was all mine." He looked up at them through his long eyelashes, practically fluttering them, almost pitiable. *Look at me, the beaten-down poor relation, simply* forced *into an extramarital affair.*

Luis threw out another line. "Did anything change when you found out Ashley was pregnant?"

"No." He smiled, a rictus that wouldn't have fooled a five-year-old. "We were thrilled. She was—exactly what you'd expect. Full of plans to decorate a nursery and already obsessing over the right preschool."

"And Martin?"

"Even more ecstatic than she was. Another heir to his empire."

"And you?"

That smile again. Utterly fake, but no sign of real discomfort. No shifting his weight or changing the subject. Michael bet that Greg hadn't been significantly unhappy about the baby, nor had he been significantly happy. He pretended to be only because society, and more importantly the Posts, expected it.

"*So* excited." The five-year-old would be pretending to gag by this point.

Luis asked if he told Kayla of his now-pregnant wife—no—or had he *considered* telling Kayla—(obviously hell) no. "You weren't concerned that Kayla would see your picture in the society pages or something like that?"

"Yes . . . yes and no. Martin is *real* good about controlling access. The media doesn't see him unless he wants to be seen. And he got a little worse once Ashley told him about the baby."

Ashley? Not "*we* told him"? Despite himself, Michael felt the slightest prick of sympathy for Greg. Super-tight family units could be tough to crack. His own ex-wife's had definitely contributed to their break.

"So you were . . . hoping neither woman would find out about the other?"

"Stupid, I know. I *know*. I wound up in the situation and didn't know what to do. It was some stress, let me tell you."

"You 'wound up'?" Michael couldn't help it. As if asking a woman out when you were married might happen by accident, like mistaking someone else's car for yours in a crowded lot, or picking up the wrong brand of laundry detergent at Target. Luis shot him a look, so he tried his innocent expression. Wasn't he supposed to be Sorta Bad Cop?

But Luis had also grown tired of the little rascal attitude. "Tell us what happened tonight. After you left the station here."

"After I got done being *interrogated*," Greg began, then dialed it back. "I went straight to Kayla's. I knew she'd be upset after being chased by reporters like that. I'd tried to prepare her for it—they'd find out about her sooner or later—so I went to give her some moral support."

What a guy.

Luis prompted him to continue.

"She was in tears, nearly hysterical. We just held each other for a long time."

The ability to refrain from rolling his eyes had, many times, turned out to be one of Michael's most valuable talents in his duties as an FBI special agent.

"We talked about the situation. She didn't want to have to speak to the reporters and I told her she didn't have to. I got her calmed down. We had a beer."

"You did?" Michael asked. There had been only one

empty beer bottle found, the one in the garbage. He had to pin this down in case Greg tried the "too drunk to remember" excuse. "How many?"

"Just one. Actually *I* had one, Kayla had water. She drinks a lot of water."

"Okay. And you discussed what to tell the reporters? And the cops?"

"Yes—no, not like that. Not like getting a story straight—I told her to tell the truth, but only to you. Not the reporters."

What a good citizen. "She had already spoken to us. Did she tell you what she said?"

Greg hesitated, knowing hidden turns lay in his path, but his headlights could only reach so far. "Yes."

"About the day Ashley died?"

"Yes."

"Take us through that day again."

He did. This time he hadn't been working alone in the man cave workshop as he'd said before. His story now matched Kayla's, down to what they snacked on and watched on television.

Good. Now he would be on record, with a second, untrue, story.

"Did you argue about it?"

"No, how many times do I have to say that? We didn't argue about anything! I loved Kayla. If anyone had a right to be angry it was her!"

"Was she?" Michael asked. "Did she blame you for dragging her through the mud?"

"No . . ."

"We have her phone, you know. And yours."

Greg said nothing. His now-seized phone had a password, and so far he had declined to provide it.

Michael told him, "Kayla's wasn't even locked. All I had

to do was pick it up, and I saw you'd called her seventeen times today. Seventeen."

Greg said nothing.

"Sounds like you were pretty upset, desperate to talk to her. You know we're going to download all those voice-mails. Plus her emails, text messages . . ."

"We didn't argue." Of course he wanted to talk to her, knew she'd be upset, but she couldn't pick up while she'd been talking to the cops, drove home and took a shower. When she finally answered, she told him to come over. They talked, Kayla calmed down, said she still loved him. He was exhausted, fell asleep. They went over it a second time, but the story didn't change.

Michael said, "So what you're saying is, some unknown person came into a locked condo and brutally murdered your mistress while you snoozed four feet away?"

Greg seemed uncertain, unsure which way to jump. His gaze darted around, seeking inspiration or maybe rescue. "I don't understand it, either. I couldn't believe it when you guys woke me up and I saw—her."

A few more tears. Luis apparently sensed they weren't going to get any more out of him, and moved on. "We spent our afternoon following up on Kayla's account of that day, the day Ashley died."

Greg's tear-filled eyes jerked up at them in a violent spasm.

"There are some issues."

His face stilled, grief for his lost girlfriend instantly crowded out by, possibly, grief for himself.

"Are you sure that was the same day Ashley went out on the boat and didn't come back? That you sat around the workshop watching TV with Kayla?"

"Yes." The word drawn out, anything to delay the mo-ment when the dark bend in this path took him over a cliff.

"Our difficulty is this." Luis slowed his speech as well,

and Michael could swear his partner was enjoying himself. "That day could not have unfolded the way Kayla said. Unless she could be in two places at once."

Not a muscle in Greg Anderson's face twitched, or jumped, or shifted in any way. But the path ended there, and they all knew it. "I need to contact an attorney before I say anything more."

No one moved except the Naples cop in the corner, who got to his feet as if the movie had begun to roll the credits. And it had.

Chapter 32

Michael and Luis conferred outside the door of the interview room. "Finally," Luis said. "Public image be damned— he's realized the nice guy act isn't going to work. We may not be able to pin Ashley's on him, but he can't get out of Kayla's. Being found next to the body with her blood all over his hands is going to be, shall we say, problematic."

"You're the FBI?" demanded a voice to Michael's right.

A tall, gray-haired man with deep wrinkles in spa-treatment skin strode toward them in a suit, Michael could tell from years in DC, which had been impeccably tailored. Another man followed with nearly equal clothing but carrying a fashionably scarred leather briefcase. Behind both of them trailed a police officer with a uniform and an apologetic expression.

"Yes."

"This is Greg Anderson's attorney, and we demand immediate access."

"All right," Michael said mildly, and had to smile at how his prompt agreement stumped the man, even if only for a second. "Mr. Anderson has just requested an attorney, though he did not have a particular one in mind. What is your name?"

"Marty Rodriguez," the second man told them, proffering a business card. Michael took it. A glance told him the man had offices in Florida, California, and New York. How did they get inside the offices? Unauthorized personnel weren't usually guided straight back—

Luis said, "According to Mr. Anderson, he doesn't *have* a lawyer."

"He does now."

"Mr. Anderson did not mention you. We will pass on your information, and if he wants to retain you, he will be provided a phone to call you."

The gray-haired man said, "No. We'll see him now."

Luis explained with almost theatrical patience: "That's not how this works. Mr. Anderson may request an attorney of his choosing. You don't get to show up and troll for high-dollar clients. I don't blame you for trying, but you can't expect us to help."

The patrician face reddened, somewhat alarmingly. Michael guessed his age at north of eighty and his weight, south of healthy. "*You* don't get to keep me from my nephew."

Michael raised his eyebrows and Luis, his ire. Luis said, "Your nephew is a grown man and under arrest. No one sees him except an attorney, and at his request. We will pass on the information, Mr.—"

"Gyles," the man said. "Peter Gyles. You may have heard of my company, even in this backwater swamp. EntreRobotics? The foremost digital electronics group on the globe. I buy and sell people like—"

"Foremost after OakTree," Luis pointed out.

The booking officer chose that moment to retrieve his charge from the interview room, and came out towing Greg Anderson in his orange jumpsuit. Since they were only five feet away, he inevitably burst out, "Uncle Peter!" and Uncle

Peter inevitably told him to request a meeting with Marty Rodriguez, his attorney, and without a second's hesitation, he did so. In the presence of six witnesses, should that prove important, which it wouldn't.

"All right," Michael said, again as mildly as he could, only because it annoyed the hell out of Uncle Peter. "This officer here will show you to the inmate conference room and that officer there will guide Mr. Anderson."

Gyles spluttered for another moment or two about the conditions, warning that all recording devices would have to be turned off and voicing ominous predictions of the chaos that could occur should his nephew *not* be delivered to the conference room immediately and without any marks of violence. "I employ half of Silicon Valley and flew jets in the Air Force. I still have a lot of friends there, in case you think the only sword I can wield is a keyboard."

"Neither keyboards nor F14s will be needed here, sir."

Michael wouldn't have thought it possible for the man to ooze one more drop of distaste from his pores, but he managed. "Those are Navy. I flew *16s.*"

"My mistake."

And truthfully he did feel a little sheepish—men were supposed to know one fighter plane from another even if the closest they got to military service was repeat viewings of *Platoon*—but he'd be damned if he let Peter Gyles see that.

But the man moved off with his nephew and his expensive lawyer and soon the hallway stood empty of all but the two FBI agents.

"Do you know who that guy is?" Luis said, now hushed with a touch of fanboy awe.

"No."

"Genius. If Martin Post has created half the computers on this planet, Gyles and EntreRobotics has done the other half. Post is the third-richest man? He's the second."

"Good for him," Michael said, too tired to care unless it

involved the bed in his hotel room. He felt a sort of calm descend—Kayla's case seemed open and shut, the scene had been processed, the suspect in custody, now the lawyers could take over and the whole thing could move into the next stage. "But wasn't EntreRobotics the one Greg said was killing scientists back in the eighties or whatever?"

"No . . . it was EntreRobotics he implied might have killed his wife."

"Uh-huh. Should we tell Gyles how his dear nephew threw him out front and center as a murder suspect? He might put his checkbook away."

"Unless Greg was right and Gyles plans to appease his conscience by not letting his nephew go away for the crime he committed. Rich people are great at buying their way to salvation . . . though he could sink a boatload into this case and his nephew is still going down. If not for Ashley, mos def for Kayla. What? What's that look?"

"I still don't get it. Yes, we've had killers lie down and go to sleep in the same room as the body—the emotion is spent, they're resigned to their fate so they can finally relax—but I didn't think this guy was that kind of killer. If he killed Ashley—"

"If?"

"—it took planning. Thinking ahead. The coolness to keep living under the eye of her father."

"One murder too many? Broke the psyche's back?"

"Maybe . . . we still have the scene. I left a patrol guy on it."

"Yeah, but I thought you were done."

"I thought so too . . . but I think I want to go back and get that beer bottle from the kitchen garbage. Ellie swabbed it but . . ."

Luis now used his "irritatingly patient" voice on his own partner. "You think someone snuck in, put a knockout drug in Greg's beer bottle, then came back, murdered Kayla, and left again?"

"Well, if you're going to put it like *that*."

"I'm putting it like that."

"Then, yes. Maybe."

"Okay." Luis turned and headed for the exit, probably also thinking about his bed back at the hotel. "We'll have his blood tested—"

"Already requested."

"And the bottle tested too. Will that make you happy?"

"Delirious," Michael told him as they hit the parking lot, heading for the rental car through the damp sea of a Florida night. "Is it *really* always this hot here?"

Chapter 33

"He told me that," Ellie said to Rachael over the kitchen table in their temporary home. The reporters must have given up waiting for her or had never left the jail where Greg had been taken. Even the squirrels had gone to sleep. But the dog had instantly sprung into fully awake mode as soon as she entered the house, and Ellie's mind churned too busily for sleep as well. "He *said* Uncle Paul had been his doctor. No reason he and his wife wouldn't go to the same office—they didn't live here full-time then, so if she needed someone it would make sense for her to take her husband's recommendation."

Eight years ago, she thought. Ashley had been seventeen. Ellie had been twenty-two and graduating from Georgetown. She hadn't gotten back to Florida even once during this time but had stayed in touch with her aunt and uncle, often calling to talk about an unusual case, upcoming holidays, their birthdays. Paul and Joanna made it clear that they were proud of her, their sort-of adopted, sort-of daughterish person who had followed them into science, not a common

occupation in the extended family. They might have preferred her to work with the living rather than the dead, with
their philosophical bent to do the most good for the most
creatures, but this did not tinge their relationship.

They had never mentioned treating the third-richest family in the United States, but there was doctor-patient confidentiality, and according to the *Times* article, at that time
Martin might not have been so rich after all.

"I know what you're thinking," Rachael said.

"That I'm ready to warm up some of that stew?"

From Rachael's expression, it was too late in the night for
banter. "You're thinking that fatal water-related accidents
seem to happen a lot in Martin Post's family."

"That too."

"And I've noticed the cabinets of patient files in your aunt
and uncle's office slash guest room where they have so gra-
ciously allowed me to rest my weary head."

"Yep."

"And that patient confidentiality after death can be waived
for criminal investigations affecting public welfare. And we
have two dead women."

"Maybe three," Ellie said.

They both rose at the same time.

When Paul and Joanna had decamped for Guinea, they
left the house in their usual order. Via sat phone they told
Ellie to make use of it, help herself to any area or resource
the small home had to offer. That included their "office,"
which held a hospital library's worth of tomes on every
topic from toe fungus to Munchausen syndrome, case histo-
ries, anatomic charts, and a three-dimensional model of a
heart of which Ellie had always been particularly fond.

And patient files, in three vertical file drawers, each neatly
labeled with the alphabetical range of the contents: *A-F, F-N,
N-Z*. Locked, of course, as patients' information should be.

But as was his habit, Uncle Paul had left the key in the pencil tray of the uppermost desk drawer, its tag helpfully labeled *Filing cabinet*.

She pulled out the N-Z file. Kayla had been looking up Martin Post's first wife's death shortly before she died herself. Did it have a connection? Why would Kayla be interested in Deborah? Sure, she could have simply been curious about the family she found herself involved in, but at this point Ellie didn't want to dismiss anything as coincidence.

She made herself pass over *Post, Martin* since studying Martin's health would be irrelevant and stemming from mere curiosity, an unacceptable reason for violating doctor-patient confidentiality. But she plucked *Post, Deborah* from the drawer and handed it to Rachael, who settled down in Paul's chair to page through it as if it were the latest best seller.

And Ellie slid open the drawer labeled *A-F*.

It shouldn't be there—after all, her mother hadn't been a patient of her uncle's. Or was she? Her mother had been in Cleveland, but Paul might not have yet moved to Florida and met Joanna. She had never asked their personal history going back that far, and the timeline had never come up. When you're a guest, staying in a home only because of the good graces of its occupants, you don't ask a lot of questions.

Nothing under Carr. Her uncle had filed it under her mother's maiden name: Claire Beck.

She took it to the desk, sat down, and began to read, stomping down any feeling of guilt or shame at doing so.

Before Paul and Joanna, Ellie had lived with Aunt Katey and Uncle Terry in West Virginia. It had been a good time in her childhood in many ways. The couple believed in free-ranging their kids, and Ellie had never before or since had the ability to spend unsupervised time exploring how tall certain trees could grow or where the river went when it bent over the rocks. Fortunately in some ways and unfortunately in others, she had to do all that exploring with her two cousins.

Rebecca and Melissa were good girls, passed their classes, took care of their pets, loved their parents, and maybe even loved each other. But one would never have known that upon meeting them. Becky and Missy spent every waking moment locked in a frenzy of sibling rivalry with Ellie as one more pawn to be taken by the winner. The game of tug-o-war began the moment she set foot on their lawn at the age of twelve, and didn't end for three years, until she went to Florida to live with Paul and Joanna after her sixteenth birthday. Until then Ellie had to balance on the tightrope of fairness, always rigid with fear to show too much preference for one over the other, having too much fun over an ice cream sundae, choosing an afternoon movie with Missy instead of going roller-skating with Becky, or wearing Becky's old dress to the dance instead of Missy's. Any tiny misstep could cause a fall, ending with shouts and tears on Becky's part or hours of the silent treatment from Missy.

The sisters united only when they needed to pull something over on their parents, such as when Becky needed Ellie and Missy to distract their father while she listened in to Aunt Katey's phone call to Aunt Rosalie. Surely they would be discussing Becky's new boyfriend, and Becky needed advance notice of Katey's plan of attack. Rosalie would be sure to advise forbidding Becky to be within twenty feet of any male other than her father, and Becky needed the specifics to formulate a counterattack.

"We're not supposed to eavesdrop," Ellie reminded her.

"It isn't eavesdropping if it's about me," Becky stated, as if this had been guaranteed in the Constitution and Ellie would know that if she paid more attention in class. "I have the right to any information that concerns me personally."

That *did* seem reasonable, and Ellie went off to assist Missy with her task: to keep her mechanic father busy with a broken skate.

Now, sitting alongside her uncle's desk, Ellie repeated these words to herself. *I have a right to know how my mother died. I have a right to know if I had been with her.*

Yet she couldn't help but think of Martin Post insisting that he had a right to bug his son-in-law's bedroom.

She opened the file.

On top she found a newspaper article about the accident, describing how on the previous evening Claire Beck, thirty-four, went off Brecksville Road near Canal, down an embankment and into the Cuyahoga River in her twenty-year-old Fairmont sedan. The reporter didn't specify that the car had been barely roadworthy but managed to imply same. This did not come as a surprise to Ellie—no one in her mother's family had ever had a lot of money. Uncle Paul and Aunt Joanna, being doctors, were considered "the rich ones" because they had a house with more than one bathroom.

The very short article didn't mention a child or anyone else inside the car. It reported the cause of the death as drowning. Was Martin Post screwing with her?

Ellie searched internet maps for Brecksville and Canal, but the intersection meant nothing to her. She had grown up mostly on the west side and wasn't that familiar with the eastern suburbs. It seemed a perfectly nice area, though mostly industrial. She had no idea what her mother would have been doing there, but of course she wouldn't, she'd been four. Claire could have been visiting friends or had a job there, for all Ellie knew.

When it came right down to it, she knew very little about her mother.

Her aunts and uncles had been full of pleasant stories about Claire as a child, about the stuffed cat that had been her constant companion during non-school hours until the age of nine or so, about beating her brothers at roller-skate races in the street, about how she'd had a lemonade stand every day one summer until she'd made enough to buy a bike, about how Ellie's grandmother had enlisted every other mother in the city to keep an eye on Claire's whereabouts, day and night, for fear she'd run off and join "those damn hippies." Which, truly, Claire hadn't wanted to do, despite tie-dying every stitch of clothing she had and doodling peace signs throughout each school notebook.

But Claire as an adult—nothing. And not a word about the accident, of course. No one would have spoken of the abrupt death of the child's mother in front of the child, and by the time she was old enough to ask, it didn't occur to her to do so. Her personal history had become set in stone, the roller skates, the lemonade stand, "died in a car accident," and it never entered her mind that there might be more to know. And now that she wanted to ask, no one was available. Her grandmother long dead, Uncle Paul across an ocean. The other siblings, Katey and Rosalie . . . they would at least know if she were in the car, wouldn't they?

Then she ran right into the wall that sprung up every time she went down this path—why was this even important? What would it matter why her mother had been on that road or if Ellie had been in the car with her? Nothing would change. Her mother would still be dead.

But she kept reading anyway. The sheet seemed to be her uncle's scrawled notes regarding her mother's autopsy, and dated the day after Claire's death. The accident had occurred at night, so the autopsy would have taken place the next day. Paul must have spoken to the doctor or at least someone at the coroner's office to get the basic facts. The notation *CCCO* would mean the Cuyahoga County Coroner's Office, since they were still on the coroner system then. Next to *COD* Paul had written *closed head injury*.

But—cause of death was supposed to be drowning.

Hematomas forehead and—a scribbled word she could not make out.

The swelling on the forehead did not surprise her. She had seen the same subdural injury in many drivers—the car made a sudden stop by hitting a wall or a tree or another car, but the body kept going at the same momentum, and the head slammed into the steering wheel. That could have caused unconsciousness, caused her not to rouse when the car began to sink. That might explain Paul's notation. Or something had gotten lost in translation.

The next few pages, the remainder of the file, were copies of her mother's medical records from a doctor's office in Parma. Ellie skimmed them, not finding anything of particular interest. Apparently her mother had been a healthy thirty-four-year-old, having given birth to one child. The only surgeries were wisdom teeth out and an appendectomy at fifteen. Allergies, erythromycin, which Ellie had inherited. Complaints: depression. Prescriptions: imipramine.

Her mother had been on antidepressants? No one had mentioned depression along with the bike and the stuffed cat. But, again, not the sort of thing you'd talk about to a small child.

But did it have anything to do with the accident?

Was it even an accident?

Ellie rocked her chair back onto its rear legs, something she hadn't done since her teens. What was it about going back to a childhood home that made you regress to that age? She balanced with much less confidence than she'd had then and searched imipramine on her phone. The dosage prescribed to her mother had been very low. Still—was there any chance it could explain how her mother had driven her car into a river at a time of year when weather should not have been an issue? And maybe with her toddler strapped into her seat?

Stop it. One mild prescription and you're constructing an entire workup. Many, many people use antidepressants to get through a tough time. Ellie ought to know—Lexapro had helped a great deal during her divorce.

No one had ever said much or expressed great admiration for Ellie's father, so most likely the marriage had been in trouble, and with a toddler in the mix. A mild antidepressant didn't seem out of line.

Your uncle let me know she died. We'd met at his office.

Stunned by the idea that she had been in the car when her mother went into the river, Ellie's mind had skipped right over that sentence. They had *met*? Surely Claire had visited family members over the years, but Ellie had never heard details of these visits. They had never seemed important.

Martin said Ellie had been an infant, so around thirty years ago. Claire would have been thirty-one, and Martin, twenty-five, a budding genius, not yet rich nor famous but on his way—very unlike Ellie's father. Ashley hadn't been born. Had Martin been married at that point?

And Claire had been quite beautiful, the kind of woman a man would remember passing in a doctor's waiting room years before. Or had it been more than that?

And what could any of this have to do with two dead young women and missile defense?

Chapter 34

Ellie's gaze escaped across the table to where Rachael read. "Finding anything?"

"Not sure. There isn't a lot in here."

The file wasn't any thicker than her mother's . . . apparently Paul or Joanna kept their records pared to the bone. Rachael summarized Deborah Post's history: "Largely unremarkable, allergic to eggs, had a tubal ligation at thirty after Ashley's birth, taking a mild dose of lisinopril for high blood pressure. From the visit dates I'm guessing Paul and Joanna were not her primary doctors and she saw them only if an issue developed when in town: bronchitis, a urinary tract infection, a rash."

"A rash?"

"Contact dermatitis," Rachael clarified. "Poison ivy or some such."

This made Ellie aware of her itchy wrist and she scratched at it, told herself not to do that and then did it anyway. Of over twelve thousand insect species in Florida, at least eighty were the biting kind, and all of them considered her a delicacy. "Is there an autopsy report?"

Rachael handed her several sheets of paper, stapled together.

Deborah's report appeared to be more thorough than Ellie's mother's, but then it had been a different pathologist, a different state, and Ellie's mother had not been the wife of the third-richest man in the country. Ellie wondered why Paul even had the report in his possession, but then he would have been provided one before the inquest. An inquest occurred only rarely—no doubt another effect of the victim's wealth.

Most of the information seemed unremarkable. Healthy though fashionably underweight, and one kidney seemed significantly smaller than the other. There could have been a number of reasons for that. Pieces of the organ went to histology, which prepared sections thinly sliced enough to view with a transmission microscope, but the pathologist found no significant issues. Brain normal except for the two cranial fractures with minor subdural swelling.

Ellie examined a grainy copy of the X-ray and the notes. Two thin fractures along the right side of her skull, slightly behind the temple, both linear but not parallel. Neither were supposed to be fatal but created an aneurysm-based compression. Cause of death: drowning. Just as the newspaper article had said, she fell at her pool and, disoriented, could not get out of the water. "That sounds reasonable," Ellie said.

"Except why would she have *two* fractures? Falling once, anyone could do. Falling twice, hitting the same part of the head hard enough to fracture it even slightly, not so much."

"She could have received both fractures at once, falling on some part of the diving board that had two non-parallel protruding edges. We have no idea what the pool area looked like—they lived in Marco Island then, a different house."

"Two fractures on her right temple," Rachael repeated.

"Right where a left-handed person would strike her with an object like a golf club, or a walking stick."

"Or where a right-handed person would attack from behind. *Or* where a woman might slip and screw up a high dive with disastrous consequences." Now Rachael rubbed her eyes. "But I don't find any notations where Deborah complained of dizzy spells or balance issues. An 'aneurysm-based compression' would have developed immediately *after* the cranial fracture, not a condition that would have existed beforehand. Unless she had some sort of berry aneurysm that had been affecting her and the fall burst it, which then caused even more dizziness to the point that she fell in the water, if not already *in* the water, and lost consciousness.

"It makes me crazy to work with so little information."

"Me too. Do you think your aunt and uncle could tell us more if you spoke to them?"

"*Could*, yes. *Would* is a whole 'nother matter entirely. He's really strict about this sort of thing. I was kind of hoping to slink back to DC before he discovered the filing cabinet breach."

"Tell him it's all in pursuit of justice."

"Not sure that will do it, but it's worth a try." She let the chair drop to the floor and dialed the international number at which she could reach Paul and Joanna—after a fashion. A tinny, robotic voice told her to leave a message, and she asked them for a return call and specified that she needed to ask about the Posts. Paul and Joanna worked in an area so remote that it might be days before the message reached them, and then more days before they could respond, but they had no choice. They needed information from a reliable source, because, she said aloud, so far they had only the cheating Greg, an eight-year-old newspaper article, two dead women, and Martin Post.

"Who," Rachael said, "has too many women drowning after head injuries around him."

Ellie's mind went back to her mother's case. Too many women drowning after head injuries *period*.

"What are you reading?" Rachael asked, apparently only then noticing that Ellie held a different file.

"My mother died because her car went off the road into a river. I was four. Martin said my uncle said that I was in the car as well, but I have no memory of that. Or *had* no memory, until a few months ago when Michael pulled me out of the Potomac." The water, warm but still chilling, the mud sucking her downward under its surface, the feeling of blind panic—suddenly she could picture another time she'd felt the same: a cracked car window, water inside the car up to her car seat and rising fast. The door opened, hands unbuckled the straps that held her, lifted her to safety. "But am I really remembering that or is it something my mind made up? And who pulled me out?"

"Who do you think that could have been?" Rachael asked, her voice as soft and probing as a therapist's.

My father, Ellie thought, but not ready to voice it. Who else?

Had he been in the car? Or had he caused the crash?

And why did he save her only to abandon her a few days later, especially after those cryptic last words? "No matter what they say, this isn't my fault."

Rachael let her muse for a while before prompting: "So— what now?"

"I wait for Martin to keep his end of our bargain and root out every document in existence that dealt with my mother's case. And I have some questions for my uncle that aren't about Deborah Post."

"Good luck. You know . . . before you go down this road—"

"Make sure I want to know?"

Rachael nodded.

"I do." Ellie looked across at a framed photo on her uncle's desk of her mother and all her siblings in one big group shot, goofy teenagers mugging for the camera. "No matter what I find out."

She gave up and went to find some Caladryl for her wrist before climbing into bed.

Chapter 35

Girded with two cups of coffee in her stomach and one more in a travel mug, Rachael showed up at the medical examiner's office a professional fifteen minutes before the scheduled autopsy of Kayla Parker. Once again she encountered Michael Tyler and Luis Alvarez in the disrobing area . . . or robing area, as they all donned enough white synthetic materials to enter a hot zone. The separation from her son, sleeping in a strange bed, the bizarre puzzle of one young woman's death and the murder of another right under their noses combined to put her usual optimism right out of kilter. It didn't help to see that the FBI agents seemed to feel as crappy as she must look.

Her brilliant greeting: "Morning."

Their equally astute replies: "Morning." A statement of fact, not quality.

She downed the rest of her liquid caffeine and did not confess to the HIPAA violation of looking at Deborah Post's medical records. She would if it came up, but right now there seemed more important topics. "Did Greg expand on his statement? What did he say?"

Michael shrugged. "Only what I told you before. He went to Kayla's to apologize for upending her life, etc. They didn't argue, he had a beer, he was exhausted and fell asleep. The last thing he remembers is her sitting on the love seat watching the news coverage. Then nothing until we woke him up."

"I don't get it. He and Kayla work out a detailed alibi for Ashley's murder, and *that's* the best he can come up with for Kayla's?"

Luis said, "Maybe Kayla was the brains of the operation."

Rachael said, "That's an idea . . . but whatever else Greg might have been, he wasn't dumb. Of course the same could be said for Kayla, so . . ."

The same pathologist who had performed both of Ashley's autopsies appeared, ready to perform Kayla's, and they dutifully followed her into the brilliantly lit room. As before, Luis preferred to stay near the door, avoiding not only the dead young woman and the motor vehicle accident victim on the next table but a third case at the other end of the room. The badly decomposed body had been found after two weeks of mail and newspapers piled up, and she either disliked air-conditioning or it didn't work. In Florida, where summer lasted until winter. Even from twenty feet Rachael could see a wash of maggots roaming the corpse.

The county had a busy morning, so the doctor made do without a diener. To help out, Rachael volunteered to do the grunt work, like making the Y-incision and snapping the ribs open to the chest cavity.

Willing, yes, but not eager. From Ellie's vivid description, Rachael felt she knew the flustered young woman. Not for the first time she understood why family members reacted so badly to the idea of an autopsy. To take a body as nearly ideal as Kayla's and purposely dismantle it seemed horrible.

But as always, she focused on *why* they were doing it. Kayla should not be dead, and Rachael must give her this one last chance to speak her protest: *Why did this happen to me? Find out why this happened to me!*

She intended to.

First, she photographed Kayla's body from head to toe, with close-ups of each rare imperfection in the skin. Then she and the pathologist examined the injuries, the three gashes in the scalp; they inspected the blood-crusted hair and cuts so deep the cranium gleamed white through the gaps, looking for trace evidence. But the marble statue had not crumbled. Rachael had brought the copious pictures she and Ellie had taken of the statue, including a ruler to illustrate the scale. She knew the doctor would prefer the actual item, but fingerprints and contact DNA on its surface took priority. Moving it from place to place and in and out of a bag, even handling it carefully, even grasping by the edges of the wings where fingers wouldn't have the space to deposit prints, all that formed too much of a risk.

Its dimensions did indeed match—the long side of the rectangular base measured four inches from corner to corner, and so did two of the gaping wounds. The third formed more of a puncture, deeper in the middle, consistent with the corner of the base.

The pathologist asked how much it had weighed.

"I'd say ten pounds, easy."

"As good as a dumbbell."

Rachael agreed. "Swing it a little and it could easily fracture a skull."

"Is that what killed her? Was it instant?" Michael asked.

"We'll get to that," the pathologist said, unhurried. The head usually came last in the autopsy regimen. The FBI agent would have to wait.

They examined Kayla's hands and scraped under her fingernails, though there were no signs of defensive wounds or any defense at all—no broken nails, no hairs caught in the fingers or in the three gold rings. The pathologist used a syringe to collect vitreous fluid from Kayla's left eye to help narrow down a time of death, since its potassium level would increase after that time. Rachael noticed Luis cringe and turn away, strolling toward the other end of the room until he caught sight of the decomposed body's maggot collection and did an abrupt pivot.

Kayla wore only shorts and a tank top without shoes or socks—doing them a favor in a way. Rachael well remembered working in DC in winter when a victim would come in swaddled in a thick coat, hat, gloves, boots, two shirts, sweatshirt, jeans, and long johns, and all of it would have to be examined, photographed, bagged, tagged, and stored. Though that work usually fell to the forensic scientists, Rachael had discovered there were few items on earth heavier than a knee-length, leather, soaking-wet-from-the-snow man's overcoat.

A disposable, plastic-backed paper sheet had been laid on the floor, and on this they spread out each item of clothing as they removed it from Kayla's body. Black stretchy shorts and a white tank top. Soft lacey panties and a comfy stretch bra. The panties did not have any apparent semen stains, but they and the shorts seemed damp from more than the humidity of the body cooler and smelled of urine—not uncommon for the deceased.

Rachael photographed each piece, paying particular attention to the tank top. Small bloodstains scattered down the right side, a few on the front but most on the back. It could be difficult to tell with cloth that shifted and bunched up and clung to the contours of the body, but the spots seemed consistent with the injuries in Kayla's scalp. She was hit and the tiny blood droplets fell downward.

She explained that to Michael, who silently leaned over

her. She also found it interesting that the swipe of cloth immediately under the arm had no spots at all.

"A void," Michael said, using the correct bloodstain pattern interpretation terminology.

"Yes, maybe. As if her arm had been at her side."

His words were grim. "She didn't see it coming. Probably from behind?"

"That would be my guess. There's not enough blood here for her to have been upright very long after those injuries. Any wound takes a moment to start bleeding, so impact patterns are often the result of the *second* blow—blood has gathered on the surface and the weapon strikes it. She's hit, she puts a hand to her head, it comes away bloody, he swings again. My guess would be if the first blow didn't knock her down or at least to the side enough that the blood fell to the floor and not onto her clothing, then the second blow laid her out. The third blow came after she had fallen to the floor. It all must have been quick. From the position of the body . . . she didn't have a chance to turn around, much less defend herself." Rachael felt a surge rise in her chest, but didn't have time for anger. The autopsy had to move on.

She removed the rings, and the tiny gold butterflies from Kayla's pierced ears. These also went on the sheet with the clothing.

She and the pathologist examined the rest of skin for injuries, bruises, recent scars, and found none. Puncture marks or abscesses that would indicate drug use, found none. Swellings that would indicate trauma, tumors, or hernias, found none. Tattoos, none.

They examined each orifice of her body for foreign matter, particularly the three openings in her groin and the pubic hair there, looking for signs of assault or semen. Nothing.

Next they washed Kayla's body, using the metal spraying hose that extended from the sink unit in long snaking loops and a squirt bottle of blue dishwashing liquid. It took some time to gently work the crusted blood out of the hair so they could get a better look at the edges of the wounds.

As the pathologist photographed those wounds and shaved the hair around each one, Rachael made the Y incision, using a scalpel to slice through the skin from each shoulder to the breastbone and from there straight down to the groin. Globules of yellow subcutaneous fat welled up from the underside of the skin. As strict as Kayla had been about her figure and her health, she still had some fat—it would be very unhealthy to have none at all.

The long-handled shears that most people used to trim small tree branches made nearly the same sort of sound when they bit through the ribs. Then she and the other doctor ran their hands around Kayla's inner organs, checking for abnormalities. Since there had been no apparent trauma to the torso, they didn't expect to and didn't find evidence of injury.

The lungs were gleaming and healthy, with no evidence of smoking. Rachael made a small incision in the pericardium, the membrane surrounding the heart, noting the amount of fluid that oozed out. Too much fluid put pressure on the heart, eventually kept it from expanding, but that hadn't happened here. The heart had no defects—the chamber walls were at their normal width, the coronary arteries pliable and clear. Kayla's heart would have kept beating even with the brain in trouble, generating its own heartbeat until the loss of blood slowed it down and the stilled lungs starved it for oxygen.

The pathologist pulled out the stomach, holding the limp sac over a plastic quart container and snipping it open with a scissors. From its size Rachael didn't expect much and, indeed, not much came out. Kayla may have been too upset or too pressed for time to eat. The doctor poured part of it into a smaller vial for toxicological testing and dumped the rest on the cutting board.

Normally Rachael hated working with gastrics, but she felt particularly interested in this one. She and the doctor bent over the board.

The doctor pushed at small flakes with one finger. "Oatmeal?"

"Looks like. That would explain the granola bar wrapper in the garbage. I guess that constituted dinner."

The doctor said, "*That* was dinner? That's why she looked like she did and I look like I do." And she used the spray hose to rinse off the cutting board.

The kidneys, liver, ovaries, and uterus were likewise without defect. Kayla had not been pregnant, nor did they see any indication that she had ever given birth.

Rachael sliced through the scalp, taking care to avoid the injuries, and used the chisel to separate the skin from the bone of the skull. This also held no surprises. Underneath the three gashes, broken blood vessels had formed small clots and jagged fractures lined the cranium. The bone had been more than fractured—it had been crushed.

Chapter 36

More cleaning and photographing, and then Rachael took the bone saw and made the cut through the bone, a neat circumnavigation of the top of the skull. After that she used the chisel again to pry the dura mater, the cover of the brain, until it released from the inside of the bone of the cranium—which promptly came apart in six pieces once freed.

Rachael arranged these pieces on the "gray board" to photograph—the matte, neutral color minimized issues of reflection and color fidelity.

One blow had only caused a hairline fracture, but the other two had cracked the thick bone all the way through. A piece had entered the brain and had to be teased out as well, and then the brain separated from the spinal cord for its appointment on the cutting board.

At first Rachael saw nothing unexpected; large hematomas had squeezed the brain until it died, essentially, and the shard of bone stuck in it didn't help. The pathologist spread the parts out, the cerebellum, the cerebrum, the pons, and began to dissect.

They called the brain "gray matter" since that's exactly what it was—a solid gray mass with an edging of white, convoluted into a landscape of valleys and furrows, all gently rounded to an innocuously bland exterior. *What it really is*, Rachael thought, *is a black box, a benign disguise hiding every mystery.* After centuries of study, it stubbornly kept secret how its synapses and cells and membranes combined to form thought and memory and personality, how it all actually *worked*.

Again, she and the pathologist bent over the cutting board, examining each section. Aside from the expected physical damage, no anomalies presented themselves. Once through the cerebellum the doctor separated the right and left lobes of the cerebrum from the small mass of glands dangling from its lower surface. The hypothalamus and the pituitary, plucked from the tiny pocket of bone behind the nasal cavity. There it had been well protected from the assault, except—

Rachael leaned forward until her nose came nearly within kissing distance of the tissue on the board . . . not that it mattered since her face shield formed a barrier between her and the dissected parts. "That look strange to you?"

The pathologist did the same and they clunked heads. "Kinda."

Their interest attracted Michael, who had stayed well out of hose-spraying range. He gingerly crowded in. "What? What do you see?"

Rachael could hear the uncertainty in her voice. "Not sure. Her pituitary stalk looks a little weird. Could be a genetic defect since I don't see any damage."

"No tumors, or injury," the pathologist muttered.

"What does that mean?" Michael asked.

Rachael assured him, "Probably nothing—it's just interesting, that's all. It couldn't have caused her skull to become bashed in, that's for sure. The pituitary makes hormones that control and regulate bodily functions—growth, development, and function of sex organs, all of which"—she gestured toward Kayla's poor, ravaged body—"had obviously been fine."

"Thyroid," the pathologist said. "But that's in the anterior lobe."

She cut the anterior lobe of the pituitary gland into sections. Rachael couldn't see anything wrong with it. Then the posterior lobe, which looked acutely undersized to her.

"Odd looking," the pathologist said.

Michael had continued to hover. "What is odd? And what would it affect?"

"Vasopressin and oxytocin," Rachael said.

"And—?"

"Oxytocin tells the uterus and breast muscles to contract, which is important during childbirth and breastfeeding."

"Not relevant to her," the pathologist commented. "Not so far."

"And vasopressin regulates how the kidneys reabsorb water from the body."

Michael said, "I thought the point of the kidneys was to get *rid* of the water."

Rachael had to smile. "Well, yes, but only what we absolutely don't need. Our bodies are all about water—maintaining just the right amount is vital. Too much can kill you just as too little can kill you. If the kidneys don't reabsorb some, we'd just pee it all back out."

Luis spoke up, still from his safe place by the door. "I thought vasopressin was taken for high blood pressure."

The pathologist said, "No, low blood pressure. It increases the fluid in the body."

"Oh . . . by the way, Doc, those things—they're coming closer."

The three at the cutting board turned. The maggots from the decomp had fled their source, discouraged by the soap and the water. They had climbed over the sides of the gurney and fallen to the floor or inched down its legs. From there they had spread across the linoleum, expanding in a three-hundred-and-sixty-degree corona, one millimeter at a time. Luis watched this nearly microscopic zombie invasion with a kind of horror.

"Huh," the pathologist said. "Yeah."

Rachael said, "Long ago we used to put bodies like that in the long-term storage freezer, kill all the insect life before starting the autopsy."

"That sounds like a great idea," Luis said.

"It delayed things, since first you had to wait for everything to freeze and then for everything to thaw."

"I got time."

"And the effects of freezing changed too many factors of the anatomy."

Luis stared at the decomposed body. "I don't think that one would care. So instead you let them roam around?"

The pathologist's attention had returned to the pituitary's posterior lobe. "Yeah. They'll just kill them all, disinfect the place when we're done."

"Don't let them get near the clothing," Rachael told him. Luis glanced at his bootyed feet, considering his options for defense, and she turned back to the dissected tissue.

Michael summarized: "So this isn't important."

"Not to you," the pathologist said.

"It—" Rachael stopped, and straightened.

The pathologist continued dissecting. Michael watched Rachael. "What?"

"Well . . . if this undersized pituitary caused vasopressin issues, she could have had CDI. Central diabetes insipidus."

"She had diabetes?"

"Not like we usually think of it, not diabetes mellitus, an insulin deficiency. Central diabetes insipidus—it might explain some things. I had a victim like this once in DC, with hypertonic dehydration."

"English, please. *What* would it explain?"

"Her pantry. And her water bill."

Michael said nothing, but the way breath puffed under his mask told her he had had enough anatomy lessons for one day.

"Okay—if she had CDI, her kidneys couldn't concentrate the urine because the pituitary wasn't sending vasopressin to tell them to do so. So she would just keep passing dilute urine and not retaining enough water. Lack of water retention would create dehydration—and that can cause arrythmia, seizures, confusion, even coma if it goes on long enough. Kayla didn't show any signs of that, had a normal life and a steady job, so *if* she had this she kept it under control. She had learned to keep drinking to keep from dehydrating, and had to keep peeing because she kept drinking."

She watched Michael's expression as the tumblers fell. "That's why the cases of water. And the water bottle I sat on in the car."

The pathologist snorted. "Everybody's got water. This is Florida."

"True," Rachael said. "It might be excessive. It might be routine storm preparation. But the water bill on top of it—"

"We'll see what the slides tell us," the pathologist said, meaning the sections of the gland she would send to histology for microscopic sectioning.

"Sure," Rachael said. "We could do genetic testing as well. But at the end of the day it's simply interesting. It didn't kill her."

The pathologist moved on to the pons and the rest of the

brain stem that linked the brain to the spinal cord. "If she does have that, though, wouldn't she have been on vaso-pressin? You didn't send her meds with the body."

Rachael hastened to assure her: "We didn't find any. I checked the bathroom, the kitchen, her purse. Nothing."

"Huh."

"Guys," Luis said again. "They're getting closer."

Chapter 37

After she'd rescued Kayla's miniscule amount of clothing from the encroaching horde and sealed the items in paper bags for the police lab technicians to examine, Rachael took the blood and tissue samples to the courier for immediate transport to the Locard. She had sent vials of Greg's blood and urine, and called to wake up their chemistry professor to beg for the rush of rushes. But Sam, a young woman with hair the color of green apples, had not been asleep but out at a location with extremely loud music. Happily, she didn't mind ditching the place for a little overtime.

Several cars followed Rachael from the secured lot at the back of the medical examiner's office—reporters, she figured, but that was okay; they formed an orderly and calm progression as she obeyed all traffic laws. Reporters didn't frighten her as they seemed to unnerve Ellie. Rachael felt only a stab of pity . . . this had to be superbly tedious, following people around for hours in the hopes that they might do something interesting.

Back at Paul and Joanna's house, she and Ellie had a video call with Sam. The gas chromatograph-mass spectrometer sat on the counter at the chemist's elbow. On the surface, it seemed inactive. Inside, it hummed with activity, volatizing Greg Anderson's urine sample, preparing to tell them if it contained anything other than the usual creatinine, chloride, and potassium compounds.

"It's not done yet," Sam told them immediately. She had begun to show the effects of a long night. Skin shiny, eyes drooping, she twirled one kelly-colored strand around her finger.

"Okay," Rachael soothed. "More is coming, but not for you. I'm going to ask Laila for genetic testing, but it's not urgent."

"How come no middle of the night call for her?"

"Because it didn't kill her—and you weren't sleeping anyway."

"That's because *I* have a social life," Sam sniffed. "What do you have in mind?"

"I want to test Kayla's samples for mutations in the vasopressin-neurophysin two gene."

"What is that?" Ellie asked.

Rachael explained her theory about the water bottles and water bill.

Sam yawned, exposing one gold tooth. "Wouldn't it be simpler to just ask her doctor?"

"Well yeah," Rachel laughed, "if you want to do it the *easy* way. But we didn't find any meds, and she was otherwise so healthy. She might not have been even seeing a doctor. If it were a very mild condition, she might not have even known she had CDI."

"Still worth a try to find a doctor," Sam said. The GC-MS beeped, and she clicked a few commands on the screen.

Rachael said, "I know, and Kayla seemed pretty organized. She's got to have medical records, receipts, something. Wish I'd paid more attention to her filing cabinet."

Ellie said, "We could also ask her family—have they found

any next of kin yet? I emailed Michael the info from Contacts."

They had downloaded the phone, Michael had told Rachael earlier, but Kayla *hadn't* made any convenient entries for aptly named family members. She tended toward nicknames like Snuggle and Princess and, interestingly, Sponger. And police hardly wanted to call each one to say something like: "Hey, did you have a kid/sister/ex-wife named Kayla? Yeah? Well, she's dead."

"Not that I've heard," she told Ellie. "I'll ask to get back into Kayla's place sometime. It's not pressing anyway. She certainly didn't die of dehydration."

Sam moved her laptop so that they could read the GC-MS results for themselves. Ellie and Rachael crowded their own laptop screen, hoping the information could tell them why Kayla's boyfriend had flown into such a rage that he killed her, and then decided to take a nap.

Mild EtOH, or ethanol alcohol, from the beer—.04 percent weight by volume, hardly enough to send the guy into a drunken rage or make him pass out.

"What's that?" Ellie asked, pointing to a peak. "Is that imidazole?"

"Yeah. That's awfully high." Rachael squinted. "1.48 nanograms per milliliter. Did Mr. Greg have a cold? Take decongestants?"

"I never saw a sniffle. He could be taking one of the imidazoles for migraines . . . Now I wish I *had* looked in his medicine cabinet when Dani offered."

Rachael raised one eyebrow, but said only, "If any day of his life could bring on a migraine, that day would be yesterday. He gets outed with the mistress, finds out his alibi for his wife's murder is toast, and then wakes up next to her body."

"Michael didn't mention any complaints. And I'm sure

Greg would pull out chronic migraines if he had that in his 'poor me' arsenal. Is that tetrahydrozoline, that imidazole?"

"Looks like it."

Ellie spoke in a rush. "We need to see what was in that beer bottle."

"The swabs labeled *bottle*?" Sam asked. "Ran that this morning. Nothing—GC said water and a touch of alcohol and hops."

Ellie's shoulders slumped. "Just a rinsed-out beer bottle."

Rachael said, "Michael and Luis got a few prints off it, though. Kayla's and Greg's, big surprise. Why—what are you thinking?"

"It's a crazy idea, but what about the eyedrops in Kayla's bathroom? All it would take is a few drops in Greg's Irish Pale Ale to make him sleepy."

"The *Wedding Crashers* prank!" Sam crowed with renewed interest.

"Yeah, but unlike the movie, it doesn't give one diarrhea. It causes light-headedness, drowsiness, slowed breathing. A strong enough dose can cause death. I've read of at least two murder trials using tetrahydrozoline poisoning. The stuff's perfect—legal, innocent-looking, perfectly safe in the eyes but lethal in the digestive tract."

Rachael said, "I read some nightclubs have banned eyedrops along with guns and drugs. It's the new date-rape drug. Alcohol catalyzes it, and suddenly the victim feels as if they've drunk twenty more drinks than they actually did. The whole prior evening is a blank."

"But," Ellie said.

"But," Rachael said. "Why would Kayla put knock-out drops in her own boyfriend's beer, which sent him into an alcoholic frenzy of murder with a convenient side effect of amnesia?"

"Maybe a third person was there, took the opportunity to

doctor Greg's drink, and then set him up as the scapegoat for the dead Kayla—"

"It had to be someone both Kayla and Greg were comfortable sitting around and having a beer with. Which, I would think, leaves out Martin Post."

Ellie agreed, propping her chin on one hand. "Man, this makes no sense. Unless Kayla doctored Greg's drink because she felt afraid of him, to immobilize him while she— what, called the cops? Then he starts to feel the effects, realizes what she did, and kills her in a fury. Still can't overcome the effects, and falls asleep."

"Except," Rachael said.

"Except," Ellie said, "who rinsed out the beer bottle? If Kayla served it in a glass, where's the glass?"

"Dishwasher?"

"She cleaned the glass *and* rinsed out the bottle before he felt woozy enough to get angry at her? Maybe."

Now they both leaned their arms on the table. "Maybe" didn't bring much satisfaction.

"You two are fun," Sam said, "but I think I'm due for lunch and a nap."

Rachael's finger hovered above the Disconnect button. "Thanks very much, Sam. Sorry to interrupt your partying."

"Eh. It was bland anyway." The screen went blank.

"If that was a dud of a party, I'd hate to see a happening one."

Ellie asked her about Kayla's phone and laptop.

"Ah, yes. Michael gave me some discs with the downloads." Rachael dug through her shoulder bag until she found them. They popped the disc with Greg's phone into Ellie's laptop and Kayla's into Rachael's. Together they skimmed through the data.

They read in silence for a while, then Ellie griped, "His texts are all over the board. Video game scores to whom I assume are his friends, meeting coworkers at HQ, links to virtual meetings, dinner plans with Ashley."

"Confirming appointments with Martin. It looks like Kayla"—Rachael waved a hand at the other screen—"shows up July twenty-third of last year."

"That's what they both said," Ellie confirmed.

"Before that hers were all about what's in stock, what's being delivered, drinks with friends, movies with friends, what the Kardashians are up to, and trying to find one more bottle of Hot Poppy. I assume that's nail polish."

"I see. And does that change after Greg enters the picture?"

"No. She still prefers the Hot Poppy to the Perkily Pink." Ellie chuckled.

"Her other messages did not change, friends, chats, but also exchanges with Mr. Anderson."

"Wait. He used his own phone to text his mistress? Under Ashley's and Martin Post's very noses—not to mention Deborah's?"

"Oh, they were clever—look. They kept the language neutral. She showed up in his Contact list as *KT* with a sunrise emoji. No profile photo. No lovey-dovey stuff—she tried that in the beginning but he deleted those—see, these highlighted lines are the deleted texts the police tech found. Looks like after a while she stopped bothering. No sexting, no dick pics, spoke only to arrange a time to 'exchange codecs' or 'work on the dither applet' with a time, sometimes a day. No location."

"Okay," Ellie said. "And little Kayla didn't figure out the guy was married? Sure."

"The code got blown a week or so ago. They stopped talking about codecs and applets."

"Yeah, I see." Ellie read from Rachael's screen, then her own. **"Kayla: Just saw u on news! U R MARRIED??? Greg: I'm**

so sorry, crying emoji—oh, I'll bet he was. **Kayla: To that girl who disappeared? WTF?"**

Rachael said, "Must have been a shock to see him on the news."

"Kayla: What r they talking about? How could u do this to me? Greg: We need to talk. Kayla: We CERTAINLY DO!"

"Understatement of the year," Rachael muttered.

"Greg: I wanted to tell u. I heart u. Kayla: Does anyone know about me? Greg: small gap of time, then, **Meet me."**

They maintained radio silence in the days after that, with only two more messages, both from Kayla to Greg and both saying **Call me!** Then came the previous morning when Kayla went to visit her lover at their private place and instead had a Locard scientist, an FBI agent, and an irate father-in-law jump into her vehicle. She must have found a moment to text him from the police station: **The cops r talking to me!**

Then, last night: **Call me!**

Then, nothing.

"Wait," Rachael said. "Let's go back a bit."

They reviewed the messages around the day Ashley disappeared. The day before, Greg had texted: **1:30. Kayla: K.** On the day of, nothing, Rachael noted. "Because Kayla was busy at work all day like her coworkers said, or because she was with Greg at the unit like he said?"

"Excellent question. I would tend to believe the coworkers, who have no reason to lie, as opposed to Greg, who has a very *strong* reason to lie. But is there any chance they got the days mixed up?"

Ellie said, "Michael and Luis watched the store video."

"Was the time right?" Rachael wondered. "Most of the people with video surveillance systems don't know how to work them, never set the right day or time, or at a minimum never update to daylight savings time."

The next day, **Greg: Let's meet to work on the metas.**

Kayla: 1? Greg: K. Sporadic exchanges continued for the next three days until Kayla caught sight of Greg on the news, pleading for the return of his wife.

The tone of the exchanges didn't change one iota after Ashley's disappearance, Rachael pointed out. "I still think little Miss Kayla had to know her man was married, but she may have told the truth about not knowing it was to Martin Post's daughter."

Ellie pondered that, wondering how, if true, the fact might figure into events, if at all. Then they scrolled through Greg's photos and emails, an avalanche of information nearly as unhelpful as his messages to Kayla. Pictures of Ashley, selfies of them both, copious pics of his Bugatti's sweet interior, a random shot of an outside bistro table covered in empty beer bottles and the remnants of chicken wings. The emails bounced around as well, notes from Martin about CurrentSDI, from Ashley detailing dinner plans and reports from doctor's visits, even a few from Dani about a charity event the previous month at which the family needed to put in an appearance. Many others, dealing with such high-tech topics that the two women could barely understand the language as English. If the FBI was looking for corporate espionage, they would have to have their own tech guys spend a week or two with Greg's emails.

Kayla and Greg hadn't emailed each other at all. Kayla's missives were purely social, chatting with friends about Naples nightspots, days at work, and hurricane predictions. Her photo library held numerous selfies of Kayla in coquettish poses and expressions, or enjoying a girls' night out. None of Greg.

Ellie said, "How did he explain that? He's camera shy? In the Witness Protection Program? Or did he just pick up her phone when she went to the bathroom and delete them all?"

"From what I've seen of Greg, I'm sure he had an explanation."

"I'd love to hear it. All right," Ellie said. "We need to get back to that apartment. Find her medical records and grab that bottle of eyedrops to work some fingerprint magic on. Check the dishwasher for beer glasses. Speaking of prints, did they get any from the murder weapon?"

"Greg's. In blood. Still waiting on DNA, but since only Kayla bled at the scene, it seems a foregone conclusion."

"So, we got him," Ellie said. She didn't sound triumphant.

Rachael wondered if Ellie still wanted to believe in the handsome man's innocence, or if triumph would exist only if Kayla's life had been saved. "Pretty much already had him. Hard to explain being found next to the body with her blood on your hands, and your fingers on the weapon."

"Open and shut," Ellie said.

"Open and shut. Except."

"Except for Ashley," Ellie asked aloud. "How did he kill *Ashley*?"

Chapter 38

Ellie broke the crime scene tape to enter Kayla's apartment, having discussed this entry with the extremely bored officer on duty in the parking lot. Michael had cleared their visit.

The apartment seemed much more cheery in the day, with sunlight streaming through the windows and bouncing off the cream upholstery. Ellie hadn't thought much about Kayla having a corner place, so that large windows next to both the television and over the dining room table ushered in some feng shui. Only the stains on the area rug and smell of dried blood belied the peace.

Rachael took the filing cabinet while Ellie went to the kitchen garbage. She hadn't examined every single item in it the previous night, interested only in the most recent items, anything that might be relevant to the crime—signs of Kayla having had a meal or snack with her killer, bloody towels from that killer cleaning their hands. Ellie now knew how the granola bar fit in and of course the removed beer bottle. Under the wrapper she found a browned apple peel, an empty bottle of nail polish, a crumpled, expired coupon for Aquafresh toothpaste, an unidentifiable glob of some dairy product, and a tiny, stiff plastic wrap such as the kind used as a seal for cosmetic products. Ellie had broken enough nails trying to open lipsticks, mascaras, and antibiotic ointments to know.

She had to hold her breath to keep from blowing it out of her palm, noting how the tiny clear scrap tapered along its length. It looked, in fact, exactly like what the tamper-proof seal from a tiny bottle of eyedrops would look like.

She dropped it into a very small paper bag, leaving the bottom of the bag fluffed outward to minimize rubbing against the wrapper. Fingerprints, or contact DNA if there were no prints, might prove interesting . . . *if* Greg had actually been drugged by his own victim.

The dishwasher held dirty dishes, three bowls and a plate in the lower rack and four coffee cups and six drinking glasses in the upper, a bread knife plus a handheld juicer with dried orange pulp caught in its sieve. Everything had been placed in a most-closely packed arrangement, like molecules in a liquid. This time Ellie carefully picked up each mug and glass to examine. Each had residue and fingerprints that no one had made any attempt to clean off. She sniffed each one, picking up only orange, or coffee, or nothing at all. No beer.

No other items seemed any more relevant today than they had the night before. No bloody paper towels—but then Greg hadn't washed his hands, he'd been found with Kayla's blood still on them. And there hadn't been a single smear in any sink.

Between the two murders, they now had two weapons— the statue and the broom handle—with the victim's blood and Greg's fingerprints on them. Greg might have been a whiz at coding video graphics, but as a killer he couldn't get past the first level.

Ellie moved to the bathroom and collected the bottle of

eyedrops that so interested her, dropping it into another very small paper bag. She examined the medicine cabinet items again, but nothing jumped out at her.

She joined Rachael in the office and wondered again about the lonely Android charging cable, lying next to the equally empty OakTree cable. She and Michael and Rachael hadn't paid much attention to it the previous evening, since schoolkids now had more than one mobile device, but now she wondered: shouldn't they have found another Android mobile *something* around? But they hadn't. Not in the apartment, not in her car; Luis had even gotten to Ulta before they closed to clear out the little cubby where Kayla stowed her bag during shifts. The cable could belong to an old device, but Kayla seemed too streamlined to stand for an unnecessary cable cluttering up her work space.

The victim's tidiness extended to her file cabinet, where among hanging folders labeled *Rental* and *Income Taxes*, Rachael, cross-legged on the floor, had found one marked *Medical*. She pointed out the more interesting contents as Ellie settled beside her.

"Right on top, a receipt from Kayla's last visit to a Dr. Brandon Pine, a checkup with lab work from four months earlier. Kayla's blood pressure was 115/74, temperature of 97.4 degrees, height, weight, so on. Kayla had had no complaints, but look at this."

She held out the paper, pointing to a written notation under *Other diagnoses*. In a barely legible scrawl the doctor had written: *CDI*.

"Wow! You were right."

"I know."

"You're grinning."

"I am. With the same ridiculous triumph as when I know the answer to a really obscure *Jeopardy!* question. But here's her lab results."

Ellie read the entries. Urine osmolality, less than 300 mOsm/Kg. Plasma copeptin less than 2.6 pmol/L. "Uh-huh . . . and that means?"

"Nothing. It's normal. Which leads me to *this*. This Walgreens patient information sheet has a prescription for Kayla, .5 mg desmopressin, a vasopressin analogue."

Ellie said, "So Kayla *had* been on meds."

"Exactly. But where were they now? Greg didn't have an opportunity to take them away. *If*, just for the sake of argument, Greg was drugged and framed, then why would this other killer take them? Vasopressin has no street value."

"She wouldn't run out of them." Kayla might have been a young, pretty girl who sold makeup, but that didn't make her brainless. She seemed to have led a very well-ordered life and took interest in matters more weighty than finding the right shade of lipstick . . . though, to be fair, the perfect shade *could* prove a long and difficult quest.

"No. From the date on the sheet, if she had been taking them correctly, Kayla would have been only halfway through the bottle."

Ellie shook her head. "An inexplicable little mystery."

"But, technically, an irrelevant one. Greg wasn't drugged with vasopressin and Kayla didn't die of CDI. We can, when we have time, drop by Dr. Pine's office to find out more about Kayla's somewhat obscure condition, but—"

"There's no guarantee he'd talk to us." Confidentiality regarding a patient's medical records existed in a somewhat fluid legal state. Generally, according to HIPAA—the Health Insurance Portability and Accountability Act of 1996—confidentiality did not expire upon death and doctors were prohibited from revealing medical information to anyone other than the patient's "personal representative." This representative could be Kayla's next of kin or executor of her estate, or the person she designated when she filled out that sheaf of papers a doctor's office usually handed to any new patient when they walked in.

The police might need to ask the doctor for the name of the representative if they continued to strike out on finding a next of kin. The FBI agents had spoken to Kayla's co-workers and hadn't reported any luck. Luis had told them, as nearly as any of the people at Ulta could recall, Kayla had never spoken of family other than to say they "weren't close." No one knew if she'd been born in the area or, like so many other Floridians, transplanted herself at some point. Apparently one had even said, "She was such a good listener—I'm going to miss that so much."

Of course HIPAA also allowed release of records to persons involved in the decedent's care or in payment for their care, and to law enforcement with a court order or perhaps just a written request. Other than to find next of kin, though, she doubted their curiosity about Kayla's CDI would be considered sufficient cause.

"Unless we find something amazing on that bottle and wrapper, it looks like Kayla's murder is as open-and-shut as it can get," Ellie said.

"Time to get back to the one that isn't."

Chapter 39

From Kayla's apartment she and Rachael first turned south to deliver the bottle and wrapper to the print unit at the police department, then went north up 41 to get to the Post estate. Only this time instead of letting the guard wave them through the gate, Ellie parked in front of it.

Clouds roiled with more than the usual afternoon thunderstorms. The outer bands of tropical storm Hazel had reached southwest Florida, sprinkling rain, stopping, starting again.

The guard on duty watched her approach, his eyes widening only slightly at this breach in protocol. She doubted he would find two clearly unarmed females, ones he had admitted before on Martin Post's say-so, a serious threat, but also doubted he would have kept this job if he didn't take *every* threat seriously.

"Ma'am?" he said, a number of questions contained in that one word.

Ellie said, "Hello. We would like to see the camera feed, if you don't mind. I mean we'd like to see what all your surveillance cameras see. Their view."

She was talking too much, but he didn't blink. With a

wave he guided them in and over to the dizzying array of monitors. Those had been installed one after the other in a straight line, along the desktop and below the windows, forming a horseshoe shape around the ergonomic desk chair. This way the guard could monitor the screens and the windows at the same time. And the windows, Ellie guessed from the slight distortion, were bulletproof.

A hallway directly behind them had a door on either side, maybe a closet and a bathroom. It led to a back room with a large window. Apparently Martin believed that all the video cameras in the world couldn't take the place of a decent window. Ellie agreed.

Isaac let Rachael sit in the desk chair while he stood. Only one chair, because this central point of access was not a place to sit with coworkers and jaw about last night's game. Nor could he sit still and monitor the bank—he'd have to constantly scan from side to side. Maybe that helped them stay alert on slow days.

Most of the screens showed trees, trees, trees and water, the street, and more trees. With the constant breeze off the Gulf, the fronds moved and waved and sometimes flopped in front of the camera's protective bubble. "How do you keep up with the foliage?"

"It's a constant battle," he admitted, in a surprisingly friendly tone. Perhaps he didn't get many visitors. "If we see leaves consistently blocking the scope, we have the landscapers go out. They can usually take care of it with a ladder and some pruning shears, but it's getting the ladder out there in the first place, fighting through the pepper trees—that's the hard part. It's even worse when they have to clean the bubbles. They have to hang over the wall with rags and a spray bottle."

"Seriously?"

He shook his head. "Tech can't solve *every* problem."

Each camera swung from side to side in a slow arc, sweeping the areas in front of the walls and, she could see from studying each screen in relation to the ones adjacent, doing a good job of overlapping their views to cover every inch of the perimeter. "Did he clear the land outside the wall when he had the estate built?"

"Yeah, quite a bit of it. But stuff's grown in over the years, can't help it. In this state, the stuff you don't want grows like a weed. But if you want a daffodil or a decent tomato, forget it."

Ellie found the spot where she had gone over the wall the day before—had that only been yesterday? She recognized the drooping branch of the live oak, the slight clearing with the stump she had used, still upright in the center. No reason to think that because she had breached that point, it meant an intruder had as well. But the screens to the left also showed fairly clear areas until the lens landed on open water. A clever assailant—who had already checked out the presence of cameras—could have clung to the wall and ducked under their view up to the clearing, if they—

"Could someone have come from the water?" she asked aloud.

"What?"

Could, she asked, someone in scuba gear swim up to where the wall met the water, slink along it to the live oak, wait for the camera to swing away, and use that five seconds to shimmy up the branch?

She expected the guard to raise an eyebrow and scoff: "*Seriously?*" But his face stilled, his gaze turned inward, going over the scenario in his head. She wondered if he were replaying past Seal Team missions to find examples.

"Possible," he said at last. "But highly unlikely. There's no beach, just rocks and silt and rough surf. They'd have to be one hell of a swimmer—which I guess they would be to get there in the first place—and then they'd have to come up in exactly the right spot, which isn't easy to do from under the water when there's no landmarks around. There's no light pollution, either, so it would be a real nightmare at night."

"I'm thinking during the day."

"Oh. Slightly easier, but only slightly. It's all mangroves. That would provide cover for them to get out of the water, but then they'd have to fight their way through a briar patch of roots and branches that's going to rip all your equipment off. *I* wouldn't want to do it." That seemed to settle the matter for him. "Besides, Martin and then the FBI already checked all the video to see if someone jumped the wall and stowed away in Mrs. Anderson's boat. But there was nothing."

Ellie considered this. "I know you've probably been asked this ten times already, but did anyone else come onto the property that day? Any deliveries?"

"Nope. An Amazon package for Mrs. Post, that I took from the driver—like the size of a shoe box—and the cook, Mrs. Carrolla. She came in about eleven and left just after three. That's normal for her on days when Mr. Post doesn't want her to make dinner."

Rachael asked, "The day before? Guests? Deliveries?"

Ellie had a cartoonish image of someone smuggling themselves inside an oversized carton . . . surely such a large estate would lay in large amounts of supplies. But the guard continued to shoot down her ideas. She finally thanked him and she and Rachael returned to the car.

At the entrance to the Post home, they waited for someone to appear inside the glass door and allow them to enter the relief of air-conditioning. No one did.

Ellie rapped her knuckles on the glass, a tentative knock. Thunder rumbled in the distance—deceptively, because a second later the sky lit up like a nuclear flash and cracked with a single, deafening peal that shook the ground beneath them.

"Shit!" Rachael burst out before the sound could fade. "I can't believe you keep telling me that's normal."

"It *is* normal."

"Maybe we should ask Deborah," Rachael suggested. "Before we melt."

"From the heat or the rain?"

"Both."

The doors slid open, and Ellie thought the house assistant had heard them until she saw Tomas on the other side.

"Hello, Doctors. Dani asked me to let you in. She'll be down in a minute."

Down from where, the bedroom? It was cliché and unfair of her, but Ellie couldn't help wondering. He really *was* handsome. "Dani told me you're the contracting officer."

"Yes." He waved them toward one of the leather couches.

"This must be one of your more difficult assignments," she went on, blatantly fishing, though for what, she couldn't say. A connection to Kayla Taylor? Or whomever Kayla might have been working for?

"Oh my gosh, is it."

"Dani says you're the linchpin to the whole process. The most important person."

He chuckled, his gaze falling in modesty. "Technically, I am. Which is nowhere near as fun as it sounds. I'm a hero if things go well and the DOD feels it's made the right purchase. But if not . . ."

"You have to coordinate all these tests and demonstrations?"

"Starting from step one. I have to document everything, so that if anyone's unhappy afterward I can show why I made the decision I made. I have to determine if the company knows what it's getting in to, how much of their operations they're going to have to devote to the contract. It might be much more than they realize and they'll need to suspend work in other areas—do they really want to do that?"

Ellie glanced at Rachael. That put a different slant on his conversation with Dani in the garage.

"I have to know all the relevant laws to make sure that nothing happens to violate any, on the company's end, in terms of contracting regulations. I have to make sure there's no undue influence on anyone's part. I'm here to be a check and a balance, while the Army brass just wants to know 'can this company solve my problem, and what's it going to cost?' It's their job to focus on their needs no matter how Martin might be grieving right now. So I feel terrible for going on with this test after Ashley's death, but it has to be done. Brilliant girl."

Rachael sat up. "Did you meet Ashley?"

"Yes, of course. She largely wrote the capability statement for OakTree."

Dani approached from a hallway, blinking in mild surprise at their arrival. She wore a sleeveless top of some thin, chiffon-like material and lightweight pants. For such a slender woman she never seemed to get cold—or perhaps never stopped moving long enough. "Dr. Davies, Dr. Carr. How are you?"

"Just fine. How are you holding up?"

A sad smile marred the woman's perfect skin. "Well, you know. Best we can. I'm afraid no one's here, really—two of the cleaning crew and Terrance from Oaktree, finishing up what Greg was supposed to do."

"He's who I need to see," Tomas said, and bid the doctors goodbye.

Dani barely acknowledged his leaving. "Martin is at the Ritz giving a presentation to the committee before they caravan over here for the test. I have to leave for a fund-raiser for the Guatemalan plant. Terrible timing, but it's such an important project."

More important than the secure defense of the United States? Ellie's surprise must have showed on her face, because Dani said, "I know. I can't decide if I'm bailing because I'm a wimp or because I'd only be in the way." The stress of the past few weeks showed in the crinkles around Dani's eyes and the fresh scrape on her arm, perhaps from more garage construction projects. *This is how we cope with stress.* Even the rash on her arm seemed redder, angrier. "I just know that if it fails, I don't want to be here. And if it succeeds, it won't matter if I'm here or not."

Was she *afraid* of her husband? "I'm so sorry to bother you. I was hoping to see Ashley and Greg's bedroom again. And perhaps the boats."

A perplexed frown, but Dani had probably developed a high tolerance for random and perplexing requests. She waved at the vast entryway. "Certainly. You can find your own way? I really do have to—"

Rachael assured her. "Yes, absolutely! We don't want to hold you up. I'm not even sure what I'm looking for."

"Does anyone?" Dani hustled off, leaving them to find their own way.

Chapter 40

As it turned out, they had been a little too quick to turn down any offer of assistance, and wandered through a game room with a pool table and pinball machines, then a suite of meeting rooms before finding the huge pool with the aquarium bridge. Even then Ellie steered them into a wrong turn, ending in a vast library that she coveted even with its modern design. If she had Martin's money, she'd have made it incredibly old-fashioned, with heavy wood shelves and those rolling ladders to reach the top ones, instead of gleaming white laminate and not an overstuffed couch in sight. But Ellie put this criticism aside and managed to find the Post version of an in-law suite, otherwise known as the Ashley and Greg wing.

It had changed since her last visit. The bed had been stripped of its sage silk clothes, and bare pillows lay abandoned on the mattress. Ashley's nightstand had not been touched, but a cardboard box sat on the floor next to Greg's, the Grisham thriller on top of the neat stack inside. Only the lamp remained and the drawer, open and empty.

"Wow," Rachael said. "If my husband and I could have lived in a place like this for free, we might still be together."

"Ditto." Ellie checked the closets, if one could call those large and perfect areas by such a mundane name. Ashley's walk-in remained untouched, but half of Greg's items had been removed from their hangers and folded into freshly assembled packing cartons. All the footwear had already been boxed with *Shoes* scrawled on the side in Sharpie marker. Clearly, Greg Anderson would not be returning to the Post estate under any circumstances, no matter what the justice system ultimately proclaimed him to be. Ellie could not blame Martin Post for that.

She figured the aforementioned cleaning staff had started this process, not Martin. Not because he had "people" to handle painful tasks, but because if Martin had done it, the clothing would not be folded so neatly.

This also made it more difficult for her to search through Greg's belongings, so she temporarily gave up on the closet and joined Rachael in the bathroom, which, thankfully, the cleaning crew had not yet touched. Messy, compared to the rigid order of the rest of the estate, though tidy compared to many of the victims' homes Ellie had seen in her work.

"This is gorgeous," Rachael said of the marble and bowl-like tub. She stood at Greg's medicine cabinet, examining each item in turn.

"It's identical to Ashley's, except without the floor-to-ceiling windows. Maybe Greg didn't trust one-way glass."

"Maybe he hadn't been given a choice."

"Good point. *Ashley* was the family member here. Greg? Only an in-law. Ashley got the bathroom with the view. She probably got her choice of which side of the bed to sleep on. Find anything?"

"Not so far. No prescription meds, not any illegal ones. No opioids, male enhancement pills, antibiotics, or cocaine.

Not even the odd baggie of marijuana. Whatever else Greg Anderson might be, he isn't a drug addict."

"Or he figured his father-in-law might regularly search his room?"

"Maybe. But you didn't find anything at his storage unit either, did you?"

"Nope." Ellie searched through the drawers. Greg had been a little better than Ashley about trying new products, tending to stick to one brand of shampoo and shaving cream, but he also left the bottles and razors scattered over the counter when they clearly had designated holders on a shelf at the base of the mirror.

Other than an education in the vast choices now available in men's styling products, she found nothing of interest. Nothing that would interact with tetrahydrozoline sufficiently to make him forget killing his girlfriend, or cause tetrahydrozoline to show up in his system. He didn't even have eyedrops among his supplies.

Ellie's phone binged. She checked her text. "It's Michael. The only prints on the bottle are Kayla's and the wrapper had only smears."

"Huh," Rachael said.

"Indeed. It doesn't *prove* that she spiked her boyfriend's beer for no apparent reason—"

"But it certainly indicates that no one else did. But why? What possible motive could she have had?"

"Revenge? She thought, like most people do, that it would work like on TV and only give him a bad case of the runs? A relatively mild punishment for turning her into the national poster child for *home wrecker*."

Rachael opened the last cabinet. "Or did she know exactly how the stuff would work and wanted to knock him out to, I don't know, search through his text messages? Put him in a position where he needed her to take care of him, proving how much more loving and nurturing she could be as opposed to the spoiled Ashley? Incapacitate a violent man so she could escape?"

"Or, Kayla had used the eyedrops herself because she needed them after crying all day, and Greg had ingested tetrahydrozoline from some other source."

"But *what* other source? And I still can't wrap my head around Kayla's missing meds. That desmopressin should have been in her apartment. Especially if Greg had killed her—he didn't take it away because if he'd left the apartment, he would have stayed gone instead of coming back to be found next to the body. But if someone else killed her, why, of everything else there, would they take her pills and not her purse or her phone?"

Ellie gloved up and plucked dirty laundry from the hamper, holding each piece as far away from her as she could. "Unless this killer who isn't Greg *did* take her phone—her *other* phone, the missing Android."

"Why?"

"To hide the connection between them. Call history, text messages. It was a burner."

"If she had a burner, why wouldn't she use it to text Greg?"

"She didn't need to. Martin or Ashley wouldn't be checking *her* call history. They didn't know she existed."

"Okay." Rachael stood, and ran one hand through her hair. "So Kayla had this Android burner—which we still can't prove even exists—to hide her communications with the person who killed her. Whom did she need to hide from? Greg? And if she and Greg were conspiring to have an affair, then what did she and her killer conspire about? Killing Ashley?"

"Maybe. Or maybe *she's* the corporate spy Martin has been looking for. Not Greg, but someone who had access to

Greg's thoughts, workshop, and phone." Ellie thought this through. There had to be more to Kayla than really nice cosmetics. "Maybe someone from Peter Gyles's camp. He couldn't get his nephew to turn on Martin, or couldn't trust Greg—*not* the world's most convincing actor, not up close— to pull it off. He needed someone once removed, someone who didn't live under Martin Post's watchful eye."

"Someone who, according to what the agents relayed from the girls at Ulta, was all about the money. She wasn't going to get it from Greg, not with that prenup in the way."

"So she found another way to cash in on the situation."

"Or," Rachael said, "they killed Ashley, but couldn't get what they wanted. Maybe they couldn't break the encryption on her laptop or whatever. They approach Kayla after she finds out who his wife had been, and she's now aware that her boyfriend's income is going to dry up."

"But if her true employer, Gyles or some other tech company, killed her to tie up a loose end—why take her meds?"

Rachael stood in the middle of the room, staring at nothing.

Ellie thought hard as well, but try as she might she could see no connection between Kayla's obscure medical condition and the corporate espionage theft of a national defense system. "I got nothing. There's too many maybes. I think we need to go back to Kayla's apartment *again*. Maybe she kept the bills for the burner in another place. If we could get the number, then the carrier could—Rachael?"

Rachael hadn't moved.

"Rachael?"

Suddenly she spoke, but not to Ellie. "Deborah?"

"Yes, Dr. Davies?"

Okay, *that* was creepy.

"Deborah, who has an upcoming appointment with Dr. Pine?"

"There are no upcoming appointments with Dr. Pine."

Ellie suddenly understood where Rachael's mind had led them. The *only* reason for anyone to take Kayla's meds was to hide a connection between Kayla and themselves.

"Okay. When was the last appointment with Dr. Pine?"

"The last appointment was June second at three forty-five p.m. Would you like me to make a new appointment?"

"No. That appointment on June second—who was that for?"

Deborah told her.

And suddenly everything made sense.

Chapter 41

On the other hand, Ellie thought, nothing made sense. Why most of all, but also how.

The sound of her feet along the boardwalk became lost in the noise of the wind shifting the mangrove trees as the air pressure dropped. She and Rachael were headed to the boathouse, returning, as it were, to the scene of the crime. Tropical storm Hazel would be fully upon them soon and they might have to decide either to stay in the boathouse and wait for a band to pass or make a dash for the house and arrive dripping. Floridians didn't bother with umbrellas or raincoats. They were a Band-Aid over a gushing artery — you would be soaked to the skin within ten feet no matter what you did, so why bother? At least the subsequent heat would dry it all quickly.

As they fast-walked, Ellie tried to call Michael, but his voicemail picked up and she didn't want to explain their theory to a recording, shouting over the wind . . . not within range of the omnipresent Deborah. She asked him to call her back and disconnected, slipping the phone into her bag.

The boats bounced only slightly more than before, the water inside kept calm by the shelter and the short breakwall outside the boathouse. The eerie quiet, the dimness of the interior still unnerved her, and still, she didn't know why. She loved boats, loved the water. The happiest part of a happy—relatively speaking—childhood had been mucking about in an old rowboat on the river in West Virginia with her cousins. From there she'd come to Naples and spent every spare minute in the warm waters of the Gulf, then moved on to summers during college in LA with her mother's cousin and his wife and two boys. The Pacific had been not as warm but much more exciting, not unlike her second cousin Esteban.

But Martin Post's words rang in her head, turning the depths to an ominous mystery: *You were in the car when it went into the river.*

She pushed it from her mind, holding the door against the wind as she and Rachael slipped into the boathouse.

But this time instead of boarding the *Phantom*, the boat from which Ashley had disappeared, Ellie jumped aboard the *Wicked*. The two boats were identical; if it were not for the names on the sterns—and the fingerprint powder still clinging to the *Phantom*—she would not have been able to tell them apart. Rigging station, grill top, helm. Pair of red and purple jet skis in their holders on the swim platform.

Ellie dumped her bag on one of the seats and dug in it for a pencil flash to examine the steering wheel, and the gunwale. Nothing to see. No sticky areas, only the grainy salt film that covered everything on or near the water.

They moved belowdecks, taking the short flight of skinny steps to the cabin.

"This is exactly like the *Phantom*," she told Rachael, "down to the kitschy decor."

Rachael, Ellie knew, had plenty of training in psychology, and that must have been why she saw more in this fact than decorating trends. "Martin keeps his gifts strictly equal between wife and daughter—whatever one has, the other must also have in identical measure?"

"Or it's simply more efficient to order two boats once you'd decided on the specs for one. This isn't identical, though." With the wind picking up, the wooden pulleys and glass floats in rope mesh decor rattled more pointedly against the wall and Ellie noticed a small block pulley where there had only been an empty space on the *Phantom*. She pulled it off its peg. It measured perhaps two inches by three by two, polished wood with a set of ropes snaking around its three wheels, and all of it dangling from a nasty-looking hook.

She handed it to Rachael, who said: "Surprisingly heavy for its size . . . add momentum from a swing or two and it could have some real knockdown power."

"Drop it into a neoprene wetsuit boot, and you had a formidable weapon. A pregnant girl caught unawares would be easy prey."

"Hence the flecks in Ashley's hair."

Ellie moved to the bathroom but had no interest in the sink and towels. Instead she unlatched the skinny cabinet in the shower door to find the cleaning equipment, same as on the *Phantom*. A spray bottle of Mr. Clean, a mop, two brooms. But the push-type broom with the stiff scrub brush for a head didn't quite match. Its handle didn't have a rubber red tip; its tip was brown. And the body of the scrub brush was yellow, not white, the bristles perfectly clean without the slightest smear of grime or tangled hair. Almost as if it had only just arrived from Home Depot.

She unscrewed the handle and showed it to Rachael.

"Right diameter. The tube wall looks a little thicker, but I can't be sure without a micrometer."

"Not that it matters, since surely this broom was purchased to replace the one used to kill Ashley."

"Doctor Carr," Rachael said, "I concur."

The boat gave a slightly stronger lurch. The heavens were beginning to open, but that gave them an excuse to wait it out and let their brains work. They had a scenario. Now all they needed was some proof.

Then someone shut the cabin door, and Ellie heard the click of its bolt sliding into place.

Chapter 42

Ellie did all the stupid things a hapless hero does in a cheap thriller: she tried the knob, pushed on the door, knocked on it, shouted "hey!" and then looked around for her phone, which, of course, rested in her bag on the upper deck. "Do you have your phone?"

Rachael pulled the slim electronic device from her back pocket, frantically thumbing commands. "I've got one tiny bar . . . yes . . . no . . . *damn!*"

Beneath them, the engine whined and the boat abruptly picked up speed. The *Wicked* must have cleared the boathouse, maybe even the breakwall. Heading straight out to sea, from the way the keel would jerk upward for a brief moment of weightlessness, then slam back down on the back side of each wave in a steady, frightening rhythm. With each plunge Ellie grabbed the counter, safety rails, anything to keep from falling to the floor. The driver headed directly into a tropical storm, knew it, and didn't care.

Ellie reached over one set of galley cabinets to the slender windows above, pulling up its lightweight blind, but from that angle she could only see the angry gray sky. She jumped onto the counter and bumped her head on the ceiling to peer through the skinny glass there, but still—only more of the same. Waves churned by the rising wind, a tanker far off to the north, a shoreline made vague through the drizzle and quickly receding. Boats had returned to their berths in preparation for the storm and they were alone on the water. What was the driver's *plan*?

The killer would have been unable to predict this. The inability to cross each T or dot each I could help Ellie and Rachael, but might also create panic and desperation—making the driver more likely to kill the two women. Whoever drove this boat would have no other choice.

Ellie stopped moving and forced herself to concentrate. They couldn't break the door down, as tempting as it sounded. Even if they did, what then? Surely the person above had a weapon.

Did they? Other than a fishing rod or one of the brooms?

In maritime thrillers, someone always wound up shot with a flare gun. But she had searched the sister ship and knew the flare gun would be stored in a red-labeled space under the steering console.

Wait—the galley was a *kitchen*.

Rachael, one step ahead of her, dove into the drawers, opening each one, but found only a set of regular table flatware and two decently sharp paring knives. She handed one to Ellie and slipped the other into her back pocket. "Don't they have anything bigger?"

"Filet knives are up on deck at the grill top."

"Accessible to the killer and not us."

Ellie nodded grimly. But she could always take a page from their book. She picked up the antique block pulley. Without the need for subtlety she didn't look for a neoprene boot to drop it in. If she had to use it, she wouldn't care if it left a mark.

The boat did not slow. Ellie had to adjust her stance and

keep her knees flexible to stay upright amid the tilt, the flight, the crashing into the water after each lift of a wave. Her heart raced along with the vessel, faster with every yard farther from shore. What would happen out there, miles from anywhere or anyone, with no one to see? Anything could—

Stop. It's already too late. If tossed overboard out here without a life preserver, we're both going to die. There's no way one could stay afloat long enough to get to anything or anyone. Stop thinking about it. "They're not moving around," she observed aloud, then kicked herself. Of course they weren't. In that storm, they'd be hanging on to the steering wheel to keep the wind from shoving them to one side. Not a time to be strolling about the deck.

"Is someone even up there? They might have repeated their trick with the dissolvable string."

The killer could have positioned the wheel and jumped off back at the breakwall. A short swim to land, go in, dry off— or say you'd been caught in the rain. Utterly believable. Though attempting to swim in these circumstances seemed more than a little nuts. "It wouldn't last long in this down-pour."

Good and bad news, if so. Good because they only had to get through the door and up to the deck to motor the boat back to land. Even if the killer had ripped off the GPS and thrown Ellie's phone overboard, at least they had a decently seaworthy vessel on which to await rescue.

Bad, however, in that they still had to get through the door. Otherwise the boat would continue across the Gulf until it ran out of gas, leaving the two women in a floating tomb until or unless a passing ship happened to get close enough to notice her. In over six hundred thousand square miles of surface, the odds were deathly bad.

Good and bad news also if the killer remained on board. Good: the killer would need the boat to get back so gas would be conserved. Plus, they wouldn't want to be gone too long, would need to return as quickly as possible *and* have one heck of a convincing story with which to explain Ellie and Rachael's rental car, still parked in the drive.

Bad, because whoever it was must have a plan to disable them even if they made it through the door.

If the killer needed to work quickly, she and Rachael did as well. Should they focus on getting the door open, with no way to defeat the opponent if encountered? Or on a killer who might not be there, while speeding toward a watery point of no return?

"Don't hesitate," Esteban had warned her. "Life is short."

And at this moment, her life might be getting very short indeed.

She moved toward the door.

"Wait," Rachael said.

Ellie turned in surprise. Rachael reached over to the sink and turned on the tap. Then she went into the bathroom and did the same, then added the shower.

"What are you—"

"Trust me."

And Ellie got it.

Back in the kitchen, Rachael pulled open the onboard refrigerator. It had been, no surprise, well-stocked, with at least a thirty-six-bottle case of water and a nearly equal amount of Gatorades of various flavors. She began to open each one, twisting the caps, dumping them upside down in the sink to let them drain as she went on to more bottles.

Ellie began to help, dropping the empties on the floor. Martin could charge her for the extra clean-up service, if she survived. The refrigerator had been running, the boats connected to constant power at the dock, and the bottles were chilled. Her fingers got cold.

Rachael tried her phone again; it refused to help. Either

they were already too far from land to get a signal, or the tropical storm had already taken out a tower.

When they had finally emptied the fridge, each opened all the other cabinets and storage areas looking for more. Ellie swept the empty bottles out of the sink and they bounced off the floor, the noise barely audible over the crashing waves and the engine's roar. If they had guessed wrong, the Post estate was going to be pretty pissed, especially after Rachael discovered three bottles of wine with fancy labels and broke off the necks with the pulley block because she wasn't about to waste time using a corkscrew.

"Those might sell for thousands per bottle," Ellie warned.

"Martin can bill me."

Ellie went into the bathroom and flushed the toilet. The flow from the taps had slunk to a thin trickle, and the toilet did not refill after it drained. She had no idea how water was managed on a boat—she'd never been on one that had a full-sized bathroom before. But surely the waste didn't release straight into the water; there had to be a holding tank, and wouldn't that be equal in size to the freshwater supply? Otherwise . . . environmental disaster.

This done, they checked their weapons, shut off the taps, and used a kebob skewer to poke the door hinge pins free from their knuckles. The door didn't move until Ellie pried it open with a cake server. Then it swung inward with an uncertain groan and Rachael jumped out of the way to let it *thud* to the floor.

The weight of the possibly watertight door sent tremors through the speeding boat, and the vessel abruptly slowed. The engine died, the sudden silence deafening. The killer had not jumped ship yet. Good news, bad news.

Ellie dropped the server, and she and Rachael went upstairs to meet their captor.

*   *   *

Michael felt only annoyance when the beefy guy at the guard shack told him, yes, Dr. Carr had arrived at the estate and no, she had not left yet. Then why, Michael pondered, wasn't she or Rachael answering their damn *phone*? Of course, the fallout shelter bunker of a house that Post lived in might block signals, for all Michael knew.

Not that he had driven to the Post place to find Ellie. No, he and Luis had come to question—confer with, he mentally corrected, doubting he had leave to *question* Martin Post—about business rival Peter Gyles, his relationship to Greg Anderson, and how much Post had known of that relationship. Luis had opined how the case had to be as simple as it appeared: discontented frat boy kills supercilious wife, then kills mistress when mistress in turn becomes inconvenient—but that still left them a long way from a conviction. Too many questions had not been answered. *How*, for instance. When, and where? A jury would expect proof of such things.

And Michael couldn't shake the feeling that this was about more than a discontented frat boy.

As the guard promised, the Locard's rental car sat outside the expensive-resort entranceway. Michael parked behind it, and he and Luis approached the glass doors. On previous visits there had always been one of the Posts waiting for them, and now Michael realized he had no idea how to get in. There were no knobs, and the electric eye ignored them. Knocking seemed ridiculous. He looked around for a button or keypad, feeling stupid to be so easily stymied.

Finally Luis found a flat, black rectangle attached to the stucco-coated concrete, and pressed the button in its corner. They waited.

Nothing happened.

Chapter 43

The killer came to meet them, waiting at the top of the cabin steps.

And snorted when she saw the door lying flat on the floor of the lower deck. "What the hell did you—Martin is going to be *so mad*! But don't worry. I won't tell him."

Ellie took each step slowly, all too aware of the Glock 40 dangling from the woman's right hand. Rachael moved behind her, clinging to the small railing.

Ellie said, "Hello, Dani."

Peripheral vision told her they were in open water, no land in sight, the boat still pitching and tilting in wild waves. Ellie's purse had disappeared from the seat, certainly thrown overboard, which meant no phone even if she could get a signal. No help to be had. Only her, Rachael, Dani, one boat, and tropical storm Hazel. And a gun.

If they weren't shot and killed, then they'd be drowned and killed, and all at the hands of this slight, beautiful woman.

Rachael said nothing. Ellie felt her boss at her shoulder, waiting for the right moment to spring their plan.

Ellie had so many questions that which to ask first fought for primacy in her head. The winner turned out to be: "Why?"

Dani kept her distance, backing against the gunwale on the other side of the steering wheel, gun not pointed—that would tire her arm too quickly—but her finger on the trigger. "Why, what? Why am I going to kill the two of you? Or why did I kill Kayla?"

"Why did you kill *Ashley*?"

"Seriously? Why *wouldn't* I kill—look, I don't have time for a long chat here. I'm supposed to be at a—"

"Charity event." Ellie noticed one other item missing from the deck along with her purse. Where there had been two jet skis, only one remained. "You're going to be late."

"Yes, and that's just one of the many ways in which you've screwed up my afternoon. I *hate* being late. I never fail in my obligations. I may be a trophy wife, but I am a damn good one."

"Sorry."

"They'll cut me some slack. Recent death in the family, and so forth. People with money always get all the slack they need."

They wanted Dani to worry, panic maybe, believe that whatever she had in mind would not work, that she might need to keep the women alive. "You won't even make it in time for cocktails. After you scuttle this, it will take a lot longer to get back on a jet ski—*if* you can do it without getting lost and driving in circles before you run out of gas. There's no horizon, no landmarks, and we've already twisted around so much since you stopped that you can't tell what direction land is supposed to be—"

"Compass," Dani said. "I'm old-school."

Ellie didn't relent. "Then, what, dump the jet ski and swim from the breakwall, or take your old route over the oak branch?"

A crack of thunder split the air, so loud it hurt the ears.

She and Dani, accustomed to the seasonal rains, ignored it, though a few spare brain cells in Ellie's head recalled how Florida led the country in deaths by lightning, with fishermen four times more likely to die than golfers. Perhaps Rachael had read the same study, since she started badly enough to shove Ellie an inch to one side.

For the first time, Dani seemed surprised, and not at the lightning. "Very good, Doctor. How'd you figure that?"

Ellie held out her own arm, its underside now peppered with small red bumps. "Poison ivy. I should have recognized it sooner, but I always sucked at botany."

Dani glanced at the matching rash on her own arm. "Is that what that is? Been driving me crazy. That's what I get for climbing trees."

Ellie wondered how to get her hands on that gun and kept talking. "Easy for a former gymnast and champion swimmer. You noticed the angles of the security cameras. From right under it, you can hear the lens shifting from side to side. You dumped Ashley in the water, took the boat back to the breakwall, tied the wheel with dissolvable string, and sent it out to sea. You swam the rest of the way in, got some scratches, bruises, from the rocks and the coral—not woodworking. The FBI agents checked the tapes for someone breaching the property before Ashley went out, thinking someone stowed away in order to emerge at sea and kill her. They got it half right, I guess, but they never checked for someone coming *back* afterward. They never checked for a stowaway from inside the estate."

Dani smiled, pleased to have her brilliance and daring acknowledged—probably one of the many motivating factors.

"Which brings me back to *why*. Why Ashley?"

"Why *not* Ashley?" Dani asked again.

Rachael asked, "Just resentment? The money? Or are you a spy for EntreRobotics?"

"Yes, yes, and no. *Just* resentment?" She raised her voice

to be heard over the wind and the splashing of the water. "Of the crown princess? The pampered little darling heir and Chosen One? The acolyte so perfect, so dedicated, that she never even realized her only identity had been breathed into her, a doll fashioned in his image? Why would I be *resentful*?"

"I can't imagine." Ellie couldn't keep the sarcasm out of her voice. It didn't seem prudent, given how Dani's fingers tightened on the gun.

"But no, it wasn't just *resentment*. It's the damn money. How stupid are you that you can't figure that out? Do you know what he's *worth*?"

The bucking of the boat gave Ellie a reason to glance around as she clutched the grab bars along the console. The GPS seemed to be working; built in to the dashboard as it was, it couldn't be ripped out except with a crowbar. Above it, two hollows served as cup holders, one currently displaying Dani's ever-present water bottle.

The weather band faded. For a brief moment the Gulf seemed to calm, and the air got quiet.

Rachael asked, "What's your long-term plan? Are you going to kill Martin too?"

Again, genuine surprise. "No. No, I *like* him continuing to invent lucrative things. I have to swallow my pride a lot, yeah, but I can live with that. I could even live with Ashley—she was too clueless to get angry at. And when we got married," she went on, a reflective tone creeping into her voice as if she'd never thought this through before, "she was in college, so not really a problem, just put up with her on vacations, etc. Then college ended, okay, a couple years, and she met Greg, was getting married. I thought, great, she can go off and live her own life, happy for her, best wishes. But then she *still* won't leave, wants to live with Daddy! Who *does* that?"

Dani had said Martin would be home soon. Ellie hoped

that had not been a lie. Surely he would notice their rental car, that both women were missing. This boat's tracker would work now—he'd had the battery replaced. Would he have seen to that detail even while occupied with his daughter's murder and a new missile defense program?

Hell, no.

"And then she's going to have a *kid*? A *new* heir and Chosen One? Who's going to need nannies and cars and colleges? No, thank you. Something needed to be done."

Ellie didn't waste time discussing the ethics of murdering a pregnant woman only to avoid having to share one's billions to pay for Stanford. She focused on logistics. Dani, the architect of the nearly perfect murder, would relate to logistics. "It was risky. Getting out to the boathouse without Ashley glancing out a window and noticing you."

"She wouldn'ta cared. And what would be weird about me taking a break from my charity busywork, anyway? It's easy to do that stuff in advance, easy to make it look like I'd had my nose to the grindstone the whole time."

"What if the cook came in to ask if you wanted anything?"

Dani shook her head, or might have—hard to tell with wind whipping her hair. "She doesn't come in until after eleven, and staff *never* interrupts unless they're summoned. Martin has them too well-trained for that."

"So Ashley headed the boat out to sea and you, what, put the pulley in the diving sock and snuck up the stairs? You're so lightweight—"

"Thank you. It isn't easy to maintain. I don't think I've had a full meal in fifteen years."

"—that she didn't feel your steps with the rocking of the boat at anchor. Or did you pop out and say hi?"

"Never saw me. She was sitting on this bench here, back to me. In the shade, of course, protecting her delicate little skin."

"You hit her with this." Ellie held up the block pulley on its chain.

Dani could not be more proud of her work. Even sideways rain smacking her in the face didn't dampen her delight. "Got her in one. Laid her out—she didn't feel a thing, the little shit, because I'm a nice person."

Rachael clung to a roof brace to keep her balance. "Why stab her? You could have just dumped her over—"

"Also not easy. She was eating for two, all right—gained thirty pounds at a minimum."

"—instead of bringing along the sister brush from the *Wicked*, unscrewing it, stabbing her, throwing that away, and then carefully unscrewing the one on the *Phantom*, with Greg's prints on it, to dip in the blood. How did you clean up the blood, anyway?"

"I didn't." The rain swelled, heavy drops that increased to a deluge within a single second. All three women moved inward, one step only, under the slight shelter the hardtop afforded.

Dani had to raise her voice in a shout to be heard over the pounding of water against water. "Didn't need to. It does *this* every friggin' day!"

Ellie shouted as well. "Why frame Greg? The prenup made sure he wouldn't have walked away with cash."

Dani shrugged. "Backup plan. I had no idea if the body would turn up or in what condition, or if the boat would be located. It's supposed to be unsinkable." She hefted the gun again, but didn't point it at Ellie or Rachael. "I guess we'll find out."

Without turning her head, she thrust her arm out over the water and fired twice. She didn't have to check if the bullets penetrated the boat's hull—even in the nonstop motion Ellie could feel the vibration of something more than waves. Dani was trying to sink the boat.

But water slowed bullets considerably, and if it were a

hollow point type it might shred. The shots *could* have gone through several layers of construction without serious damage. Dani didn't lean over to check. She had also left plenty of ammo still in the clip.

If the *Wicked* went down, how long could they last out here? There were life jackets below, but staying afloat would be only the first hurdle. The Gulf spanned a vast area and other boats would be scarce for hours, maybe days. Search and rescue would not be active during the storm, and they would have to get to the women before the sharks did.

How many rooms would Martin have to search before checking the boathouse? What if he asked—

And she knew why Dani had suddenly decided that Ellie and Rachael had to die.

Martin Post finally answered the door and let Michael in, Luis beside him. "Good afternoon. I hope you're not here to tell me Greg has been released."

"No, sir," Michael said. "I see Dr. Carr and Dr. Davies are here."

Post was not alone. A dozen or so men in suits or military uniforms followed him through the lobby, now stopping to mill about in impatient confusion.

"Are they?" He glanced at their car, visible through the glass doors. "Fine. Do whatever you need to do. We're about to start the demo."

The young officer, Tomas, hovered at Martin's elbow. "Are you sure this is possible? It's a tropical storm, sir."

"I know damn well what it is," Martin snapped.

"I want to see it," a bald general interrupted. "Enemies halfway around the world won't hold off because of our weather. If it can work under these conditions, then—well, then we know."

"Exactly."

"Why is Dr. Carr here?" Michael asked Martin.

"I don't know." He walked away, slightly more occupied with the defense of the entire United States than the two missing scientists he didn't need anymore. The generals and politicos followed the third-richest man in the country.

Luis turned to his partner.

"I know," Michael said. "But if the case is so complete, why is she here? To report to Post in person? Discuss her fee? I just don't think this is *quite* closed. Deborah. Where is Dr. Carr?"

Nothing.

Luis said, "I don't think she talks to just anyone, dude. You have to be—"

Deborah interrupted. "I do not have that information."

"Deborah, is Dr. Carr in this house?"

"I do not have that information."

"Is Dr. Davies in this house? Or on the grounds?"

"I do not have that information."

Luis sighed in resignation. "We'll have to look around the old-fashioned way. And let's do it fast, before the rain starts."

Chapter 44

"Deborah," Ellie said. "You were listening through Deborah, when Rachael asked who had an appointment with Dr. Pine. Just like Martin did to Greg."

"I meant it when I said I didn't mind always having to talk to Martin's first wife. I find Deborah very handy."

"She'll have a recording of my inquiry," Rachael pointed out.

Dani's smile faltered, the corners of her mouth straightening out, but not by much. "I can fix that. I'm not a genius like Martin but I can handle a few things."

Rachael continued. "You met Kayla at Dr. Pine's office. You both had CDI, started chatting—wait. You said you decided to kill Ashley because she got pregnant. But you sicced Kayla on Greg a *year* ago."

Dani lifted both hands, the gun wavering dangerously. Her words sped up. "I needed to throw a rock in the gene pool. If he hadn't bought the Bugatti I might not have been so ticked off. I thought I'd hint to Ashley that getting their own place would save the marriage . . . but she was too clueless, and Greg too good at keeping it secret. Little Kayla fit the role so perfectly. She wanted the money, followed every instruction to the letter."

"You set up the murder for a day you knew she couldn't alibi Greg."

"Again, easy—if you know Greg. She told him to clear a day to have really great sex, then, oops, I forgot I had to work."

"You weren't working *with* Greg?" Ellie asked. "He's from Gato Lago, you're from Cat Lake."

Dani went still—but not in guilt. Then she shouted in laughter. "Hah! No, I'm from a speck of a town in Iowa called Cat Lake."

"Oh." Ellie felt foolish. And wet. But she couldn't stop, had to keep Dani distracted. The woman kept edging back, toward the stern, heading for the jet skis, yet reluctant to leave the minor shelter of the hardtop. Ellie said: "How did you know he wouldn't, I don't know, stay home, or order pizza at the storage unit?"

"I didn't. Framing Greg was a side bet. If it didn't work out, no harm, no foul."

Rachael asked, "But then why stab Ashley? You could have shoved Ashley overboard after knocking her out and we would have thought it an accident like everyone else did. Why risk leaving evidence of murder?"

Dani said nothing. Pointedly. Backing out into the deluge by inches, like a reluctant swimmer easing into a cold pool.

A sudden guess hardened into a dreadful certainty, and Ellie spoke—not out of the need to delay Dani, but only to rid herself of the horrid thoughts welling up in her mind. "You stabbed her to make sure that baby wouldn't survive."

Even the rain seemed to grow quieter in the wake of this.

No one moved.

"Fishermen could have happened upon Ashley seconds after you motored away, and babies can survive for a short time in the womb. Even if by some incredible stroke of fate

Ashley survived, still—she never saw you, so no real harm done. But getting rid of the baby wasn't optional. And Ashley almost certainly would not be able to have another."

The blond woman got back on track. "I do feel bad about killing her—Kayla, I mean . . . but it's your fault."

"Ours! How?" Rachael asked. Her fingers tightened on the support pole as the boat gave a sharp, steep rock. Ellie watched Dani do the same with a simple, spare motion. They needed Dani to lose her footing, stumble, slip, but so far she hadn't come close. That former gymnast training had given her sea legs extraordinaire.

"You didn't think Greg did it," she now complained. "Everybody thinks Ashley is an accident, great. Then *you* say it's murder. Somebody had to go down for it—Martin would never rest otherwise. I needed it to be Greg."

"Who dosed him with the eyedrops? You or Kayla?"

"Kayla, duh! I wasn't there until he'd already passed out."

"Kayla never saw her own murder coming, so why did she agree to dose him at all?"

"I told her I needed to plant a piece of evidence on him, something that would definitely tie him to Ashley's death. I told her the fact that he had been released meant he might get away, and that would jeopardize her fee. She wasn't about to have that, not after she'd put a year into the project. She didn't even ask what the evidence was—good thing, since I had no idea what to make up. I really do feel bad about Kayla. She was fun, and she knew what she wanted. So few people do."

"And she knew what it was like to have CDI," Rachael said. In one motion she picked up Dani's water bottle from the console and flung it over the side of the boat.

Even with the incoming storm blowing the air around, the wall of rain visibly approaching over the waves, the Post estate still felt like a steam bath set on low. Michael's shirt clung to him and he could feel the sheen on his legs. The vigorous hike around the grounds made him sweat like a racehorse—without a ribbon, because they had not found Ellie or Rachael. Dani Post seemed to be gone as well, since the guard had not passed her through the gate.

Luis beat him to the boathouse, where he opened the door and gave a shout. "The *Wicked*'s gone."

A streak of lightning took that moment to crack through the clouds and nearly blind them. "They took the *boat* out?" Michael enjoyed the water as much as the next person, but the idea of sailing into *that* made his stomach lurch.

"Is she *nuts*?" Luis blurted. "Ellie or Dani or Rachael or all of them? Why would they do that?"

Michael didn't have an answer. Maybe Ellie had some theory about Ashley's death, how Greg had killed her and gotten back to land. But why wouldn't she have told him? And she'd lived there, she'd know not to—"Coast Guard?"

"They'd never go out in this." The finality in Luis's tone brought a chill to Michael's overheated face.

He thought. "We're on the property of the tech guru of the world. I don't care if half of Congress is waiting in his office to decide the future of the U.S., he's going to have to find our doctors first."

"You really think he's going to give a—"

"He will if his wife is on that boat too."

They turned and headed back to the house just as the first drops fell. The rain would completely ruin Michael's suit coat, but it could only improve the smell.

Chapter 45

Dani watched the flying bottle winking through the rain with a bemused look. "What'd you do that for?"

"Central diabetes insipidus," Rachael said, speaking clearly to be heard over the pounding rain and roaring wind—and to drag this out as long as possible.

Dani stilled, as much as a body could on a wildly pitching boat.

"Your pituitary doesn't send the vasopressin to your kidneys. Instead of recycling the water, your kidneys pass it right back out again. That's why you have to excuse yourself to pee every fifteen minutes—you probably have to go right now—"

A spasm crossed Dani's face, marring that self-assurance . . . but only for an instant.

"—and also why you're never without a water bottle at hand, to keep your fluids up. Right now you're becoming dehydrated from all the exertion and sweating, and as I've learned upon arriving here, the rain doesn't lessen the humidity. But with CDI it's getting worse every second."

"And you think throwing out my water bottle is going to cripple me?"

"I think throwing out *all* the water is going to cripple you." Rachael spoke firmly, with a typical doctor's confidence and gravity, the kind of tone that commands attention and brooks no argument. "Soon your mind will become confused, and your vision will blur."

Dani opened her mouth to say something. Then she shut it again.

Ellie thought—hoped—Dani had been about to point out the supplies in the cabin, but hesitated. Which meant she *did* fear the loss of all drinkable water, even if only for the next thirty minutes or so.

Which meant Rachael's play might be enough to take the game—*if* they could keep the game going long enough.

The boat did seem to be taking on water. The bouncing no longer seemed as extreme but not because the wind or waves had let up. A quick glance down the steps did not show any water in the cabin, so perhaps it leaked into an inner wall. The ballast of the extra weight made the craft sit lower in the water, increasing its stability.

Rachael said to Dani, "Yes. You no longer have a supply in the cabin. Sorry about that—now the dehydration will keep getting worse and there isn't anything you can do about it."

"I can leave right now. Goodbye, Dr. Davies, Dr. Carr."

They couldn't let up. Ellie joined in, forcing her voice to sound both calm and definite. She might not know anything about central diabetes insipidus, but she had learned the effects of dehydration during other investigations. "You won't make it. Long before you get near the shore you'll get confused, won't be able to read the compass. You'll be too tired to hang on to the handles—"

Dani raised the gun and fired.

*   *   *

"Well?" Michael said. "Where are they?"

He and Luis stood flanking Martin Post as he sat at a sort of command center inside his home, their suits dripping puddles onto the hardwood floors. A curved desk held four large monitors with razor-sharp definition and magnificent color, with a sister desk opposite to form a broken circle. Men in uniforms and nicely dry suits milled through the relatively small space, only about a third paying any attention at all. The rest checked their phones or talked golf or votes with each other in front of the vast windows, drawn to the churning sea.

Then a particularly close bolt of lightning rattled those windows, and they moved back.

"I don't understand this," Martin Post muttered. "Well, rather, I do, but—the signal has disappeared, just as it did with Ashley's boat. But in that case the tracker batteries had run down. But that shouldn't happen so quickly. I had Isaac change them. Closing the barn door, maybe, but—"

"Sir—" Tomas said, still hovering, but not close enough to touch Michael's sodden suit jacket. Its clammy weight rubbed against the back of the FBI agent's neck.

"He's busy," Michael told the kid. "Is the weather interfering with the signal? Or could someone have removed the batteries?"

"Why would anyone tamper with the *Wicked*?" Then Martin answered his own question: "Are you thinking someone has kidnapped Dani and the two Locard women? Why? Who? This is all supposed to be *Greg*."

He sounded almost plaintive, and Michael couldn't blame him.

"Sir," Tomas said again, "The committee—"

"Will have to wait," Martin spoke absently, this new puzzle commanding his attention.

Michael asked if there was any other way to track the boat. "The jet skis? What about the jet skis?"

Martin began to say "What about them—" before realizing what Michael meant, and shook his head. "I don't have any sort of tracker in them. We didn't use them for long distances, and they're cheap."

Relatively speaking, Michael thought. He wanted to shout in frustration. All this incredible technology, all Martin Post's personal power, and they would be defeated by some gray clouds and a low-pressure system.

"What's going *on*?" Tomas had finally lost both his patience and his obsequious tone.

Luis explained: "Mrs. Post, Dr. Carr, and Dr. Davies seem to be missing on the sister craft to *Phantom*. That's the boat that—"

"Dani? She's out there in *this*?"

His squeak attracted the attention of the general and the colonel, who had formed their own clique a few steps away from the lower ranks and the politicos. The general stepped closer. "What's happening, Post? Has the weather nixed the demo?"

Martin spoke with absent irritation. "No, the signals go through the clouds. My system doesn't distort—" His voice trailed off, brain cells more interested in thought than speech.

The colonel's words were less strident. "Mr. Post, we've been here for nearly an hour. If the demonstration cannot be completed because of the weather, I'm afraid—"

"You'll have to wait," Michael told him, aware that his career might take a hit for this. "We have more pressing matters right now."

"More pressing than the security of the United States?" the general demanded.

Martin didn't answer. He didn't seem to have heard.

Tomas stepped in to try and salvage the situation he had put together, speaking to the room at large. "The planned demo will show—would have shown—a test hypersonic missile from Central Command in Tampa being tracked in real time. Mr. Post's system takes in all the data reported by the satellite bounces, analyzes same in a split second. Once the object is identified as a missile, the coordinates are sent to Vandenberg and they shoot up an interceptor to take it down."

Luis, apparently, couldn't resist a moment of distraction. "Vandenberg was going to actually shoot it out of the sky?"

The rest of the people assembled showed no surprise. The details had been spelled out for them well in advance, Michael figured, his face burning even in the chilly clothing. How to blast them from their bubble of self-interest—

Tomas spread his hands modestly, as if the whole impressive planned display was his idea. "It would be out over the Gulf. And it's a dummy missile anyway."

"You hadn't planned on a tropical storm?" the general pointed out. "If weather stymies this thing—"

"It's not the weather!" Martin exploded, without bothering to turn from his screens. Even the politicos fell silent at this outburst. Every gaze swiveled to the third-richest man in the country. Then Martin sat up as if he'd touched a live electrode.

"It's not how it's meant to work," he said, typing a string of numbers and letters so quickly the taps ran together as one continuous, nonsensical sound. "But it can. It should. If I can get the parameters in there right. It's a forty-five-foot boat, another two, say, for the engine overhang. Fourteen across. Twenty-five thousand pounds—even at fully open it's standing still compared to a missile . . ."

Luis finally dared to ask what he was doing.

"CurrentSDI." He glanced up at the agents with a surprising smile . . . or perhaps not so surprising. Michael could swear his voice held a note of pure delight when he said, "It will be one hell of a test."

Chapter 46

The shot missed, of course. Maybe because the dehydration had caused floaters or at least blurriness in Dani's vision, but more likely because a particularly violent wave struck the starboard side. For one terrible moment Ellie thought the boat would capsize, with Dani catapulted over her head. All three women had to grab anything stationary and hang on until the boat righted.

Waves sloshed over the sides, weighing down the boat that much more. The empty bottles that had been in the cabin sink floated up the steps. "We've got to get out of here," Ellie cried, though she heard the absurdity. And go *where*?

Dani didn't bother responding, simply headed for the rear of the boat and her escape hatch. This meant leaving the inadequate shelter of the hardtop and plunging—literally—into the maelstrom of water swirling in the air. Her face screwed up in virulent distaste.

Dani, Ellie reflected, should have shot them both and leapt on the jet ski the second they emerged from the cabin. Every moment lessened her chances of success, her chance of coming up with a reasonable explanation for her disappearance and reappearance. *If* anyone was even at the Post estate to notice.

Dani had hesitated, Ellie realized, because Dani was afraid.

Afraid to find out that knocking an unsuspecting and hated party on the head might be one thing, but shooting two women in the face, quite another. Afraid to cross the Gulf's pitching waves with only a tiny jet ski. Afraid to find out what the dry mouth and the muscle weakness might add up to.

So Ellie persisted. "The arrhythmia will make it difficult to hang on to the handlebars. Then the seizures will make it impossible."

Dani turned and fired again. But Ellie saw her begin to pivot and ducked behind the center group of seats and rigging station, pulling Rachael with her. Above their heads, the bullet tore through the port side seat back and showered her with bits of fiberglass padding.

She risked a glance and saw Dani busy with the ropes that held the remaining jet ski in place.

Rachael kept up the pressure, shouting to be heard over the rain. "You'll fall off, and the next wave will carry it too far away for you to ever catch it. Then there will be nothing but you and the water. With luck you'll already be in a coma by then, so you won't feel the sea drowning your lungs as you sink."

Dani fired again but absently, barely looking at them as she pulled the trigger, cover fire rather than an attempt to actually hit a target. Five shots so far—little comfort since, assuming a full cartridge, Dani would have ten more.

Ellie guessed that Rachael had vastly overstated the symptoms, more likely to occur over the course of several days instead of several minutes. But why underestimate the power of suggestion on a person desperate, frightened, in a hurry, who had been under a terrible, secret strain for over two weeks. Of course Dani's limbs felt heavy and her mind felt sluggish, but they needed her to blame that on the CDI. Maybe, just maybe, she'd get scared enough to give up.

But even if she did—then what?

Dani threw off the last of the ropes, which coiled through the water like a tangle of snakes. She didn't need strength to slide it out from between the gunwale and the engines; Gulf waters lifted it for her. The boat had sunk that much.

"We need to knock her out, find life jackets for all of us, then we can use the jet ski to tow Dani to land," Ellie said to Rachael. Dani just said it had a compass. What had seemed like a crazy idea now appeared to be their only hope. As long as they kept heading east they'd have to hit land eventually, and unlike Dani, she didn't need to go directly back to the Post estate to try to come up with an alibi. Any land would do. All Ellie wanted to do was survive.

"Great," Rachael agreed. "How do we get close enough to her to do that without getting shot?"

"Hope the storm covers me? When I move, you find the life jackets, put one on, and get one for me, one for her."

Rachael glanced down the steps, where the water level in the lower cabin had reached a halfway point, and shuddered. Ellie's plan to charge an armed woman must now sound preferable. "Not there," Ellie said. "There's more under the captain's chair."

She stood up. Rachael moved to stop her, grab an arm, then must have realized the futility of it. Shot or drowned, they might soon be dead either way.

Don't hesitate.

Ellie crossed the deck, clinging to any stationary object she found and sloshing through the inches of water accumulated. The noise and motion of the waves covered any sound she might have made, and Dani needed both hands to battle the waves for control of the jet ski. Ellie grasped the hook of the short chain, swinging the heavy wooden pulley at the end of it.

* * *

"Is that it?" the colonel asked.

A young man who reeked of too much aftershave asked, "Why are we looking for a boat when we're supposed to be looking for a missile?" Michael wanted to slug him.

"So it's radar," the general said.

"It's a scan," Tomas corrected. "The system has broken through a tropical storm to pinpoint a pleasure craft barely more than forty feet long, without motion and without a heat plume."

"That was fast," the general admitted.

"But it's a *boat*," a man earlier referred to as "Senator" pointed out. "If it was a hypersonic, we'd all be dead by now."

Tomas waited for Martin Post to respond, but the man didn't seem to be listening to them. So Tomas said, "If it was a missile it would have been fired from another continent or one of the oceans. It would be identified in seconds, with Vandenberg notified immediately."

"Unless it comes from the east," the congressman from Florida intoned. "That's why we need another Vandenberg-type base on the East Coast."

"You just want the funding channeled to Highland County," another argued. "No one in western Europe is going to bomb us."

"Want to bet your life on that?"

"Having a base just creates a desirable target. How do your orange growers feel about that?"

Michael wanted to scream, but only raised his voice. "How do we get to it? The boat?"

No one answered him.

"The *point*, gentlemen," Tomas insisted, "is that this is simply a program. The infrastructure, the satellites, are already there. In other words—"

"It's basically free," the general finished.

A silence fell, in awe of that delicious concept.

"Got it." Martin Post rose abruptly and said, "Let's go."

Michael couldn't be sure to whom he spoke but felt pretty sure it wasn't the guys in the tailored suits. He and Luis snapped into the man's wake.

"Wait," the general said. "You found a boat in the middle of the Gulf in a hurricane, using other people's satellites?"

"Tropical storm," the colonel corrected.

The general didn't wait for Martin to respond. The man showed no signs of hearing the question, only continued toward the door. "If you pull that off . . . I'd guess you've got the bid."

Tomas blanched. "Sir—surely the Coast Guard . . . couldn't you stay here and explain the system—"

Martin did pause at this, slowing his stride only long enough to glance at the men assembled. "You can take care of it. You're doing fine."

The young man gulped.

Michael followed the genius out the door.

Chapter 47

Ellie had restrained, handcuffed, shot, and even stabbed another human being at some point in her career. She'd never bludgeoned one.

She swung the block pulley with the full length of her arm, from down near the sloshing floor, up and around, then down, down to the back of Dani's neck.

But before it struck, Dani turned. Animal instinct or acute hearing had alerted her—though not quickly enough. The wood block struck her shoulder and right ear. She dropped the gun to put a hand to her bleeding ear, and in an instant the water claimed the Glock as if it had never existed. Dani moved too fast to notice. She launched herself at Ellie with a snarl.

Ellie stepped back. Dani's foot slipped against the slick jet ski seat and her shins cracked across the stern, but she managed to grab Ellie's T-shirt with both hands. Ellie tried to hit her again with the heavy pulley—and failed as her own body slammed back onto the fiberglass deck and all air left her lungs.

Dani became her second priority, breathing her first. The rain drove itself into her nose and mouth and she sucked in both water and oxygen, choked, drowning while still on the boat. Dani now sat on top of her, drawing back a fist.

Ellie jerked her head to one side so fast she heard her neck snap. Dani's knuckles caught only the side of her head, behind the ear—and a lot of the deck. Dani howled again, this time more in pain than anger.

Ellie's shoes gave her more traction against the wet deck than Dani's bare feet, and the trophy wife diet didn't leave her attacker with great bulk. She bucked hard and Dani fell to one side.

Ellie could move a lot faster without a gun pointed at her. She left Dani to shoot up and over the stern, ignoring the electric crackle and subsequent roar of the lightning overhead. The jet ski bobbed merrily just past the now half-submerged engines and she leapt for it, their only lifeline. She'd circle back to get Rachael and the life jackets and Dani. And *maybe* Dani, depending on—

Midair, a hand grabbed her ankle and she fell across the stern and engine, smashing her cheek against its cover. Her outstretched fingers grazed the rim of the jet ski, and after that, nothing but water. All around her, nothing but water, her body weightless and free.

Then a punch to her back as Dani used her as a stepping-stone to get to the jet ski. Or she simply fell out of the boat, Ellie couldn't tell, because now Dani pushed her away, down, into the waves. The *Wicked* nudged her to one side, a loose rope brushing against her wrist.

Ellie kicked, flailed, wanting only to break the surface, but Dani's hands went around her neck and squeezed, not allowing her to rise. Ellie rammed both her arms up in front of herself and slammed those out to the side, ripping Dani's hands away from her throat. Salt water immediately stung in the deep gashes left by perfectly manicured nails.

A kick upward and she felt air, managed to suck in a few molecules before a wave hit her and filled her mouth. The entire world seemed to be roaring and the water kept her blind. Something pushed her below the surface and held her there, but only as an impersonal lump.

The jet ski.

She grasped its edge, pulled her head out of the water. The mini-craft tipped wildly sideways but she didn't care. It could capsize and still stay afloat—that's what they were designed to do.

She gulped in air in hacking, gasping breaths that would never be enough, coughing and gagging and gasping in more. Then, through hazy, salt-water-stained vision she saw Dani, trying to swim in the insane water, moving around the inert engines and heading for the jet ski.

And behind her, Ellie felt a new force approach. Something else was in the water with her, large and alive.

Just as she pictured a shark, jaws gaping wide, the sinking boat bumped into her, and Rachael grabbed her shirt. Hauling her on board wasn't much of a trick—the *Wicked* had sunk so low that the top of the gunwale barely cleared the water.

Just enough stability remained for Rachael to help Ellie shrug into a life jacket.

Ellie drew in enough oxygen to shout, "The jet ski!"

"I've got it." Rachael held the rope attached to the nose of it. Dani could climb aboard, but she wasn't going anywhere without them.

Besides, something had arrested her progress. The blond woman struggled with something below the surface as the crests and troughs hid, then revealed, then hid her again.

"Dani, hang on!" Ellie called as she climbed onto the jet ski, and off the boat—though very little separated the two now. The Gulf waters began to cascade over the gunwale into the boat, the last stage of a quick end.

Its key dangled from the console, start switch molded in a bright red. *Please start*, she prayed. *Please start*.

It started. It also had a compass, large and visible, as advertised. All she needed was her partner—

The craft lurched wildly as Rachael climbed onto it from the rapidly sinking *Wicked*. She wrapped trembling arms around Ellie's waist. "There she is—"

Only ten, perhaps twelve feet separated them from the thrashing woman. Ellie turned the throttle.

And the *Wicked* sank.

One minute it was hovering, the square of its hardtop still protruding from the waves. The next, the sea swallowed it whole without leaving the slightest shred of evidence behind.

And Dani disappeared as well. Ellie thought she could see the last shadow of light-colored hair sinking through the blue depths, but that might have been a reflection of the clouds.

She must have been tangled in the ropes, Ellie thought. That's what she'd been struggling with. And couldn't extract herself before the ship that she sank took her down with it.

Neither of them had the ability to dive and recover the woman, or a place to perform CPR even if they could. Ellie felt numb from more than the cold rain.

How could she tell Martin about Dani? Not only a betrayal, but a betrayal upon betrayal of the deepest kind, the deepest cut, the deepest kill. The person closest to him had destroyed his only child and his only grandchild, in a murderous perfect storm of hatred, resentment, and greed.

When a wave tried to shove them over, Rachael's arms tightened and Ellie snapped back to the present. Dani might be gone, but they were still alive. For now.

Rachael shouted, "Where are we—?"

"East." Ellie twisted the throttle and the jet ski leapt into a wave. With an increase in speed it seemed to surf from the top of one wave only to plunge into a valley, then climb the next. The motion and the wind tried their best to peel the two women from the craft and each raindrop struck their skin like an ice-cold needle.

A light flashed, and thunder cracked through the sky in the crystal-clear notes of shattering glass. Rachael shouted, her voice a bit unbalanced, "You sure this is normal?"

"Oh yeah." Ellie spoke through gritted teeth. "Totally normal."

"And you know where you're going?"

"Trust me."

She aimed the speck of a vehicle through the pulsing waves for the coast, where soon the mirrored front of the Post estate twinkled like a diamond.

Notes and Acknowledgments

I am an omnivorous researcher, devouring information anywhere I can get it, and I utilized many and varied sources for this book. My fellow Rogue Women Writer, Karna Bodman, told me some tales of when her time in the White House took her to defense contractor presentations. My former boss, Larry Stringham, explained which military branches fly which fighter jets. The fellow Mystery Writers of America members in my Florida critique group gave me invaluable feedback.

Of course I perused a number of medical articles and especially the website of NORD, the National Organization for Rare Diseases and their information on central diabetes insipidus. However, full disclosure, the extreme physical ailments in case of dehydration would take much longer to set in than portrayed here. Also, a pathologist told me it's highly unlikely to notice such an issue in the pituitary with a visual exam—it's a very small organ.

I found the *DOD Contract School* podcast helpful, and the book *The 300: The Inside Story of the Missile Defenders*

Guarding America Against Nuclear Attack, by Daniel Was-serbly.

The information about the mysterious deaths of the "Star Wars scientists" is all true, and written about here: https://www.thevintagenews.com/2018/09/16/star-wars-program/, https://www.latimes.com/archives/la-xpm-1987-04-08-mn-185-story.html and https://cdn.preterhuman.net/texts/religion.-occult.new_age/occult.conspiracy.and.related/Anon%20-%20Conspiracy%20to%20Kill%20the%20SDI%20Scientists.pdf

I'd also like to thank my always supportive siblings and the rest of my family, my terrific agent Vicky Bijur and the staff at her literary agency, and my editor Michaela Hamilton and all the great people at Kensington Books.